Fed by the anger building i[...] forth from the steam pipes. Each new creation was larger and more fearsome looking than before. Each pulled angrily at its roots, achieving a little more distance from the curtain of vapor. Soon they would be able to sustain their reality without touching it. Fans near the stage retreated, shrieking, as the beasts struck out at them. The creatures were still insubstantial, but that could change any moment.

Calm, Liz thought, opening her arms wide. Summoning Earth Power, she called upon the element of Earth to spread out among the crowd. *Calm. Serenity.*

It was no easy thing soothing an audience of 80,000 people. Liz tapped all the way down into the bottom of her reservoir of magic to touch the outermost rows of the audience. She urged her mood of calm on the thousands of people, chivvying them to release their harmful emotions in a positive way.

As if to field-test her enchantment, a new laser-born monster, more horrible than before, with glowing red eyes and huge tusks rose up out of the steam pipes, its claws reaching for fans in the first sixteen rows. Liz was rewarded then; instead of screaming in fear, the audience erupted with glee at the exquisite complexity of the special effects, applauded appreciatively, then settled down into a quieter enjoyment of the music.

"Good God," said Boo-Boo. "Some of 'em are even foldin' their hands."

"I had some good training," Liz said, with satisfaction, "as a room monitor at a girl's school."

"That's mighty impressive," Boo admitted. "But they're tied to your emotional state now. If you get frightened or excited, sure enough, the crowd will do the same. We'd have a bloodbath."

Liz shook her head. "I am capable of retaining my cool," she said. "I *am* an Englishwoman."

LICENSE
INVOKED

ROBERT ASPRIN
&
JODY LYNN NYE

LICENSE INVOKED

This is a work of fiction. All the characters and events portrayed in this book are fictional, and any resemblance to real people or incidents is purely coincidental.

A Baen Books Original

Baen Publishing Enterprises
P.O. Box 1403
Riverdale, NY 10471
www.baen.com

ISBN: 0-671-31978-7

Cover art by Gary Ruddell

First printing, March 2001

Distributed by Simon & Schuster
1230 Avenue of the Americas
New York, NY 10020

Production by Windhaven Press, Auburn, NH
Printed in the United States of America

To Vilhelm,
thanks for finding us each
a friend.

Chapter 1

"Damn it to Hell anyway!"

Hearing the utterance of these words by the head of the United States Secret Service, his aide materialized in his office like a genie answering a magical summoning.

In actuality, the simile was not that far from the truth. The men had been together for years (a professional, working relationship, of course. It's not that kind of a book!) and the aide had long since learned that on the rare occasions his chief resorted to swearing, it was best to stand by even before being called. Even then it would sometimes be too late.

"Trouble, sir?" he said.

"Where have you been?" the chief snarled.

(See what we mean?)

"Sorry, sir. It won't happen again," the aide replied, deliberately bland of countenance.

Washington, D.C., was a city of power, both built on and undermined by petty tyrants and obscure pecking orders. One did not survive there being thin-skinned.

1

"I can't believe we're getting this dumped on us!" the chief raved. "And in an election year, too!"

The aide waited patiently. Eventually the vital points of information would be forthcoming. Trying to rush it would only focus attention on himself.

"Every no-name power monger in Washington up for re-election bugging us for protection ... not to mention the 'equal treatment' demands from their opponents ... and now we're supposed to provide protection for some foreign nut touring the U.S. And with our limited budget, we can barely—"

"Excuse me, sir, but providing protection for foreign dignitaries is a normal part of our department's function."

"Dignitaries, yes," the chief said. "Ambassadors, royalty. But this falls well outside that description. Did you ever hear of a rock group called Green Fire?"

"Yes, sir."

"You have?" For the first time in the conversation, the chief abandoned his mad long enough to look directly at his aide.

"You forget, sir, I have two teenagers at home," the aide said with a smile. "Green Fire is currently all the rage in the younger set. An Irish group, I believe."

"Well, those are the 'dignitaries' we're supposed to be providing protection for," the chief said, returning to his tirade. "At least for their lead singer. What's her name ... ?"

"Fionna Kenmare," the aide supplied.

"That's the one. Anyway, the group's about to start a performing tour of the U.S., except the lead singer has been getting threats and had a couple unverified attacks on her. Normally, I'd try to dodge it, but the Brits are taking it seriously and sending along a protective escort of their own. That means we're stuck. There's no way we're going to let someone from a foreign agency wander around over here without someone from our side tagging along."

"Excuse me, sir," the aide said with a frown. "Did I understand you to say 'unverified attacks'?"

"That's the kicker." The chief nodded. "It seems the threats she's been getting, as well as the unconfirmed attacks, have been of a psychic nature. In short, magic. Real bibbity-bobbity-boo stuff. Just what we need to help us with our leisure time problem. We're already spreading our manpower dangerously thin and— What are you smiling at? Did I say something funny?"

"As a matter of fact, sir, you've already solved your own problem."

"I have?"

"Yes, sir. You have. As soon as you mentioned 'bibbity-bobbity-boo.' It reminded me that there happens to be another department you can delegate this whole problem to."

The chief began to smile, too.

No one could remember exactly how Department BBB got its designation or what BBB was originally supposed to stand for. It might as well have stood for "Bibbity-bobbity-boo," however, because that's how everyone referred to it. That is, everyone who knew of its existence . . . or remembered it at all.

Department BBB got its start back in the '60s, roughly about the same time the CIA was conducting its clandestine experiments on the possible military uses of LSD. "Red phobia" was rampant, and all one needed to do to get funding for a department or project was to report (or speculate out loud) that Russia was already channeling resources into research of a similar vein. The thought that the U.S. might drop behind the Russians in yet another field (people were still wincing over Sputnik) loosened governmental purse strings on countless strange and dead-end endeavors, most of which, thankfully, the voting, tax-paying public remained blissfully ignorant of. Department BBB was one such project.

Anything weird and not already nailed down by another department (like Telepathy and Telekinesis) got delegated to them for investigation or experimentation. Everything from crystal power to totem animals, secret names to ethereal spirits, came across their desks or ended up in their voluminous files. They imported "experts" from every accredited earth religion (and from most that were deemed "crackpot" even by the loosely wrapped) to assist them in their quest. All in all, a good time was had by everyone concerned.

In the '70s and '80s, however, the Department fell on hard times. Waning interest in the supernatural, as well as countless exposes and investigations into needless government spending, forced major cutbacks in the program, until its survival seemed to hinge almost entirely on its anonymity.

Currently, Department BBB consisted entirely of only two full-time employees: Sherry Meyers, a middle-aged woman who used to be the mistress of a senator until he bought her silence by appointing her to the chairmanship of Department BBB; and Don Winslow, her male secretary and occasional lover. (We aren't going to try to kid you that nobody in Washington, D.C., has lovers!) These were the administrators, whose main function was to answer the phone and deal with the endless paperwork associated with running a government office. Any actual assignments were delegated to a handful of "agents" they kept on retainer.

Even though romantically involved in a haphazard, casual sort of way, the administrators were not so engaged when their phone rang. To be specific, Don was reading a current bestseller while Sherry was updating her address book.

Neither looked up when the phone rang.

It rang again.

"Aren't you going to answer that?" Sherry said.

"You're closer," Don replied from the depths of his novel.

"Yes, but you're the secretary and I'm the boss—"

Don looked at her over the top of the book.

"—the boss who signs your pay vouchers and approves your raises," Sherry continued pointedly.

The secretary heaved a sigh of martyrdom and rose from the sofa where he was comfortably reclined.

"It's probably a wrong number, anyway," he said darkly, timing his comment so it would be over before he lifted the phone from its cradle. "Department BBB. Can I help you?"

He listened for a moment, then raised an eyebrow.

"May I say who's calling, please?" Sherry looked up at the tone of his voice.

His other eyebrow elevated to join the first.

"Just a moment, I'll see if she's available."

He artfully punched the "hold" button and turned to Sherry who was already on the alert, having tracked the progression of his expression during the exchange.

"It's for you," he said, needlessly. "The Secret Service, no less."

"No fooling?" Sherry asked.

The question was rhetorical. Even though Don had a bent for practical jokes, he never sounded a false alarm when it came to the working of the department. If nothing else, he felt that to do that would be so

easy it would be beneath him. He shook his head.
Sherry's eyes widened.

"Sherry Meyers here," she said, punching in on the
call. "Yes, sir. I see . . ."

She began to quickly scribble some notes on the
legal pad on her desk.

"And when will they be arriving?"

More notes.

"Do you have a description on the agent who will
be with them?"

A few more notations and the pencil was cast aside.

"Very well, we'll get on it right away . . . Don't
mention it. That's what we're here for . . . Thank you.
Good-bye."

She replaced the phone on its cradle and sat staring
at her note pad.

"I take it we have something other than a senator's
wife seeing a ghost or having a dream that needs to
be interpreted?" her secretary said, urging her gently.

"Here's where we justify our budget for the year,"
Sherry responded, snapping out of her trance. "It
looks like we have a full-blown assignment for a
change, Donald. There's an Irish rock group, Green
Fire, that's about to start a tour of the U.S. It seems
one of their members has been getting threats and
even suffered a couple attacks. The rat in the wood-
pile is that the threats and attacks have been of a
psychic nature. That makes it our problem."

Don began to smile. "The kind we can solve without leaving the office? Good. Who's the target?"

"Fionna Kenmare."

"Fionna Kenmare? Their lead singer? Isn't she the
one with the green hair?"

"I guess." Sherry shrugged. "I don't keep up with
that world much."

"What kind of attacks are we talking about here?"

"Mysterious illnesses, disembodied voices, and cuts appearing on her arms when there's no one around."

"All of which could be staged for publicity," the secretary said with a frown. "The Secret Service is taking it seriously, though?"

"The Brits are," Sherry said through tight lips. "They sent someone to check it out, and that person is out of the running with a mental breakdown. Because of that, they're sending along an agent of their own to watch over Ms. Kenmare while she's on tour."

" . . . And if there's one of theirs tagging along, there has to be one of ours tagging along as well, right?"

"You got it in one." The department head grimaced. "Run a quick check for me, will you? Have we got anyone in New Orleans, or do we have to airdrop someone in?"

"I think . . . Let me check."

The secretary ran his finger quickly through the Rolodex on his desk.

"Here we go . . . Oh boy!" Don said, dismayed.

"What is it?" Sherry was suddenly concerned by the change in his voice.

"If you're ready for this, our agent in the New Orleans area is none other than one Beauray Boudreau."

"Beauray . . . Oh God! You mean Boo-Boo?"

Chapter 2

"Mayfield!" Ringwall shouted.

Elizabeth put down her copy of *Paranormal* magazine. "Sir?" she said, springing to her feet. Director Ringwall peered out of his office at her, his plump-cheeked face glowing pink. He was beaming.

"In here, please, Mayfield," he said.

"Yes, sir," she said, keenly aware of the curious glances shot her way by the other agents of the Office of Paranormal Sightings Investigation branch of MI-5 as she scurried in.

Ringwall gestured to her to shut the door. Elizabeth stood, breathless, on the threadbare rag rug in front of his desk. What was so exciting that it could make her notoriously moody boss smile?

"Mayfield, I don't have time to make this long. Have you heard of Fionna Kenmare?" Ringwall asked, snatching up a sheet of fax paper from his desk.

"Er, yes, sir." Elizabeth immediately drew a mental picture of a skinny woman with weirdly cut hair and

Halloween makeup. She racked her brain for specific details. "Irish. Sings what she calls acid folk rock. Something to do with magic, sir."

"That's right, *magic*," Ringwall said, with savage delight. "Puts it right into our field, doesn't it? I've got an assignment for you. We got a call, from, er . . . Upstairs. I don't need to tell you how far Upstairs. Truth is," he said, leaning over the desktop toward her and lowering his voice, "I can't. I don't know. But this is a very important mission. There is reason to suspect that this Fionna Kenmare is under some kind of psychic or magical attack. She's reported seeing bleeding cuts appear on her skin when there's nothing sharp nearby. Suffers mysterious illnesses. Hears voices. In other words, the lot, and all gloriously unproven."

Elizabeth made a face. "The cuts could be self-inflicted, sir. As for the rest . . . it'd make good publicity, wouldn't it?"

"Right you are," Ringwall said, with a curt nod. "It's certain to be nothing; it always is, but because it might have to do with the paranormal, it's us instead of the fancy boys with their big budgets and their Porsche automobiles. But not this time."

OOPSI took precedence over the other branches of British Intelligence when the mission had to do with its special field of expertise, although that garnered them no extra respect from the other agents. Paranormal investigation was still regarded as a bit of a joke. They took all the calls for the hauntings at stately houses, apparitions in churchyards, bogeys at Wookey Hole, and so on. The other agents called them the "Ghostbusters," but not with the kind of affection that meant they respected the department. Elizabeth took the slight personally, although she tried not to.

"What do you need me to do, sir?" Elizabeth asked, starting to take fire with the idea of putting a finger in the eye of the high-profile boys. *They'd* be in the headlines for a change.

Ringwall ran a finger down the fax. "Kenmare and her group are about to embark on a tour of the United States, starting in New Orleans. I need you to keep close tabs on her, at all times, from the moment she touches down in Heathrow, until she's safely on her way back to Ireland after the tour is over. How can I say this without getting the gender-equity people down my back? I want a female agent on this case, because you have to be able to go anywhere she does, any time. A male agent can't barge into the Ladies', no matter what credentials he's carrying. Do you follow me? And if the attacks should prove to be coming from a supernatural agency, then it's a cockadoodle for us. And for you."

"But why us?" Elizabeth asked, not wanting to have this fabulous plum snatched away from her, but at all costs she must be professional about it. "Surely she's an Irish citizen."

Ringwall pushed a fingertip toward Heaven. "Ours is not to question Upstairs, Mayfield."

"No, sir," Elizabeth said, letting her mouth snap shut on her next question. She was agog with excitement. "Please go on."

"The whole thing is absolutely hush-hush. We are not to appear to be working in this matter. Only Kenmare and her immediate intimates are to know the British government is involved. You'll be working with an American agent." When Elizabeth inadvertantly made a face, Ringwall actually looked sympathetic. "Sorry, lass. The Yanks insisted on having a finger in the pie. But it's *your* pie. You decide how far they can push it in."

"Yes, sir!" Elizabeth said. Her pie! How marvelous that sounded. Well, she'd be very careful about anyone shoving in an unwanted digit. Ringwall stood up and extended a hand.

"Your briefing is being prepared now. I'll have the courier meet you at your flat to deliver it. Jump to it! You've got two hours to pack and get to the airport. You'll receive your ticket at the information desk." He picked up the telephone and dialed an internal number. "I'm calling a car for you from the motor pool. You'll never get a cab at this hour of the afternoon."

"No, sir," Elizabeth breathed, watching with awe as he spoke tersely into the mouthpiece and replaced the receiver. "Thank you for giving me the chance, Mr. Ringwall."

"I'm sure you'll do well," Ringwall said, nodding significantly and touching the side of his nose with his finger. "We're all counting on you, Mayfield." The director put out a hand to her. Elizabeth shook it energetically. "Good luck."

"Thank you, sir," Elizabeth said. Her head was quite spinning with joy, fear, and lists. She had so much to do. In only a little while she'd be on her way to her first international assignment! What should she pack? How much could she take with her?

Ringwall's voice penetrated into the whirlwind of speculation bumping around in her mind. She looked back.

"And, Mayfield, don't let the woman out of your sight, whatever you do. As I told you, this assignment comes from Upstairs." He pointed toward the ceiling. Elizabeth nodded reverently.

"What's all that about?" asked Michael Gamble, springing out from the wall behind Ringwall's door the moment Elizabeth emerged. He was a fellow agent, nice to look at with his shock of dark hair a la Tom Cruise, but prone to popping up almost under one's nose. He trailed behind her as she hurried to her desk.

"I've got to follow an Irish singer around and see if she's being haunted by something from the unknown," Elizabeth said, yanking open her desk drawer for her purse and briefcase. She might as well tell him; he'd uncover it soon enough from office gossip as soon as she was gone.

"What, not another alleged poltergeist?" Gamble laughed derisively. Elizabeth made a face at him. "Is her boyfriend beating her up, eh? Sifting through her purse while she sleeps?"

"Need to know, Gamble!" Ringwall's voice roared from the office door.

"Yes, sir," Gamble said, disengaging without a trace of guilt, and sliding smoothly back into his desk chair. "Bugger all. Good luck, Mayfield."

"Thanks, mate," Elizabeth said. With her possessions in her arms, she bumped her way out toward the lift to wait for the car.

Gamble's attitude was similar to the others in the small branch, and to everyone else in British Intelligence. The government most fervently did not believe in magic. They felt there had to be a mundane explanation for anything that happened. Even that which was completely inexplicable was told off as having a cause that they were not yet able to ascertain, just that it wasn't and never could be magic. Well, they were wrong.

Elizabeth often wondered what Mike and the others would say if she told them that she knew poltergeists and visitations and, indeed, magic, were real. An admission like that would tag her as a genuine loony, and she'd lose the credibility she had established painstakingly over the last six years. Salaries in the public sector were by no means generous. She needed to stay on the promotable track in these budget-conscious days. So she laughed when the others laughed, and made disparaging comments about the trippers who mooned around Stonehenge and Britain's other mystic sites. All of them had their government-issue wands, bells, and censers, and an officially sanctioned grimoire full of exorcisms, invocations, and exhortations that everyone used but considered to be a huge joke. The spells didn't work for most of them. Any actual effect was put off to coincidence.

If the official word was that these things did not really exist, it was fine with her. Some day the opportunity might come along that would prove to the scoffers once and indisputably for all that magic was real. The best way to do that would be to find some real magic and bring it to her superiors' attention. But her superiors, like the rest of the world, did not really want her to find any. It was much more comfortable to keep the department going on speculation, hope and fear.

She hoped sincerely that the Irish singer was not really mutilating herself, or being attacked by another person whom she was shielding. In order to justify OOPSI's actions—and budget—Elizabeth needed to produce results of some kind, but on that point the department was torn. To uncover magic would justify their funding forever, but they were not prepared to handle the publicity attendant on proving that magic existed. It was a conundrum. Elizabeth wanted to succeed in her mission. She half-hoped she could offer up a magical result, so that there would be less scepticism around the office, opening the door so that one day she could come out of the broom closet, so to speak, as a genuine practitioner. She suspected that her q.v. in the office files included mention of her grandmother and female ancestresses stretching back to the Ice Age, but nothing official had ever been said to her about it. The others were mostly here because they were fans of speculative fiction or wanted a cushy government position that didn't require much work except to visit suspected sites and look knowing.

In the meantime, she was on her way to her very first international assignment. Though it was only logical to use a woman to protect a woman closely, giving her the job still meant that the brass believed in her ability to do the job. She was very proud.

Proud and astonished, when, instead of the usual antique, miniature Peugeot minicab, the car that pulled up to carry her to Heathrow was a long, black limousine, the kind used to convey senior officials to white tie dinners at Buckingham Palace. The driver, an older man in a peaked cap, leaped out to open the door for her. Feeling like royalty, albeit royalty in a hurry, she jumped into the back seat. As the car pulled away, Elizabeth got a glimpse of her co-workers gazing enviously down from the office windows. This piece of luck boded well for her mission.

"Just five minutes, miss, or you'll be late for the arriving flight," the driver said as he double-parked at the kerb outside of her flat. Elizabeth hopped out the door.

"I'll hurry," she said, giving the limousine door a pat as she closed it. It was so nice to be given a bit of luxury. She glanced up and down the street. No sign of the courier as yet. It would probably be some spotty youth wearing a Day-Glo tabard and mounted on a motorbike who could negotiate the traffic faster than her car. No doubt he'd be waiting when she came down.

Although she had always regretted not being able
to have a cat in the apartment, this time she was
grateful. Now she had no need to call a friend or
relative to come and feed it, unable to explain how
long she'd be gone. At last, Elizabeth experienced the
excitement she'd always pictured when she first joined
the service. She was the agent in charge of a high
profile international case! She was still quite breathless
over the suddenness of it all.

Elizabeth ran upstairs, mentally sorting out her
wardrobe. She had no idea what kind of clothing she'd
need in New Orleans, a place whose name she recognized, but had no actual knowledge of. She had
a vague idea that it was hot there. That would be a
welcome change from the chilly London spring where
it had yet to rise above 15 degrees Celsius.

She sorted through the built-in closets in her tiny,
well-lit bedroom. Very little of her everyday wardrobe
was suitable for high temperatures, and she didn't
think that the colorful bandanna skirts and halter tops
she wore on Costa del Sol holidays would be appropriate for an MI-5 field agent on the job. Still, on
a high-profile assignment like this she could surely
cadge a clothing allowance out of the accounting
department, the better to fit in with the locals. In
the end, she stuffed her suitcase full of clean knickers
and all the protective spell impedimenta that would
fit. *Always pack your own underwear*, Elizabeth told
herself virtuously. She stripped off her dress, and put
on her most wrinkle-resistant suit, a very upper-class
skirt and blazer of a cream-colored fabric that looked
like linen but wore like iron. That was the way she
must appear to those she encountered: neat and
approachable, but inwardly tough. There, she thought,
pleased at her reflection. Ready for anything.

With a last backward look at the photograph of her

grandmother, who'd taught her everything she knew about the unseen world, she locked up her flat.

The limo driver hooted his horn when he saw her coming.

"Hurry up, miss!" he shouted.

"Did the courier come?" she asked.

"Not a sight of 'im," the man said, pinching out the cigarette he was smoking. He got out of the car and opened her door for her. "Stuck 'alfway between here and Marble Arch, I'll bet. 'E'll catch up. Come on, 'op in."

"Just one minute more," Elizabeth pleaded. She made for the bare bit of garden between two forlorn London trees that stood before the building.

Undoubtedly the limo driver had thought her quite mad standing there barefoot in the patch of earth with her arms to the sky, but she couldn't take the trip entirely unprepared. Ignoring him, she concentrated on reaching her mental roots deep into the earth and far up into the sky, making herself a conduit to gather together the two halves of energy that made up Earth power. It took a moment to ground and center herself. The familiar, warm tingle rushed along her limbs, feeling like the terror and pleasure of a steep roller coaster ride where they collided in the middle of her belly. Elizabeth took a deep breath as she joined the two elements together. She wound it into a skein of power deep within her that she could unreel at will.

Unlike the driver, her neighbors were accustomed to seeing Miss Mayfield in the garden patch recharging her magical batteries. While she stood there, feeling mystic, the power of nature flowing into her body from the earth and sky, one of the little old ladies who lived next door tottered by with her arthritic Pekinese.

"Good afternoon, Miss Mayfield!"

Elizabeth replied without letting go of the strands of energy. "Good morning, Mrs. Endicott. Lovely weather, isn't it?"

"Oh, it might be a little warmer, mightn't it, dear? Off somewhere?"

"An assignment. Official business."

"Ah," the old woman said, pulling her dog away from sniffing Elizabeth's ankles. "Have a nice time, dear."

"Thank you."

Mrs. E. tottered away. Thanking heaven for the native British tolerance for eccentricity, Elizabeth finished up storing as much Earth energy as she could take on a brief "charge," and sealed it into herself with a few more words to prevent any from dissipating unnecessarily. She'd need it to ground herself. It wouldn't do at all to find the "batteries" empty if she was forced to do any magic-working on the fly. With a smile at the driver's puzzled expression, she gathered up her small suitcase and purse, and climbed into the rear seat of the car. Now she was ready for anything.

Her triumphant mood didn't last long. She was prepared, but prepared for what? She didn't have a clear idea of what she had to protect Fionna Kenmare from. The courier remained conspicuously absent while they drove the rest of the way to Heathrow. Elizabeth kept turning around in her seat to look behind her. No motorcycle. No official car. Her heart sank.

Traffic was horrible as usual. Three miles before the turnoff for the airline terminal, the limousine slowed to a creep, then a halt. Elizabeth looked around frantically for any signs of movement.

"Afternoon rush hour," the driver said, sympathetically. "It'll get you every time."

Elizabeth looked at her watch. Forty-five minutes to go before the Irish flight arrived. Perhaps she could hurry things up just a little bit. She generally balked at using magic for personal gain, but this was in service to OOPSI, wasn't it? Rationalizations a specialty, she thought wryly, trying to recall if there was an appropriate cantrip in the office grimoire. No, of course not. Flushing poltergeists out of cottages, yes. Bringing up secret writing, naturally. Opening up traffic jams, of course not.

Time for a little impromptu poetry. "Let all cars move to there from here," Elizabeth said in a low voice, trying out the chant, "open the way to my goal clear." Not brilliant, but it should do the job of persuading everyone to hurry up just that much more. It was risky, but she could not miss meeting that flight. Repeating her chant, she released a little of her stored-up Earth power, feeling it worm its way forward along the lanes of traffic. It seemed as though it would work when the tiny psychic thread smacked into an overwhelming strong counterforce as firm as concrete that stopped it cold: England itself. Do not interfere with the status quo, the presence said. Nice girls and boys don't make a fuss.

Elizabeth groaned. One couldn't be well-mannered all the time, not with a schedule to keep. The push-push-push of greater London, as unlike the surrounding country as an ambitious nephew was from a staid great-aunt, lay behind her to the east. She appealed to it for assistance. All she wanted to do was get where she was going without inciting road rage or using up her carefully hoarded store of power.

Whether England relented or London succeeded, traffic began to break up. The taxi joined the lane of cars rolling towards Terminal One.

To her dismay, no messenger was waiting for her

there. She whipped out her small cell telephone and punched in the office number, all the while looking for a chartreuse tabard.

"This is Agent Mayfield," she said, turning her back on a young businessman in a very expensive suit who kept giving her interested glances, and raised his eyebrows when he overheard her identify herself. "The courier didn't meet me at my flat, and I still don't see him anywhere."

"Sorry, love," the receptionist said, her voice tinny on the line. "His bike broke down, so he's on the Tube. We just heard from him. He's stuck at Acton Park. He'll meet you in time to brief you at the ticket desk for the American flight. Mr. Ringwall says you're to meet the subject from flight 334 from Dublin. You'll be able to board the U.S. flight at the same time as her party, and you'll sit beside the subject until you arrive in New Orleans. You're not to let her out of your sight under any circs. Read me back, love?"

"Not in a secure location," Mayfield muttered back tersely, peering back over her shoulder at the businessman, who was leaning as close as he could but trying to look as if he wasn't.

"I'll take it as read, dear," the receptionist's voice quacked in her ear. "Good luck."

Don't let her out of your sight, the big boys said. Well, they hadn't taken luxury travel perquisites into account. Elizabeth ran along the endless corridors, and into the satellite gates in Terminal One just in time to see the famous green suede-cut, surrounded by a dense shell of fans and reporters, emerge from the jetway at gate 87, and sweep down the narrow corridor. The rest of her group, Green Fire, emerged one by one, and the crowd erupted into a frenzy.

Elizabeth tagged helplessly along all the way to Terminal Three, determined to stay as close as she could. She couldn't draw nearer without actually using some of the unarmed combat training that she had been required to learn for her job, and she wasn't perfectly convinced some of the fans didn't know martial arts, too. They looked a tough lot.

As soon as Fionna Kenmare and her party reached the American ticket desk they were ushered through check-in and baggage inspection by a member of the airline staff. Elizabeth had no choice at that moment but to abandon her vigil, because she had to find the information desk and pick up her ticket.

Only two people were in the queue at the desk, but they looked to be there for the next decade: an old lady with a very low voice who had some trouble with her luggage, and a large American man with a shockingly loud voice whose luggage had been scratched by the baggage handlers. As soon as a new clerk appeared from the tiny room behind the desk Elizabeth waved him over, showing her ID card in her cupped hand. The man's eyes lighted with recognition, and glanced from side to side. Neither the woofer nor the tweeter paid any attention.

"Yes, madam, we've been expecting you," the clerk said, very quietly. He reached under the desk for an envelope, and offered her a clipboard with a document from Central Accounting to sign. It had been faxed only moments before. Talk about cutting things close.

"Thank you," Elizabeth said briskly. She opened the envelope to double-check the flight details. "Just a moment," she said, putting out a hand to stop the desk clerk from walking away. "This is for Economy Class."

"I am following the instructions to the letter,

madam," the clerk said, looking hurt. He showed her the place on the document where "3rd" had been checked off, instead of "1st."

"But, this is wrong! I need to be in First Class."

"I'll be happy to alter it if I receive further instructions from the head office," the young man said hopefully, sounding exactly like a junior agent in a 007 picture, which is undoubtedly what he hoped. Elizabeth was in no mood to coddle him. She gave him a wan smile from the teeth out, and hurried to check in. She could not leave Kenmare alone for long. She'd have to phone from the other side of the barrier.

With the greatest of good fortune, Kenmare's party was still in the ticket hall. Elizabeth joined the mass of fans and photographers milling slowly toward the departure gate.

They sauntered, in no kind of hurry, through the express passport control, and down the hall toward the VIP lounge, still accompanied by those fans who were actually holding travel tickets. Now was the time Elizabeth must catch her and identify herself, before something else happened. She snatched up her purse from the rollers as it exited the X-ray machine, and ran toward the lounge. Just as she got there, the door was slammed firmly in Elizabeth's face. Fionna's fans, disappointed, scattered into the Duty-Free shopping area, leaving Elizabeth standing alone in front of the door.

Airport security was admirably tight, but she ought to be in line-of-sight contact with her subject. She knocked on the burgundy wood door.

Her quiet conversation at the desk inside the club did nothing except to create a feeling of smugness among the staff. They weren't about to let a lowly Economy passenger into the sacred confines even to forestall a death threat. If Elizabeth had official credentials to back up her claim, they might consider allowing her to remain in the corridor. Because of the security order keeping information concerning the mission to "need to know," Elizabeth knew she wasn't permitted to show her MI-5 badge, so she was forced to retreat out into the Duty-Free area, her cheeks burning with embarrassment. She found a point where she got a decent signal on her telephone yet could still see the door, and made her third call to HQ.

"Sorry, Mayfield," Ringwall said, ruefully. "Economy measures all round, you know. I'll try to get Accounting to alter that for you before you board, but you know what they're like. They absolutely choked at the thought of four thousand pounds for one agent's transportation. Do your best. Don't let the woman out of your sight."

"She's already out of my sight, sir," Elizabeth said, desperately. "She's inside the first-class lounge, and they won't let me in with an economy-fare ticket."

"Dammit, do what you can," Ringwall said. "You're an Intelligence agent. Be resourceful."

"Yes, sir," Elizabeth said, with deep resignation. "I still haven't seen the courier yet, sir."

"He'll be there. Probably meet you at the gate. Best of British luck, and keep us posted."

Elizabeth hung up the phone. Well, if she couldn't get in, she must monitor all those coming and going from the club, and hope the courier would arrive with her credentials so she could go inside before things went bad. She took up a position across the pedway in a bookshop with a good view of the door of the lounge. At all costs she must look like an ordinary tourist, interested in ordinary tourist things.

The magazine racks were protected by a dense wall of fellow passengers, all intent on the rows of glossy color covers. She located the fan magazines, and started to look for Fionna Kenmare's name, deciding that she would read up on her charge, and steal a march on the tardy courier. Evidently, the woman was more famous than Elizabeth realized. Articles about her appeared in every single one of the magazines. Elizabeth chose five magazines with the highest ratio of words to pictures, hoping that they would contain some actual information instead of pure public relations hype.

A couple of huge men stood up from the floor where they had been kneeling in front of the computer magazines, blocking her view, and began to discuss hard drives and RAM. Elizabeth all but dove over them to reestablish sight of the burgundy door. They gave her a hard glance, and she had to show an intense interest in the rack of crossword puzzle books to throw off any hint of suspicion. She liked puzzles, but there'd be little time for such amusements on the plane, not with an eight-hour babysitting job to get through, and a weeklong protection assignment at the other end of the flight. She chose three anyhow, and moved on to the next rack nearer the door.

An hour passed. Elizabeth felt her stomach rumble. She'd had nothing to eat since breakfast, and it was getting on towards lunch. The clerks in the bookshop were showing signs of nerves at having her hovering about for so long. They couldn't have missed her staring at the club entrance like a vulture. To calm them and her hollow stomach, she bought a handful of chocolate bars, all the while darting her head around to keep an eye on the corridor. She must be the very picture of a security risk.

Sure enough, a pair of gigantic men with that indefinable air of confidence appeared at her elbow.

Plainclothes police. The cashier must have pushed the silent alarm. Elizabeth smiled up at them with innocent puzzlement on her face as she walked up the checkout, and moved away from the shop with her purchase. She sat down on the farthest chair that would allow her to see the length of the corridor, and unwrapped a Yorkie bar. The bobbies, satisfied, drifted off. The clerk looked unhappy that Elizabeth hadn't actually gone away, and kept shooting her worried glances. Elizabeth ate her chocolate hungrily, and hoped that the courier would arrive soon. There'd be decent refreshments in the club. Maybe even a cup of tea.

An unintelligible announcement came over the tannoy, ending with the words, "boarding at Gate 21." She looked up at the overhead video screen. The word BOARDING was now flashing next to the flight for New Orleans. Only a half hour remained before departure, and there was one more security checkpoint to pass through. If she was too late they could deny her boarding. Wasn't Kenmare ever coming out?

As if in answer to her anxieties, the door burst open, and the mass of the Irish entourage surged out. Elizabeth sprang to her feet and shoved the remains of her third candy bar into her handbag.

The moment Fionna Kenmare appeared, the gang of fans converged upon her from all over, clamoring for photo opportunities and autographs. A slight, balding, middle-sized man in a very expensive dark suit, probably her manager, chided them jovially as he gestured them away so the star could walk. Elizabeth panicked. Could she get nearer? Now would be an ideal time for an assassin to strike. Any one of a million handbags or shoulder bags could conceal a weapon or magical impedimenta, without the least concern for all the innocent civilians between hunter and prey. Elizabeth tried to push her way through the group to the center, and got twenty elbows in the ribs before she'd moved five paces. Stuck between a tall young man in an Army surplus T-shirt and a woman in a rust-colored, silk Armani business suit, Elizabeth could see flashes of the long, manicured hands as the star scribbled a few tributes on ticket envelopes and magazine covers.

The mass of people gradually moved down the hallway and through the glass doors. At the gate, Fionna Kenmare and her people were winnowed out of the crowd by the airline personnel. She swept through passport protocol and onto the plane, a privilege of a First Class ticket and her famous face. Elizabeth tried to follow her, but the staff stopped her at the barrier.

"May I see your ticket, madam?" asked a nice young man with dark hair and blue eyes.

"Here," Elizabeth said, desperately trying to see over his shoulder. "But I must get on the plane *now*."

"Yes," the attendant said, very patiently. "We all saw her. But you'll have to wait for a while. Economy Class boarding will commence shortly. Will you please take a seat in the meantime?"

Elizabeth looked past him at the jetway, feeling at a loss. Every moment Kenmare was alone, disaster could strike. She thought about showing the staff her MI-5 warrant card, but that would lead to other questions which she could not answer. And the airport authority would demand, quite rightly, to know why no one had notified them that there was a "situation" in progress. Protests would be filed with the Ministry of Transport, the Secret Service, the Metropolitan Police, and there might even be embarrassing questions asked in Parliament. Mr. Ringwall would be cross. Elizabeth winced involuntarily.

She moved away from the crowd and opened her telephone.

"Sorry, love," the receptionist said, halfway between sympathy and amusement. "Your man's still stuck somewhere between Hatton Cross and the International Terminal. Track delays. You'll have to go it alone. Your briefing is being faxed to the FBI. Your contact will bring it to you at New Orleans."

"So I've got to sit an entire flight without knowing the full nature of the threats? In Economy Class? Damn all horrid bureaucrats," Elizabeth said irritably, and then remembered too late that all incoming phone calls were taped.

The receptionist chuckled. "Double on that, Agent Mayfield. Good luck."

Chapter 3

The gate attendant announced boarding for Business Class, and a dozen passengers queued up to pass through the barrier. Elizabeth blew a strand of hair out of her face as she paced, hoping she looked like no more than a typical nervous traveler. She ought to feel proud. The brass had never given her an international assignment before. This was a promotion, she reminded herself. There'd been such envy on the faces of the others in the Whitehall office that she was being sent off on a mission, with its tantalizing whiff of influence from High Places and Mysterious Danger, instead of someone with practical experience in dealing with kidnapping and anonymous threats. But all she could do was worry. Elizabeth felt a headache coming on. She had no aspirins with her. To get them she would have to go out the door through security again, leaving her post. That wouldn't do at all. She massaged the knotted tendons at the back of her neck.

The female staff member politely asked Economy

Class to board. Elizabeth presented her ticket with
hardly a look at the attendant, and ran down the pas-
sageway to the jet. She had to wait ages at the door
for the cheerful women and men in uniforms to stow
baggage and coats for their First Class charges. Standing on tiptoe, Elizabeth managed to spot the back of
Fionna Kenmare's green-dyed head as the woman
leaned over to tap champagne glasses with a big
bruiser of a man across the aisle from her. Gad, why
would anyone do that to her hair? The suede-cut was
the very next thing to being shaved bald. Elizabeth
supposed the style went with the makeup. As Kenmare
turned to signal the flight attendant nearest her for a
refill, Elizabeth got a full look at the star's face. A fine-
featured head with good cheekbones had been used
like a billboard for graffiti-like makeup. From the
eyelids to the hairline, she wore white eye shadow
overpainted with what one presumed were mystic
symbols. She had slashes of red-orange blush along her
cheekbones, and if that wasn't enough of a visual headache, her lips were sharply painted with fuchsia to
clash with the rest of the ensemble.

"Why doesn't she just hang a fireplug from her
nose and complete the picture?" Elizabeth muttered,
as the flight crew politely but firmly steered the Third
Class passengers down the aisle toward the rear of
the aircraft. It wasn't as if the woman was even much
of a singer. Elizabeth could remember hearing Fionna
Kenmare on the radio many times. She had a pretty
voice, but seemed more to be shouting her lyrics than
singing them. What good did it do her fans if they
couldn't understand the words? Or didn't that matter to fans any longer?

Elizabeth had to make direct contact as soon as
possible now. Once the pilot had turned off the

seatbelt light, Elizabeth sprang up from her seat. She excused her way out of the tight row, smiling at the man in the aisle seat, who gave her a puzzled look.

"Some people have the tiniest bladders," he muttered to himself.

Elizabeth felt her cheeks redden. Let him think what he liked. It would suit her purposes. She was working for the good of the British Empire, and such personal considerations as ego ought to be of secondary importance. It still stung. She wriggled her way up the narrow aisle toward the front of the plane. Too much time had gone by. An unknown enemy might already have struck.

Nothing in the jet made her natural sensitivity to magic come alive. The only good thing about being on board a plane was that Cold Iron would chase off the Fay. If Fionna Kenmare was under attack by one of the Fair Folk, whom Elizabeth had never seen but in which she firmly believed, she'd be safe as long as they were airborne.

The chances were much more likely that an unknown enemy was as mortal as she was, and might take advantage of the proximity and easy access. Elizabeth wound up just a tiny fragment of Earth power around her fingers and held it ready.

Using the force of her will and just a little magical misdirection, she persuaded each of the flight attendants in her cabin to look the other way as she slipped past the curtain into Business Class.

There were only six or seven people in the middle cabin. One of them, a well-dressed woman in her thirties, gave her a dirty look as she sauntered in. Territoriality, Elizabeth thought. She sent a fragment of 'fluence toward the woman, who forgot her presence and turned away to look out the window through the clouds at the fast disappearing island of Britain.

Business Class had as many attendants as Economy, but for a fraction of the number of passengers. Elizabeth had to move fast, tossing cantrip after cantrip with little flicks of her wrist, to keep the people from noticing her. So far, so good.

Things began to go awry as soon as she reached the curtain separating First Class from Business. She distracted the first uniformed man and put a neat double whammy on the next two, but she simply missed the fourth attendant, who came out of the galley just as Elizabeth reached Fionna Kenmare's row. The young woman hastily interposed herself between Elizabeth and her subject.

"Madam, please return to your seat," she said. She was British, blond, and solid, with the sort of no-nonsense manner one associated with school prefects and hall monitors.

"I just had to speak to Miss Kenmare," Elizabeth said, trying to sound friendly but just as firm and not at all lunatic. She didn't want the woman to put her into the category of insane fan. Elizabeth knew perfectly well that airlines now carried plastic straps they used as handcuffs for passengers who proved themselves dangerous. She'd never hear the end of it back in the office if she spent the flight tied up.

"I'm sorry, but that's not possible," the flight attendant said, with a practiced mix of steel and cordiality. At this moment, the other cabin staff woke up to the intruder among them, and began to move towards her. "Please return to your seat at once."

The green-headed singer turned idly to see who was leaning over her. Without interest, she went back to her drink, her magazine, and her stereo headset, without saying a word. The blond woman looked from Kenmare to Elizabeth with her lips pressed together

in exasperation. Elizabeth suddenly thought it was
better to retreat than explain.

"I'm so terribly sorry," she said. "I thought it would
be all right." She turned on her heel and marched
with dignity toward the back of the plane. A better
opportunity would come along later.

"Oh, God, not you again," Fionna Kenmare said
in an amused whinny, when Elizabeth reappeared next
to her an hour later. With her slim, blunt-tipped
fingers, she picked up a cocktail napkin, one with a
ring in the center from where her drink had been
resting, pulled a pen out of her pocket, and signed
it. "I'm after giving you points for the Lord's own
tenacity, lady dear." She extended it to Elizabeth, who
reached for it automatically, then was outraged at
herself and at the ego of the woman who assumed
she had stormed the barricades for an autograph.
Reasserting her professional persona, Elizabeth summoned up the words of a protective cantrip her gran
had taught her as a child, hoping it would come out
sounding like embarrassed gratitude. It would at the
very least alert her if something happened to
Kenmare. All she needed to do was touch the other's
skin. . . .

As soon as her fingertips closed on the damp
morsel of paper, the First Class attendants abandoned
the caviar cart and champagne bottles, and converged
upon Elizabeth.

"Madam!" the British woman exclaimed.

Distracted, Elizabeth sprang upright, still holding
onto the seatback. The attendants, accustomed to
dealing with intruders, expertly pried her loose. Elizabeth, vainly trying to complete the words of the spell,
thrust out her free hand to reestablish contact. The
first woman, a British woman about ten years older

and an inch shorter than she, took her wrist firmly
and turned it aside. The burst of power misfired. Now
Elizabeth had offered protection to the seat beside
Fionna Kenmare's. The big man had been holding her
hand. Would the Law of Contagion, an ancient prin-
ciple of magic, extend the benefit to Kenmare because
of the touch?

"Now, madam, this won't do at all," the attendant
said. She tucked a hand around Elizabeth's upper arm
and steered her backwards. "Please return to your seat
at once."

"But . . ." Elizabeth said, attempting to break free,
realizing that no argument that followed would be as
convincing as the first word.

"We are very sorry, but this area is reserved for
our First Class guests," said the taller attendant, a
black American woman with exquisite cheekbones and
pale hazel eyes, in which Elizabeth could see blunt
determination behind the affable exterior. "We are
sure you understand."

"But . . ."

"This way, madam," the older woman said, holding onto her as she moved inexorably in the direction of the gray curtain. Elizabeth glanced back over
her shoulder. The green head had disappeared back
into the gray leather cocoon. Fionna Kenmare had
already forgotten her existence. No, that wasn't true.
She was sharing a merry laugh with her seat companion over the persistent intruder. At least the
woman was unharmed, and amused.

Her captors urged Elizabeth into the Business
cabin. Once she was in their jurisdiction, two more
attendants took charge of her at once. *They* had a
sharp word with the woman at the head of the
Economy cabin, whose cheeks turned a discreet but
definite red. That flight attendant marched Elizabeth

back to her row and lectured her while she sat down
and buckled herself in. Elizabeth was to stay in her
seat, except when nature absolutely dictated that she
rise. Then, she was not to pass beyond the curtain.
She would only use the lavatories at the center and
back of the section. If she tried to get through the
curtains again they would invalidate her ticket and
send her back to London on the first turnaround
flight.

"Yes, madam," Elizabeth muttered, trying to retain
some dignity, but it was impossible. Unhappily, she
conceded the battle, and settled down for good
between her smugly grinning seatmates, and snatched
a magazine out of her bag to shut out their grinning
faces.

Bother the attendants for chasing her off
Kenmare. If she tried it again the airline would
assume she was some sort of threat herself, and
she'd have to go home. What would her bosses say
when they knew she hadn't been able to keep her
subject under her eye, even though it was absolutely,
positively not her fault? The aborted cantrip tingled
at the end of her nerves like the irritation from a
plucked-out hair. Her fists clenched in reaction. She
looked down, and a smile spread slowly over her
face. Never mind. She had the napkin that Fionna
Kenmare had signed. By the Law of Contagion, she
had made all the contact with her subject that she
needed to.

She uncrumpled the square of paper and touched
the squiggle of green ink. Yes, there was enough of
a link to build upon. Thank all powers, but the point
of a pen was a great focus for the soul, however little
conscious attention Fionna Kenmare had put into the
autograph. Elizabeth put a fingertip down on the end
of the last wild flourish and concentrated. Reaching

into the reservoir of power inside her, Elizabeth brought to mind the words that would form a protective ward to send past the curtains to hover around Fionna Kenmare until they landed. It was a very minor magic, as fragile a line as the one drawn with the pen. She felt it catch, and concentrated deeply. Faint as a heartbeat, she sensed the other woman's emotions: worry, excitement, but boredom overwhelming all else. Elizabeth urged the little spell to wrap itself around Fionna and keep her safe. The trace of worry lessened slightly, as the cantrip took effect.

Elizabeth put the napkin away. She had done the best she could, under the circumstances. The only thing that comforted her was if someone was threatening Fionna Kenmare, unless he was flying in First Class, he didn't stand a chance of getting to her until they landed in New Orleans.

With nothing else useful to do, Elizabeth began to read the fan magazines. She had little hope of getting a clue as to the peril facing Fionna Kenmare that had caused Upstairs to take such immediate action from the full-color public relations hype, but it was worth a try. Opening the first one, she began doggedly to read.

Fan digests were as disgustingly simpering as they had been when she'd been buying them as a preteen. She thumbed past photo after undistinguished photo of unwashed hair, made-up faces, and pierced outcroppings of flesh, until she found the article she wanted.

The "real-life, totally true" bio of Fionna Kenmare sounded like a load of rubbish, not even as good as the cover stories MI-5 made up for the agents going on undercover assignment, which were always unlikely in the extreme. And they dealt very delicately with the subject herself, suggesting she was worthy of the reader's sympathy and admiration.

Fionna, one columnist tenderly offered, was orphaned as the result of a blast from a bomb during the sectarian troubles in Ireland. Elizabeth tried to remain unbiased, but an opening like that raised her hackles. Fionna was raised by a poor, disabled auntie in a cottage that didn't have running water or electricity until the girl was ten. Her first instrument had been an old penny whistle that she taught herself to play by listening to the birds singing outside their window. Without glass, no doubt, Elizabeth thought, snorting, as she turned the page. No doubt the mattresses were stuffed with straw and discarded Superquinn bags.

As a child, Fionna earned a meager supplement to their family assistance grant by playing pipe music outside the pubs and stores. She had found her first guitar on a dump. The strings had been chewed by rats, but she swept and cleaned house for a music teacher for six months to earn a new set. Elizabeth frowned, doubting sincerely that strings cost *that* much. By dint of sheer talent, Fionna Kenmare had pulled herself up from direst poverty and into the eye of the world. She'd dyed her hair green so she would always remember her roots.

And leaves, too, Elizabeth decided, eyeing the shocking green pate in the accompanying portrait. Sympathy was an emotion unlikely to be roused by the image of the aforementioned star wearing a mystic robe cut from khaki camouflage material and wearing a tongue-out grimace that would have scared away space aliens. But what was the source of the mysterious threats inferred by her supervisor?

"Magic has always been so important in Fionna's life," gushed the columnist in the second magazine's article, accompanying an even more weird photo. In this one the star clutched a dissipated black cat and a cross-looking black rooster with a red comb.

Magic important, eh? More so perhaps than even Fionna anticipated, Elizabeth thought. But she didn't know why MI-5 was involved at all. All of the complaints Mr. Ringwall had told her about could have been the result of drug-induced hallucination. The problem seemed more like a matter for Interpol or a good therapist. Chances were that she'd never know who or why was sending down pressure from Higher Up.

"Hey, that's Fionna Kenmare," said her seatmate on the aisle, who was an American man about her age. He aimed a thumb at the picture and spoke to Elizabeth out of the corner of his mouth. "I thought I saw her get on the jet. Did you see her, with the makeup and the hair and all that? Cool, huh?"

He grinned at Elizabeth, who smiled weakly back. Should she confirm the star's presence, like any other fascinated passenger, or ought she to keep the information to herself? After all, this man might be part of the unknown threat.

"I don't know," Elizabeth said, affecting an innocent expression. "You see, it looked like her, but it could be anybody under that makeup."

The man brightened. "You mean, like Kiss? Wow, what if that's her double, and she's traveling incognito? Wouldn't that be something?"

"That'd be something, all right," Elizabeth said, and wished with all her heart that the Service had thought of it first. Draw attention away from the target, and give them something else to look at. But misdirection wouldn't fool a magical foe. Probably the attacks on Fionna Kenmare were part of a great big publicity stunt. That wouldn't wear well Upstairs, since they'd been forced into acting *sub rosa*, and committing a field agent plus the requisite monetary outlay. If it turned out to be a hoax, she, Elizabeth, would be the scapegoat because the office had to spend half its meager budget on a trip to America. She'd better not go too far on her new wardrobe. Having swallowed the obligatory camel, the department was likely to choke on a gnat, no matter how fashionable or appropriate.

She tried listening up the cantrip-formed link, to find out if anyone was meeting Green Fire in New Orleans. No luck. All she got was a kind of psychic static. Too much Cold Iron and too many people were in the way. She was lucky that the spell had fired up at all. Not three hours on assignment, and Elizabeth had already lost control of the situation. No more. The moment they landed in New Orleans, she was taking charge.

The First Class passengers, Keenan among them, were far ahead of her in the gateway. The VIP treatment began again at once. A reptile-like transport was waiting for them.

Chapter 4

As 9:00 P.M. Central Standard Time approached, the preliminaries of touchdown seemed to go on forever. Out of the constricted portholes, Elizabeth watched twilight advancing slowly across the flat, flat plains of the central United States. The chief flight attendant showed a lengthy video on the wild night life in New Orleans, followed by an information film on how to pass through Customs and Immigration into the United States. By the time the landing gear crunched and ground its way out of the belly of the plane, Elizabeth was wriggling in her seat with impatience. She forced her way out into the aisle as soon as she could, and hurried off the jet in the wake of tired business people and families pulling rolling suitcases.

The First Class passengers, Kenmare among them, were far ahead of her in the gateway. The VIP treatment began again at once. A jeeplike transport was waiting for the star and her entourage. With a roar and a honk, the car zipped into a U-turn and sped away down the tiled corridor of the terminal. Elizabeth ran along behind, but it swiftly outpaced her and vanished into the crowd. More bollixing. *Wait* until she got that London courier alone. She'd make sure he wished he'd never been late for anything in his life!

She didn't manage to catch up with the party until past Immigration, when Kenmare and the others were waiting for a limousine at the curb outside in the hot, sticky evening. The American courier must have missed her, too. She'd have to face the singer without her credentials.

"So it's you again," Kenmare said with high good humor as Elizabeth arrived at her side. "I'm sorry to be inhospitable, but it's been a long flight and I drank far too much. I'm too tired to socialize just now, lady dear. I'm glad to know such a perseverant fan as you, and I hope I'll see you at a concert some time." And with that she turned her back.

Frustrated, tired, and disheveled, Elizabeth stalked around her until she was face to face. She didn't know how prissy she sounded until the first words were out of her mouth.

"Miss Kenmare, I am Special Agent Elizabeth Mayfield. I have been assigned to you by the British government as your security escort for the duration of your tour through America. I believe you were told to expect me. I would appreciate it if you would stay within reach of me at all times. I have been informed you have been the victim of certain attacks. I can't protect you if you will not cooperate. You must understand that I speak with the full force of the British government."

Fionna Kenmare stared her squarely in the eye, while her whole body swayed slightly, as if that focused gaze was the only thing holding her steady.

In an entirely different voice, devoid of the folksy Irish accent, she said, "God, you're the same shirty prig you were back at University, Elizabeth. Will you never get over being hall prefect?"

Elizabeth goggled. With the utmost self-control, she pulled her jaw back into its upright and locked position.

"Phoebe? Phoebe Kendale?" she hissed. "Is that *you* under that awful paint job?"

Suddenly, everything became clear. Elizabeth knew who it was Upstairs that had set the wheels in motion and put the pressure on from Whitehall: Phoebe's daddy. Lord Kendale, one of the very great muckety-mucks in the Ministry of Defense, wouldn't hesitate to call in favors from companion services to protect his only daughter. Fionna Kenmare had a legitimate Irish passport, but Elizabeth was able to make a shrewd guess how she got it. Phoebe's mother was Irish. Under laws which had only recently been changed, Phoebe was entitled to apply to the Irish government as the immediate descendant of a citizen. She must have changed her name at the same time. It wasn't illegal, so long as she wasn't defrauding anyone. Her father must have been mortified that his child had thrown over her allegiance to the Queen while he was a trusted member of her very government. Fionna Kenmare was vocal in interview and song as favoring Irish independence. Lord Kendale would have insisted on that veil of secrecy that was drawn over Fionna Kenmare's past. No wonder the bio had read like something out of *Girls' Own Adventure* magazine. The reporters hadn't a clue.

Fionna/Phoebe looked at her in horror, realizing that she'd let her secret slip.

"Shh!" she said, clapping her hand over her mouth and whispering through her fingers. Her ridiculously made-up eyes were huge. "Secret identity. Come on, be a sport, Liz. Don't tell."

"I won't," Elizabeth whispered back, "but you do have to cooperate with me. I'm here to protect you."

"Protect away," Fionna/Phoebe said airily, fluttering both hands. The accent came flowing effortlessly back, and the consonants rolled together on her tongue. She had so ingrained herself with the Irish persona that not only didn't the accent slip when she was drunk, it became even more flowery. "I'll not stop you. In fact, I love a party. I love all mankind, all the world." She was three sheets to the wind, Elizabeth realized, and taking on more sail all the time. The bodyguard took a few steps forward to catch Fionna and hold her steady. She leaned back against him and caressed his cheek with a languid palm. "And Lloyd will look after me, won't you, looove?"

Lloyd Preston wrapped one arm around her lean waist. Elizabeth saw the possessive look on his face, and knew she had to get him on her side if she was expecting not to be locked out of dressing rooms and stage wings, accidentally on purpose. In all the wide angle photographs of Fionna, the dark-haired, thick-eyebrowed man had been an aggressive presence hovering at her shoulder or in the background.

"You do understand that I've got to investigate any threats," Elizabeth said over Fionna's head to him. "I'm just here to do a job, same as you."

The man growled. "I know about you. I can do all the protecting she needs. Go home."

"That isn't possible," Elizabeth said. She cleared her throat and pitched her voice higher. "I will be riding with Fionna and you in your car to the hotel."

"Not a chance, sunshine," Preston said flatly.

Elizabeth fixed him with the stare that she had

perfected in years of cadet service to teachers and school librarians.

"I know who you are," she said with great confidence, although all she had to go on was the information she had gleaned from reading the glossies. "You've been with Fionna for two years now. It's been . . . rewarding, hasn't it? If something happens to her, that'll be the end of it for you, won't it? You can't guard her against supernatural attacks."

"And you can?" Preston regarded her with suspicion and dislike. The feeling was mutual. Elizabeth knew his type. He was the kind of big brute who got loud and dangerous in pubs, and waited for his mates to quiet him down so the police wouldn't have to come in and arrest him when he beat someone bloody. The short, dark-haired woman with the peculiar eyeglass frames standing with the roadies was keeping a close, anxious eye on them, and looked as if she was going to rush in at any moment. The good-looking, brown-haired man at her side put a hand on her arm. They must be familiar with Preston's blustering.

"Come on, children!" the manager said, clapping his hands together to break them up. "We're all tired. Here are the cars. Fionna, Lloyd, and myself in the first car . . ."

"And me," Elizabeth said.

"And who the hell are you, duckie?" the manager said, wheeling on her. He was a dark-haired, well-built man with a clipped beard. He looked about twenty-eight, except for the fine creases in his skin next to his eyes and mouth, which suggested he was actually in his middle forties.

Elizabeth pulled him away to a handy overhead streetlight, and showed him her badge from OOPSI.

"Ah," the manager said, his eyebrows climbing high

on his forehead. "I'm one of those people who doesn't need to be hit on the head with a brick, love. I *believe*. I absolutely believe. Of course you'll join us. I'm Nigel Peters, ringmaster of this circus. Glad to have you here." He clapped his hands again. "Everybody! The band in car two. Everyone else in car three. Anybody else will have to cab it, I'm afraid. I think these bloody hearses only seat sixteen."

There was a strained guffaw from a couple of the roadies, each of whom had charge of what looked like a container-load of baggage. Elizabeth hadn't properly appreciated how much of an entourage or how much equipment a musical group needed on tour. She suddenly realized that every luggage cart on the pavement belonged to Fionna's group. The manager snapped his fingers, and the porters started loading the parcels and cases into the boots of the limousines. With little shooing motions, he steered each person toward his or her assigned car.

Elizabeth had much to think about as the limos arrived, each stretching on and on like a clown car at the circus. My heaven, but American cars are BIG, she thought. With the hall-monitor training foremost, she managed to help shift everyone in the parties into the cars, got Fionna, her bodyguard, the manager, the publicist, and herself into the first, and away they went. As soon as the car was moving, Fionna slumped into the corner of the plushy seat, and reached out a languid hand. Lloyd Preston automatically dug into his jacket pocket and brought out a cigarette and a fancy gold lighter.

"Thanks, dearie," Fionna said. Elizabeth studied her.

Well, well, Fee Kendale. She and Elizabeth hadn't seen much of one another since coming down from St. Hilda's College, Oxford. They'd been friends then, but had lost touch immediately after graduation. Her family said she had gone abroad. How interesting that it had turned out to be true, although she wasn't as far away as her father had made it sound. What's more, it easily explained what must look to an outsider like a coincidence. Lord Kendale knew Elizabeth was in the Secret Service; he even knew which branch. She ran into him occasionally in the corridors of power, and he always remembered to have his secretary send her a card on Christmas and her birthday. She only hoped that he hadn't exaggerated the nature of the threat just to get an agent on the case whom he knew he could trust. And he'd known perfectly well where Phoebe had been all these years she was supposed to have been "abroad." Elizabeth wondered how many of Fionna's entourage knew that their rebel star was really a British debutante of the most drearily respectable antecedents. Well, mostly respectable. They *had* been up at St. Hilda's. Elizabeth grinned.

Phoebe had been intractable even as a child, always going her own way no matter how much her father pleaded with her. It was going to be hellish keeping Fee from slipping away from scrutiny when it became onerous, but now Elizabeth had a weapon she might be able to use over her to keep her in order: her deeply dark, secret past.

As the airport disappeared from view, Elizabeth realized with a shock that she had forgotten to look for her U.S. counterpart. After the Phoebe/Fionna bombshell, it was small wonder, but the omission was devastatingly unprofessional of her. Still, no one had attempted to contact her. Oh, well, too late to go back now. Her connection would have to catch up with them at the hotel.

Chapter 5

"Will you stay off me bleedin' heels?" said the slim, green-haired woman, rounding drunkenly on the blonde woman in the crumpled suit behind her.

A big, dark-haired man wearing a white linen sports jacket over an immaculate T-shirt and jeans cut between the two of them and put an arm around the tall woman, who was recognizable anywhere as Fionna Kenmare, the acid folk rock star. The blonde woman, shorter by several inches, had a good, strong chin and steady, gray eyes. She looked as if she could put up a good fight but was choosing not to.

Beauray Boudreau watched them make their way from the file of limousines that had pulled into the underground garage of the Royal Sonesta Hotel on Bourbon Street. Fionna Kenmare staggered over the threshold into the hotel, and the large man steadied her. Behind her, the woman in the suit maintained a calm expression, but her eyes sparked to show that she was fuming mad. Boudreau followed them inside, past the uniformed doorman, who stared with open admiration at Fionna Kenmare all the way up the stairs to the lobby. The star tottered toward the deep armchairs upholstered in cherry pink. She flung herself into one and stretched out a languid hand to the dark-haired man in the expensive suit.

"Nigel, be a dear, sweet man, and check me in, will you?"

"Of course, Fee, darling," Nigel said, with nannylike solicitness. He asked the woman on the other side of the desk. "Sweetheart, can someone get my friend there a drink? And one for me, too. It's so bloody hot here we're evaporating."

"I'll have a waiter come by right away, sir," the young, black woman said, smiling.

It took Elizabeth a moment to sift the hotel clerk's words into a sentence she could understand. The honey-sweet, slurred accent was no easier to understand than broad Irish. The clerk behind the dark-stained wooden desk picked up a phone and tucked it into the angle of her neck and shoulder while she flicked through the sheaf of reservation slips Nigel Peters handed to her.

Yawning into her hand, Elizabeth stood back a little ways to keep an eye on Fionna while the group checked in. She'd get a room, take a quick shower to sluice off the grime of travel and wake herself up, then call in to HQ. It'd be nearly four A.M. at home. No one would be there, but the switchboard operator could take her message. She cringed at the notion of stepping back out into the saunalike atmosphere, but she needed to connect with solid earth. Now that she was back on the ground she needed to recharge her magical batteries. It would take special intervention to keep from falling asleep while she set up security for Fionna/Phoebe's room. A handsome porter in green livery and a white stock at his neck came over to smile and gesture toward her small suitcase.

"I'll keep it, thanks," she said. He nodded and dipped his head in a little bow as he moved on to the next person in the party, the slim, balding man, who gestured toward a heap of document cases.

A tall, good-looking blond man emerged with alacrity from the offices behind the desk and bore down upon Fionna, who had absorbed her first drink and was waiting for another.

"Miss Kenmare!" he said. "I'm Boaz Johnson, the evening manager of the Royal Sonesta. How do you do?"

"I'm well, thank you so much, dear man," Fionna said graciously, offering him a languid hand.

Johnson beamed. "We're so happy you're here. We'll make sure your stay is just as comfortable as we can."

"I'm sure you will, you dear man," Fionna said. "Nigel! Mr. Johnson, this is Mr. Peters, my manager. The two of you work out the knotty details, won't you?"

"Why, of course," the manager said, shaking hands with Peters. "I'd be honored to take care of your arrangements *personally*."

The pretty desk clerk smiled with a quirk of her head that might have been a shrug. Every Englishman loves a lord, Elizabeth thought wryly, and every American loves a celebrity.

Elizabeth could not believe how hot it was in New Orleans. Intent on her mission she'd been almost oblivious to the first blast of steaming air as she had set foot outside the airport terminal. Compared to the interior of the air conditioned limousine, the street and the hotel lobby were sweltering. She picked at the sodden collar of her suit while she looked at the people around her. She'd never been to America before. All she knew about New Orleans was what she'd seen in movies like *The Big Easy* and *Interview with the Vampire*, both insufficient research, no matter how you looked at it, for the actual place.

It was curious. In London, home of the punk movement, Fionna Kenmare's weird makeup stood out a mile. Here in New Orleans, she was just another passerby. On the drive through the French Quarter from the highway exit to the hotel, Elizabeth had already seen men with multiple-color-dyed hair, women wearing gaudy body painting and not much else, and at the last intersection, the limousines were halted to allow passage to an entire jazz band dressed in rose-colored suits, led by a man carrying a frilly parasol. The lobby was full of local color, too. Elegant businessmen and businesswomen rubbed shoulders with odd characters dressed in tie-dyed scarves and picturesque rags.

Fionna received her second drink and her square plastic key, and rising to her feet with balletic grace hammered into her by lessons from Miss Felsham at Congreve School, swept toward the lifts, followed by the hulking form of Preston. Elizabeth started after her, her mind full of cantrips and hotel security codes. Peters caught up with her within a few steps.

"Give the girl some privacy for a while, can't you?" he asked in a whisper, tucking his head down next to hers. "It's been a long flight."

"I can't," Elizabeth said, just as quietly. "Not until this mission is over and she's safely back home."

Peters sighed. "I figured not. Good enough. Look here, I'm putting your room next to hers. Second floor. Separated only by a wall, all right?" He held out a key to her. "On us. What do you say? Otherwise this lass can't guarantee you're even nearby. We've blocked the whole wing."

"Very good of you," Elizabeth conceded, accepting it. She could almost certainly have bullied her way onto the same floor with the help of her American connection, wherever he was, but Elizabeth was grateful that Fionna's manager, at least, was cooperating willingly with Intelligence. It would make things far easier in the long run. She could save what was left of her energy for making security arrangements. Mr. Ringwall would probably be pleased at the cost savings. The room tariff was remarkably expensive, even by London standards.

Preston, the security man, was still shooting daggers her way. Her very presence was an affront to him. Well, if he could scare away bogeys, she wouldn't be here!

Her legs felt heavy and tired as she followed Fionna toward the lift alcove. She watched the singer saunter with ease, as if she had not been up all night, had not spent nine hours cramped in a plane. Of course, one of the two of them had been in a First Class couch, with attendants to rub her feet, while the other had been stuffed into a lightly-padded sardine can with two other people. Her old school chum, Elizabeth thought with amusement. Who'd have thought it?

She was not the only person watching Fionna make her grand way through the lobby. Suddenly, one of the odd characters appeared at Elizabeth's elbow. He gave her an engaging grin.

"One weird lookin' mama, ma'am," he said. Elizabeth gave him a weakly polite smile, and continued walking. Fionna vanished around one of the faux marble pillars flanking the far end of the lobby. Elizabeth hurried to catch up.

"How long you think she takes on painting up every morning, huh?" the character persisted, striding alongside her. "Every little line like that takes time."

"Look," Elizabeth said, spinning on her heel. She gave him the full headmistress's voice, starting low and threatening to rise to the painted plaster ceiling. "If you do not leave me alone I'll summon hotel security, and have you thrown out of here." She glanced toward the desk, where the young woman was already helping someone else to check in.

"Oh, you don't want to do that, Liz," he said, shaking his head, stepping up so he was level with her. "Make things rougher for you and me."

Liz? Elizabeth stared. "How do you know my name?"

The man put out his hand. "Beauray Boudreau, ma'am. Call me Boo-Boo. I'm supposed to be working with you. Didn't they tell you?"

"You?" she asked. The man had very intense blue eyes that beamed with sincerity and savvy. His sharp cheekbones and nose outlined a mouth that was thin-lipped but quick to smile. His wrists and neck were whipcord thin, and they disappeared into a disreputable, ragged hunting jacket that might once have been khaki. His jeans were untidy and threadbare, and he wore sneakers without any socks. His blond hair was very short, but the severe cut didn't lend him an iota of respectability. "You're with the FBI?"

"Yes'm," he said.

"Oh! Well, yes," Elizabeth said to this apparition, trying to collect her thoughts. "They did tell me there'd be someone working with me, but they didn't say what—I mean, who."

Boudreau laughed heartily. "Don't blame you none for being skittish. You're new around here. I know

a lot of visitors think all of us Americans must be
gangsters or hillbillies, but we're more than we seem.
We're kinda used to it. Oh, by the way," he reached
into one of the dozens of pockets that made up—
nearly held together—the body of the hunting jacket.
He presented her with a manila envelope that had
been folded twice to fit in a pocket. "Here's your
dossier. They said you'd be wantin' that first off."

"Thank you," Elizabeth said, examining it surrep-
titiously to make certain there were no insects clinging
to it. She glanced quickly back toward the reception
desk to see if there was any reaction to her and her
odd escort. No one was paying any attention. New
Orleans must see people like Boudreau slope in and
out every day. She started to open the envelope flap,
keeping the edge close to herself so Boudreau couldn't
see in.

"Some mighty interestin' readin' in there," he
continued, conversationally. "I'll just look forward to
chewin' it over with you, when you've had a chance
to clean up."

Elizabeth noticed the adhesive strip had already
been broken. She stared at him, outraged. Putting a
finger in her pie without permission! "How dare you
read my briefing before I do! I'll tell you what I think
is appropriate for you to know."

"Ah." Boudreau tipped his head back and half-
lidded his eyes so they glinted with blue fire. He no
longer looked like an innocent street lunatic. He
looked like a fully aware and possibly dangerous street
lunatic. "I'm so sorry, ma'am. I thought we was supposed to be sharin' information. I'll just be sure to
remember that for gettin' you around the city and
all, tellin' you only what you need to know."

Elizabeth was instantly contrite, and wary. She
didn't need to have his meaning spelled out for her.

Cooperation. Hands across the water. Special relationship between Great Britain and the United States of America. She was in a strange city, and she needed this strange man to help her complete her mission. He knew it, and she knew it. She took a long breath. Time to start over.

"I am so sorry," she said. "I am not thinking. I'm exhausted, and it's been a trying day. HQ threw me in at the deep end. I was assigned to this only just before the flight left."

"And it's wrong of me to be so inhospitable," Boudreau said, bowing low so that the frayed end of his sleeve brushed her shoes. "We'll get your bag up to your room. You have a chance to wash up, and then we'll tell each other things."

"This is Mr. Boudreau. Mr. Boudreau, Mr. Nigel Peters," Elizabeth said, effecting introductions in the hotel bar an hour later. They had taken a very private table in the Mystic Den, and she had searched it carefully, using the bug detector from Q Division, her training from OOPSI, and native talent inherited from her grandmother.

"Call me Boo-Boo," the American agent said, shaking hands with both of them. He had a grip like a bench vise, Elizabeth thought, carefully counting her fingers when she got her hand back. "I'm what you might call a free-lancer for the Bureau, Department BBB."

Elizabeth felt her brows go up. "A free-lance agent?"

Boo-Boo leaned back in the elegant brocade-covered chair, looking like a bedraggled cat toy at a cotillion ball. "Works out good for all of us, ma'am. I got some trainin' from the best people down here; an interest of mine, even a natural talent, you might say." A meaningful glint from those very blue eyes, and Elizabeth thought she understood. "The Department can use that, and they don't have to keep a permanent office. That's good for their budget. They keep me on retainer, and that does me some good. I keep an eye on things for them down here, and they call me when they need me. I'm a sworn agent."

"Yes, well," Peters said, clearing his throat. He lit another cigarette off the end of the first and stubbed out the butt. Elizabeth could tell he didn't have much confidence in the American's professionalism. Neither did she, for that matter, but necessity ruled in this case.

"I think we oughta go over security arrangements," Boo-Boo said. He pointed at the envelope at Elizabeth's left hand. "We don't need to discuss what's in there. All of us already know."

The British agent nodded. She had read the dossier while changing clothes in her charmingly elegant room, and then got immediately to work. Everything that she had guessed was confirmed by the confidential briefing. Lord Kendale was concerned for his daughter's safety, based on Fionna/Phoebe's complaints of magical attacks. He would not, could not dismiss them, and neither should the agency. The report had been updated while she was on the plane.

The one thing about the case that Mr. Ringwall had not mentioned that really worried Elizabeth was that there had been an MI-5 agent assigned to the Kenmare group before her. Twenty-four hours before, he had been found wandering half-naked up Dublin's Grafton Street, babbling about little people—odd, but not inexplicable. The agent's . . . indisposition was the reason Elizabeth had been sent on in such haste. There still was no explanation as to what had struck him mad in the middle of the Dublin shopping

district. Tests so far had turned up no traces of drugs
or physical trauma. Elizabeth gulped. The mission was
already sounding more dangerous than she had feared.
Was she up to a mission like this? Peters and
Boudreau were both studying her, waiting for her
input. She must continue to present a professional
mien, no matter what.

"MI-5 has no conclusive information as to the
source of the attacks on Ms. Kenmare," Elizabeth
said, "but we are prepared to protect her to the extent
of our powers."

"Us, too," Boo-Boo said. "Even if it turns out to
be a wild goose chase. Better that than real trouble,
although my superiors won't like it much."

"Look," the manager said tentatively, eyeing them,
"I don't know what I'm getting into now. I don't want
two governments angry at Fionna, but I don't want
her hurt, either. Do you think the things that are
happening are real, or not?"

The two agents exchanged glances.

"Won't know until they strike again," Boo-Boo said.
"We've got to keep an open mind about that until
we see for ourselves."

"Whether the attacks are of paranormal origin or
not," Elizabeth said, "if we are to believe her, and
I am inclined to do so, someone or something has
targeted Fionna Kenmare."

"Right," said Peters grimly. "Then, security's the
main concern."

"Right," Elizabeth echoed. She accepted a gin and
tonic from the waiter, and paused until he was out
of earshot. She turned to Boo-Boo. "You already
know how many people are with the party. Three
band members, twelve permanent roadies, Mr. Peters
here, her personal bodyguard, publicist, special
effects woman, technical director, the costumer, and

the makeup artist. None of them appear to have any connections with the United States other than professional contacts in the business, particularly Michael Scott, who is known as the Guitarchangel. He had quite an independent career going earlier in the decade, two platinum albums, and all," Elizabeth finished hastily, lowering her face so the others couldn't see it. She had hardly had to refer to her notes for Michael. She'd been a big fan for years. Working in proximity to him was going to be distracting.

"The keyboard player, Eddie Vincent, was well known in the American group Skywatch, a Christian rock band. He began to play with Fee—Fionna around five years ago." Better be careful about her old friend's secret identity. There was no telling whether she had enraged someone by her masquerade as a starving Irish waif and what they might do if they found out she was no such thing. "Voe Lockney's only been with her for two years. He replaced her last drummer . . ."

"Former boyfriend," Nigel said, dismissively. "They broke up, and he couldn't handle being around her. Too bad. He was stellar."

"How many other newcomers?" Boo-Boo asked.

"Because of the labor laws, we've had to hire most of our backup staff here in the States," Nigel said, taking a healthy gulp of his drink. "It's all I've spent the last three weeks doing. Six musicians, three backup singers, a couple dozen grips and technicians. They're really out of the picture. Most of them haven't even met Fee yet. They've been working with our stage manager, who's been here on site for a week with most of our techs. Only the key personnel flew in with us this evening."

Elizabeth dismissed the newcomers from her

calculations. If they'd had no contact with Fionna Kenmare in Dublin, they could not have been responsible for the previous attacks, or the mysterious indisposition of the other agent.

"The costumer," Elizabeth read from her jottings, "Thomas Fitzgibbon, came to her from the West End theater scene. Did a lot of work for Andrew Lloyd Webber's Really Useful Company. Kenneth Lewis, lighting engineer. A New Yorker, he last worked in some off-Broadway theaters. Laura Manning, the makeup artist, is also from the West End. The special effects designer is a woman, too, Roberta Unterburger."

"Call her Robbie. She hates Roberta," the publicist advised.

"Yes," Elizabeth said, writing it down. "She's from Marin County, California, three years ago. They've all been with her for at least two years, predating the first attack by at least fifteen months."

"We didn't hear anything from our end, either," Boo-Boo said. "Any problems on your end, Nigel?"

"None," the manager said. He leaned forward, placing his open hands palms up on the table in appeal. "They're all good people. They like being part of the Fionna phenom. She's got something special. People gravitate towards her. She's been sort of protected by her fans."

"It sounds as if someone loony has broken through that cordon," Elizabeth said, matter-of-factly. "Possibly someone with special abilities. That's yet to be determined. I'm here to see that nothing more happens."

"What can you do?" Peters asked, his fists closing reflexively. Elizabeth shook her head.

"If someone tries to get to her again, we can detect him, or her, or it. I've examined her room. There are four doors to the suite itself, the one from the hallway on each floor, and one from the suite to a balcony and the pool on the third floor. One of those doors leads into my room, and I'm prepared to repel attacks. I've seen to it the other doors are securely locked, and warded."

"What'd you use to ward?" Boo-Boo asked.

Elizabeth eyed him, wondering just how far she could trust him. "Who brought you in?" she asked, suddenly.

Peters looked from one to the other, puzzled. "The FBI brought him in, you know that."

"No, that's not what she means." Boo-Boo gave her that easy smile, his eyes glinting. He understood. "She wants to know how I qualify to ask her questions." He leaned over so that his mouth was close to Elizabeth's ear. "A welcoming woman who smiles," he told her. She closed her eyes, relieved, and continued the litany.

"Where was it?" she whispered.

"In the heart of the world," Boo-Boo said, formally.

"Where was the moon?"

"Shining over our heads. And her name was Elmira."

"All right," Elizabeth said, relaxing. She recognized the name. Boo-Boo was not only qualified to help the department, he knew something about her grandmother's ancient tradition of magic as well. It would be easier to confide in him, because she wouldn't be breaking solemn oaths to tell him. She sat up. "I'm so sorry," she told the manager. "Department business. I used an . . . Earth-Fire ward, tapping into the hotel's electrical system."

Peters looked bewildered, but Boo-Boo nodded. If he was up on New Forest magic, he'd have recognized the reference to a Ward of Vulcan, from the Trilistene Grimoire of 1585, with modern variations that obviated the need to burn charcoal or use a focusing lens to provide the fire power.

"That'd give anything trying to pass it a mighty hotfoot," he said approvingly. "I mighta put down an Earth-Water combo, but that could get messy. What about the windows?"

"No problem. I left them so they can still open—it's so bloody hot in this city—but air's the only thing they'll let in."

Boo-Boo grinned. "You should see it come summer, ma'am. This is just warming up."

Nigel Peters reflexively unbuttoned the collar of his shirt. "Warm! If it were any hotter you'd have to mop me off the pavement."

Elizabeth referred to her notes again. "There wasn't time to bring much from the department, so what I have with me is rather a hodgepodge of government equipment and personal tools. What OOPSI does run to is a decent line of general issue psychic monitors. I've left some concealed amongst Fionna's personal effects to warn us if anyone is staging an attack using her own possessions. I've also been down to the kitchen to arrange for food analysis before any room service order is taken up to the suite. The only employees who will have contact with any of the band or the stage crew will be ones I have vetted personally. You can't concentrate on the arcane and overlook the mundane. Have I missed anything?"

Boo-Boo's slow smile spread across his face. "No, ma'am. You're plenty efficient."

With a smile for the compliment, Elizabeth read off the last of her shorthand notes. "And, finally, escorts to and from the New Orleans Superdome. I'll need the limousines here at least twenty minutes ahead of time to examine them for traps or tricks."

"As you wish," Peters said. "But that's not until

tomorrow. Fee's itinerary doesn't have her doing anything until the morning, and that's just publicity. I'll have the cars here for you to inspect ahead of time. No trouble there. Until then, there's nothing more for us to do. She'll be perfectly safe here in the hotel overnight."

"Oh, I don't know about that," Boo-Boo interrupted them, rocking his chair back and forth on its rear legs. "While I was waiting for you all to come down, I saw her and that big fellah turn out the door and light out down Bourbon Street."

"What?" Elizabeth and Nigel exclaimed in unison, leaping to their feet. Boo-Boo didn't move.

"Why didn't you stop them?" Elizabeth demanded, staring down at him. If this was an example of American agents, then they were sloppy, haphazard, and careless. No wonder they were always having troubles over here.

"Nothing strange by me," Boo-Boo said, looking up at them with a hurt expression. "Most folks who come to town want to see the Quarter, and all. Plenty of interesting night life. Finest music in the world. Any bar you go into probably has at least one live musician. Usually a band."

Elizabeth felt herself swaying slightly with exhaustion. "But it's past twelve," she said. "The bars will be closing."

Boo-Boo shook his head. "Ma'am, bars around here don't close until at least dawn. Some of 'em don't open until midnight."

"We've got to catch up with them!" Elizabeth had a vision of Ringwall's ruddy face turning more purple than usual. "Right now!"

Boo-Boo rose slowly to his feet, shaking his head at the haste with which out-of-towners seemed to move.

"Well, all right, ma'am. Whatever you want."

Chapter 6

Elizabeth had barely taken three steps outside before she was drenched in sweat. The heat and humidity of New Orleans wrapped itself around her like a hot, wet blanket, all prevailing and merciless.

Pausing in an attempt to orient herself while fighting off a sudden wave of dizziness, she turned to her companion, only to find him chatting with the doorman she had passed without really noticing.

"Hey, Boo!" the uniformed man said. "How ya doin', man? Ah didn't see you come in."

"Came in off Conti," Beauray was saying, all the while exchanging a bewildering series of handshakes and palm slappings with him. "No sense fightin' the crowds if you can walk inside."

"You got that right!" the doorman responded, throwing his head back in an exaggerated laugh. "How's that pretty lady of yours these days?"

"Mean as a snake, and that's a fact!"

"Umm. Mr. Boudreau?" Elizabeth began. "I hate to interrupt, but . . ."

"Be right with you, darlin'," Boo said, holding up one finger in restraint. "Say, Willie. Did you see a cute little thing come out of here a while back? Green hair?"

"Hard to miss her," the doorman said, nodding. "She and the folks she was with headed up Bourbon towards St. Anne. Lookin' to party would be my guess."

He made an offhand gesture to indicate the direction.

"'Preciate it, man," Boo said, holding up his hand for a parting palm slap. "Got to roll, now. You tell your lady that Boo said, 'Hey,' hear?"

"Later, Boo!" the man said, waving, then returned to his duties with an aloof, deadpan expression.

"Sorry 'bout the delay," Beauray said, putting a hand lightly on Elizabeth's back and steering her into the street. "I figured it would be worth the time to be sure we was lookin' in the right direction."

Thus began one of the strangest, most memorable walks of Elizabeth's life.

The world-famous Bourbon Street was closed to vehicular traffic at this hour, but was nonetheless choked with pedestrians. At first, Elizabeth was overwhelmed by a kaleidoscope of apparently random noise, music and lights.

"NO cover charge! NO minimum drinks!"

" . . . feelin' tomorrow, just like I feel today!"

"Spare change?"

"Oooh, Darlin'! Lookin' GOOD!"

" . . . Can't touch this!"

"Lucky Dogs! Get your Lucky Dogs! Right here!"

Within the first block or so, however, a certain order became apparent to her in the seeming chaos.

Most of the crowd were tourists or sightseers. They traveled in groups or pairs, lugging their cameras or hand-cams with them like identifying badges. While some of them wore three-piece suits that marked them as conventioneers, the majority were decked out casually in shorts, new T-shirts sporting New Orleans designs ranging from the silly to the obscene, and some of the most ridiculous hats it had ever been her misfortune to see. They moved at a leisurely pace, stopping often to look in windows, listen to the music radiating forth from various bars, or to take pictures of each other standing next to street signs, the little tap dancing kids, or even trash cans.

"Table dances! World famous love acts! NO cover charge!"

"Crawfish! Best eating in the Quarter!"

" . . . Hey now. Jump in the river now . . ."

"ICE cold. Get your ICE cold Coca-Cola here!"

In the space of a few blocks they had walked from Conti, Bourbon Street featured at least eight bars with live bands and/or singers, eight more with recorded music blaring from speakers, six shops featuring exotic dancing or other delights ("wash the girl of your choice!"), more than twelve souvenir shops selling masks and feather boas, coffee and beignet mixes in yellow cans, hot sauce with health warnings printed on the labels, metallic-covered plastic beads in a rainbow of colors, and the ubiquitous tasteless T-shirts. Every one of the shops overflowed with tourists.

Overhead on the first- and second-floor balconies (second and third floors here in the U.S.; Elizabeth realized they counted things differently here), stood crowds of men and women brandishing plastic cups full of beer. People in the dense crowd below shouted up to them, and threw bead necklaces up to the women on the balconies. When one flushed girl in her twenties had collected an armful of necklaces, she hiked her shirt up to her neck. She wasn't wearing anything underneath it. The crowd erupted in cheers of joy. New Orleans was more wide open than Elizabeth had ever dreamed.

This part of the city resembled an undermaintained amusement park. Worn, broken pavement, cracking paint, wrought iron twisted like lace and painted in muted colors. Men held up signs that advertised psychic readings, draft beers for $1.00, or that the end was near. Walls sported unexpectedly bright colors, yellow, purple, moss green, Venetian red. Buildings proudly displayed brass or ceramic plaques describing their origins, name, function, and first owners often dating back two hundred years or more. London could take a cue from the Big Easy's excellence of labelling. World War II had been over for more than half a century, yet the city seemed still to be trying to misdirect invading Nazis.

There were others in the crowd besides tourists. Some, like the shills outside the restaurants and topless bars or the couples selling roses from pushcarts, were obviously workers, not unlike the mounted, uniformed police who sat at each intersection like watchtowers in the flow of humanity. More subtle were the gaudily-dressed individuals who strutted stylishly up and down the street, stopping occasionally to pose for pictures with the tourists in exchange for tips. Also workers, but self-employed, not salaried. Then, there were what could only be thought of as "locals," making their way through the crowds with bags of groceries or baskets of laundry, obviously running household errands even at this late hour. It was an interesting reminder that the French Quarter of New Orleans was a functioning community where people lived and worked, rather than a planned, constructed amusement park.

Even more noticeable to Elizabeth, however, was

that of this latter, non-tourist population, it seemed that at least two out of every three knew her escort.

"BOO-RAY! What's happenin', man?"

"Hey, Boo! Where y'at, bro?"

"Boo, darlin'! When you comin' by again?"

Every five or six steps, Boudreau was pausing to wave at someone or to exchange handshakes or greetings. Despite her impatience to be on their mission, Elizabeth could not help but be impressed with how well-known Beauray was, though she was a bit taken aback by the volume of the hailings . . . by both meanings. That is, they were not only numerous, they were loud!

People down here seemed to do all their conversing, not to mention their casual greetings, at the top of their lungs. If they happened to be across the street, on one of the everpresent wrought-iron balconies, or half a block away, it didn't really matter. They just reared back and shouted a little louder, neither minding nor caring that dozens of total strangers were forced to listen in to every word. It was completely different than anything in England, even in weekend street markets. Elizabeth put the fault down to the French influence that had founded New Orleans in the first place.

"Do you think we'll be able to find them?" Elizabeth said, making an effort to wrench Beauray's focus away from his friends and back onto her and their assignment.

"That depends. Do you happen to know if the folks we're lookin' for have eaten recently?" Beauray asked, leaning close to her so she could hear him over the street racket.

"Not really, no," Elizabeth said. "Why?"

"Well, it'll be rough findin' 'em if they've holed up in a restaurant somewheres," he said. "There're almost as many restaurants as bars in the Quarter, and it's hard to see into most of them from the street. If they're just wanderin' or stoppin' off once in a while for a drink, we should be able to find 'em with no problem."

"They seemed to have virtually ongoing food service in First Class, but that was hours ago," Elizabeth said. "I don't know what they had to eat up there, but the food in Economy Class was pretty ghastly. I ended up making do with a few candy bars, myself . . ."

Beauray halted in his tracks and cocked his head at her.

"Is that what's wrong?" he asked. "I must be goin' crazy, forgettin' my manners like that. Here I am draggin' you up and down the street, and all the while it never occurred to me to ask if you was hungry. I thought you were lookin' a mite peaked."

"I'm not really all that hungry," Elizabeth protested, embarrassed by the sudden attentiveness. "I don't think my stomach will catch up with me until tomorrow."

Beauray squinted at her, the blue laser beams boring into her eyes. "You sure?"

"I'm fine. Really," she insisted, though touched by his concern. "Tell you what. If it will make you feel better, I'll have another candy bar. They do sell them here, don't they?" she asked, playfully.

Beauray studied her for a moment, then shrugged.

"Well, as soon as your stomach catches up with you, you've got to promise to let me treat you to some of our fine N'Awlins cookin'. In the meantime, though, if it's a candy bar you want, I've got just the thing for you."

Taking her by the elbow, he steered her off the street and through the door of one of the numerous

T-shirt shops that prospered between the bars and dance clubs.

The icy blast of the shop's air conditioning was such a welcome relief from the saunalike streets that for a moment Elizabeth thought seriously of asking Beauray to continue the search alone while she waited here. A few breaths later, however, her sense of duty and her companion returned to her at the same time.

"Here. Try one of these."

He thrust a cellophane envelope into her hands, containing what looked for all the world like a light brown cow pat . . . from an unhealthy cow.

"What is it?" she asked, trying to keep the suspicion out of her voice.

"They're called pralines," he said. "It's a favorite candy in these parts. Go ahead and try it. They're good."

Unable to think of a graceful evasion, Elizabeth unwrapped his offering and took a cautious bite.

It was heaven!

Like most of her countrymen, Elizabeth had an incredible sweet tooth, and the candy she was now sampling was like nothing she had ever had before. It tasted almost like pure turbinado sugar, but with a smoother texture; like a very sweet toffee, but soft, and had a goodly dollop of chopped pecans mounded in the center.

"Are you sure you wouldn't like something more solid to eat?"

Beauray's voice brought her back to her senses, and she realized guiltily that she had wolfed down almost the entire praline in a very few bites.

"No. This is fine," she said hastily. "You're right. They're quite good."

Her companion frowned at her for a moment more, then shrugged.

"All right. If you say so," he said. "I surely do want to see you some time when you do have an appetite, though."

Elizabeth was inwardly writhing with embarrassment over her brief display of gluttony as they made their way back out onto the street. She was not, however, so uncomfortable as to fail to mark the location of the store in her mind. Before her stay in New Orleans was over, she planned to stock up on a few boxes of those pralines. Delicately, she licked her fingers, and smiled blithely at Beauray. Maybe they even had a mail order business so she could order more from England. A few of these would go a long way toward sweetening Ringwall's sour temper when she gave her expense report.

Music, music was everywhere in this city. Fee drifted from door to door, borne on an energy wave that carried her along the street without feeling its cobbles under her feet. The crowds were thick, but no one bumped into her. Fee found herself walking to the beat of the music pouring out of doorways, down from balconies, unexpectedly around corners from impromptu groups who had sat down wherever the muse had struck them, never paying attention to the people passing by. She might have been alone in this mob of people who were simply enjoying themselves.

She almost wished she was.

"Wait up," panted Robbie-cursed-Unterburger, striding to catch up with Fee and Lloyd on her short little legs. They'd almost lost her in the last crowd clustered around the entrance to a blues bar. They hadn't, more's the pity.

All of them were toddling along back there, her band, Green Fire, and her chief techies, but Fee resented Robbie most of all. She was so wet. The girl wanted to get close to Lloyd, and it killed her that she couldn't. You could see the pain and frustration in her eyes. Too bad. Lloyd belonged to Fee. Such a hunk, and so good when it counted. Like later on, if the music continued to turned her on as it was doing right now.

The blare of horns and pounding of drums and pianos pouring out of storefronts interrupted the eternal argument going on between the members of the band. They were always getting into it. You would never know that they were the best of friends, the way they sniped. It was as though Fee had three little brothers, though every one of the men was older than she. She was their leader, literally, figuratively and spiritually. She liked to think of herself as guiding them—although this was where she and Eddie disagreed the most. He could be so . . . Christian sometimes, positively pushing all the guilt buttons from her Church of England upbringing.

She let the sounds of New Orleans carry her along. This was so primevally strong, almost cavemanlike, smooth and rough at the same time, like the best whisky. The music filled her head. She scarcely felt the pavement under her feet. She breathed it in like the air, letting it take her where it willed.

"Let's go in somewhere," Fitzgibbon protested.

"No, Fitzy," Fee said, holding up her hand like an Indian scout. "Not until I find the right place."

"I want a drink," Voe said.

"You always want a drink," Eddie complained. He was *such* a Puritan, worse than Lizzie Mayfield. How very strange to have her appear out of nowhere. It was like old times having her around. How things had changed. Back then, they were earnest young women trying to earn degrees, and pretty good friends, really.

Now Fee was rich and famous, and Liz was—what, a spy? But they still had something in common: magic. Fee pouted. Not that Liz truly believed in the connection. Not yet. But she would.

"Come on, my feet hurt," Pat Jones, the publicist, complained, falling a few feet behind on the narrow pavement. Some of the others joined in the grumbling.

"Enough!" Michael ordered them, spinning around quick as a snake striking. "You know there's no hurrying her."

A long way off, a plaintive note rang in the hot, moist air. Fionna raised her head, like a hunting dog hearing the horn. She smiled at the faint sound. "That way," she said.

It may have been due to the sugar rush from the pralines, or just that she was starting to relax a bit in this new, strange environment, but soon after merging onto the street again, Elizabeth found herself seeing the Quarter in a whole new light. To be accurate, she found herself feeling it differently.

There was an energy here, a pulse of life that blended with the beat of the ever-present music, at the same time exciting and relaxing. Attuned to Earth Magic as she was, Elizabeth was startled to find herself involuntarily drawing power from the streets . . . something that she rarely if ever could do in a city. She had been prepared for New Orleans to be different, even frightening. This new aspect, however, took her completely by surprise.

"My grandma and your grandma . . . Sittin' by the fire . . ."

"Gotta cigarette, man?"

"Carriage rides! Right here, folks!"

Even the scattered fragments of music and street

pitches were taking on a different sound to her. Rather than sounding like random noise, they were like the fleeting bird calls in a heavily wooded area. True, they were still uncomfortably loud, but no longer the jarring, almost threatening cacophony it had seemed at first. She would have liked to relax and enjoy the experience, if not for the fact they still hadn't found Fionna.

"Either we've missed 'em, or they turned off somewhere," Boo said, coming to a sudden halt. "Let's double back and see if we can sniff out their trail."

Elizabeth realized they had reached the end of the brightly lit section of Bourbon Street. Beyond where they stood, the bars and shops gave way to shadowy private dwellings and dark storefronts. Definitely not an area she would choose to walk in alone at this time of night, and therefore a doubtful section in which to look for their wayward charges.

Nodding her agreement, she turned and let Beauray lead her back the way they had come.

He was still pausing occasionally to talk to people on the street, but now she was seeing more of a pattern to it. Some people who hailed them, he simply waved to without breaking stride. A few he would deviate from their path to approach by himself with greetings or questions. Only rarely in their stops would he introduce her to whomever he was speaking to, like the slender black man with a feathered cowboy hat and a carved, decorated walking staff, or the short, heavyset woman wearing a voluminous dress and long, braided hair. Amidst all the apparent freewheeling casualness of the Quarter, she could now see there was a closely defined pecking order. In many ways, the loud, raucous greetings masked a very subtle rendering of passing honors and acknowledgment of status. From what she could see, her companion was generally held in high regard in this colorful, close-knit community. With this awareness came a new resolve on her part to take closer note of those he made a point of introducing her to.

Close to the river, the mist swirling around their feet in the yellow lamplight, Fee heard the mellow strains of a fiddle and the plunk of a guitar swim up through the constant undercurrent of jazz pouring out of the storefronts. It was an omen. Irish music welcoming her to New Orleans. An *omen*. Fee was a great believer in portents. She turned right into a brick arcade. The flyers and maps on the cool walls definitely spoke of Fenian sympathies. Little pamphlets advertised talks by noted Irish philosophers and historians, as well as performances by Celtic musical groups.

Halfway between the entrance and a white fountain in a courtyard were two doors. To the left she saw a bar, with men in T-shirts watching a television set. It was from the right that the music was coming.

She pushed open the door just as the lights in the large room were coming up. A handsome, brown-haired man was sitting in the stage area with the guitar on his lap, singing in a warm tenor a song full of poignant longing. From the door, Fee joined in, lifting her high clear voice even over the amplified instruments of the rest of the players. The musicians stopped, surprised. The house lights came up, illuminating the bright green hair and black silk tunic blouse of the woman at the door. A murmur ran through the audience as they recognized her and the band.

"Mind if we sit in?" Fee asked.

"I think we've got 'em, now."

Beauray turned from a quick conversation with one of the corner hot dog vendors.

"According to Steve, here, they headed down Toulouse toward the river. Says he didn't see 'em stop at the Dungeon or Molly's, so I think I've got a pretty good idea of where they're goin'."

He gently took her elbow in his hand and steered her through the crowds on the sidewalk and down one of the side streets that crossed Bourbon.

It was remarkable. A scant half block off Bourbon, the whole makeup of the streets changed. Instead of crowds and music, bars and souvenir shops, the atmosphere was quiet nearly to the point of being meditative. There was only a light scattering of people, mostly walking slowly in couples or sitting on balconies talking in low tones. The streets were lined with clothing stores displaying handpainted fashions in the windows, small, comfortable-looking restaurants, and lots and lots of antique shops. Still, the energy she had felt on Bourbon was present, only mellower and more low-key.

She finally remarked on this to Beauray. "I'm surprised," she said. "I wouldn't have expected to find a creative power like this in such a famous tourist area."

"Oh, it's here, all right," Boo said, seeming pleased that she'd noticed. "It's my personal belief that a lotta folks are drawn here because of the spiritual energies, whether they know it or not. It's probably why we have so many writers and artists livin' here, not to mention all the musicians."

He gestured back the way they came.

"'Bout five or six blocks from here is Congo Square where Marie Leveau used to hold her big voodoo celebrations. Two blocks to our left is Jackson Square and the St. Michael's cathedral, that the pope visited back in the '80s when he was tourin' the U.S. And, of course, there's the river."

"The river?"

"The Mississippi River," Beauray said, with a smile. "The biggest in the U.S. It's about two blocks ahead of us now. If it were daytime, you could hear the calliope music from the paddle-wheelers playin'. I'll tell you, New Orleans is full of history and ghosts, but where I feel the energies most is standin' up on the Moonwalk there and watchin' the river roll by. That water has more history and energy in it than we can ever hope to imagine or draw on."

Their quiet conversation was interrupted by a group of noisy youths who rounded the corner heading toward Bourbon, laughing loudly and brandishing their plastic cups while supporting a comrade between them who appeared to be unconscious or grievously ill.

Elizabeth wrinkled her nose in distaste as she watched them pass.

"Doesn't that bother you?" she asked. "I'd think the people who live here would be outraged at the number of tourists who just come here to drink."

Beauray glanced back at the group as if seeing them for the first time.

"Naw. They're just havin' fun," he said. "You see, folks come here to have a good time. If they drink a little too much or sing their way down the street, it's no real problem, so long as they aren't hurtin' anyone. Besides, tourist dollars are what keep the Quarter green. If you think that's bad, you should see this place durin' Mardi Gras."

"If you say so," Elizabeth said. "I'm still surprised at how tolerant everyone seems to be."

Her companion threw back his head and laughed.

"Heck, the French Quarter has a history of nearly two hundred years of carousing, kept women, pirates and duels. It's a little late for us to start pointin' fingers, don't you think?"

Not knowing quite what to say to that, Elizabeth changed the subject.

"Where is it exactly we're going?" she asked.

"Well, knowin' the general direction they headed, I'm playin' a hunch," Boo said. "There's an Irish pub just up ahead called O'Flaherty's. It has live music . . . very ethnic—Celtic—and the entertainers are real friendly about invitin' other singers up on stage with 'em. I'm bettin' that if your crew is lookin' to have a drink, it's a natural place for them to stop."

Almost as if summoned by his words, the faint sound of guitar music reached them, followed closely by a ringing female voice raised in song.

"I think you're right," Elizabeth said, quickening her step. "That's Phoebe . . . I mean, Fionna's voice now. I'd recognize it any—"

She broke off suddenly and came to an abrupt halt as the lyrics of the song became clearer.

"*But my sons have sons . . .*"

"What is it?" Boo asked, peering at her carefully.

Elizabeth said nothing, but stood listening in frozen outrage until the last few lines of the song had finished, to be replaced by enthusiastic applause.

"Are you okay?" her companion pressed.

"It's nothing," she said finally, shaking her head. "It's just . . . that song. It's an old IRA song. Very seditious. It's called 'Four Green Fields,' and it talks about the Irish rebellion, essentially promising that it will never end. Considering how many people have died in Northern Ireland, both Irish and English, it's generally considered to be in poor taste and is seldom sung publicly. I'm surprised that it's something Fionna would sing."

Or, more accurately, that Phoebe would sing, she thought, but held her silence on that score.

"I guess we're a bit more liberal about our singin' over here," Beauray said, obviously uncomfortable. "I'm sorry if it upset you. If it makes you feel any better, folks sing songs about pert' near anything around here, includin' our own wars."

"As I was sittin' by the fire . . . Talkin' to O'Reilly's daughter . . ."

The music had started again, but this time it was a bouncy drinking song.

"It's nothing, really," Elizabeth said, forcing a smile. "Come on. Let's go in and join them."

As they sat at the bar in the back of the club keeping a leisurely eye on their charges at play, however, Elizabeth found it wasn't as easy as she hoped to shrug off the shock of hearing Phoebe Kendale singing that inflammatory song. How could people do that, she asked herself over and over again, dwell on bitterness and hurt? Peace was being negotiated in the province, to the delight and relief of both sides. Why constantly encourage people to vengeance and killing when the same energies could be channeled into healing and calming?

The warm energy she had been feeling while walking through the Quarter had fled. Instead, she felt cold and alone, despite the people at the tables and her companion sitting next to her. She tried to be glad that Fee was safe. Her old friend was very good at what she did. Funny how their lives had taken such different turnings. Fee's couldn't be more public, and Elizabeth's couldn't be more private, but there they were, joined together because of magic. She frowned.

"She's safe here," Boo said, only slightly misinterpreting her thoughts. "You don't have to worry about anything gettin' at her in here."

"I know," Elizabeth said distractedly. She pushed aside her feelings of discontent and concentrated on her job instead. The place *was* safe. How Fee had chosen it Liz couldn't say, but there was a measure of benevolent magic cast over the bar. They played fine music, and the drinks were good, too. The only disturbance present was what she had brought along with her.

Long after midnight, the group staggered out of O'Flaherty's and turned down Toulouse heading back toward the faint thread of music on Bourbon Street. Elizabeth had tried several times to beard Fionna/Phoebe, but the singer had been on stage with the musicians almost nonstop. On the way back to the hotel, Elizabeth tried getting her attention.

"Fee, listen to me," Elizabeth said. "You must stay put in the hotel in between rehearsals. It's for your own safety."

The other woman paid little attention. She was tripping along on air. Her performance had been a triumph. Another good omen for New Orleans. She was *so* glad she'd come.

"Fee!"

"It's Ms. Kenmare to you, Mata Hari," Lloyd said, nastily.

"She . . . she gave me permission to call her by her first name," Elizabeth said, keeping her promise to Phoebe in mind. Lloyd might have overheard their earlier conversation at the airport, but there was no reason to let all the city know Fee's secret. The streets were by no means empty even at that late hour. "Fee, you can't go walkabout in a strange place. What if something had happened?"

"Something did happen," Fionna/Phoebe said, seizing Lloyd's hand and swinging it like a child. "I was *great*! We were all great. I had a *wonderful* time. Didn't we, boys?" she called over her shoulder. No one answered her. Voe looked like he had a headache. Eddie grimaced disapprovingly, and Michael was above it all, striding along with a proprietary glance in each of the establishments they passed as though sizing them up for purchase. Elizabeth tried again.

"In future please let me know before you go out," she said, just as Fee swung into an enveloping embrace with Lloyd in the shadow of a barred doorway lit by neon. Elizabeth dodged around a man wheeling a double bass down the sidewalk to remain close to her. "I have to accompany you. I can't protect you if you persist in skipping out of the places I've checked. Things could have gone very badly back there."

Fionna and Lloyd snuggled together bonelessly into a single mass as though they were made of putty and started kissing. Elizabeth felt embarrassed interrupting. Fee wasn't listening anyhow. With a sigh, Elizabeth dropped back a few paces.

"Never mind," said Beauray. "You can't keep her in a glass case. We'll just have to keep a closer eye on her. That's why you have me."

That wasn't very much comfort. Mr. Ringwall would have expected a British agent to cover every eventuality personally. She was afraid she wasn't holding up her end very well, though she was glad to have Beauray around to help.

When at last she had seen her charge stowed away and the door warded with every seal at her disposal,

Boo-Boo escorted Elizabeth to the hotel restaurant for a well-deserved bedtime snack.

"C'mon," he said. "I know the night cook. It'll perk you up."

Over a soothing bowl of jambalaya and some intensely good coffee in the nearly empty dining room, they discussed amulets and the physical component of spells, things that were covered neither by promises to her grandmother nor the Official Secrets Act.

As Elizabeth had suspected, Boo's myriad pockets were full of little bits of this and that. They reminded her of her grandmother's living room cupboard with the hundred tiny drawers. As they talked, he produced thread, feathers, pens, chunks of rock, even a dried lizard. Most of it was just what it appeared to be, but various small packets, wrapped in hanks of dirty cloth or folded in worn envelopes, gave off an intriguing glow to eyes that could see it. In the spirit of hands across the water, Elizabeth turned out some of the contents of her handbag for his inspection, all personal goods, but kept back the government-issue spell components. She suspected Beauray was doing the same.

"Y'know, if we're goin' to be workin' together so closely, I think you ought to call me Boo-Boo," the American agent said, putting away a couple of anti-clumsiness amulets made of copper and white thread.

Elizabeth gulped coffee, feeling it revive her a little. "If you wish, Boo-Boo."

"And I'm goin' to call you Liz," he continued. When she looked at him sternly, he smiled. "Elizabeth takes too long to say, 'specially if we get ourselves in a jam."

"It's not the usual thing," Elizabeth began. She almost said that this was her first big field assignment, but bit back the words. She was supposed to be in charge of the operation, after all. He might not respect her as much if she admitted her inexperience. "This is an important mission for me. I can't just . . . loosen up."

"You're in N'Awlins now," Boo-Boo said, winningly. "You just about have to. Y'all ought to take it easy. Go on. It'll be easier than you think."

"Well, all right," she said dubiously, rolling the name around on her tongue. "Liz." But she liked it. She hadn't had a nickname since school. "Yes, why not?"

"That's the spirit," Boo-Boo said, leaning back in his chair. "I think we're goin' to get along just fine."

Elizabeth decided it was time that she set a few things straight. "So long as you understand that I am in charge of this mission. Fionna Kenmare's case was assigned to me."

Boo-Boo's eyes glinted their fierce laser-blue at her though his voice stayed mild. "I hate to correct a lady, but you don't have any jurisdiction here without my say-so."

"What? My government asked for your assistance, not to take over!" Liz heard her words echo against the far walls of the room and dropped her voice. "This is my case."

"Well, y'know, there's national sovereignty to consider," Boo-Boo said. "If it was happenin', say, in the British Embassy, that'd be one thing. But we're right here in my city. If y'all want to go home on the next plane it'll be tomorrow afternoon. 'Course, y'all will miss the concert, and that'd be just too bad." His blue eyes flashed with fire. Liz realized that he could make good on his threat. Mr. Ringwall would go apoplectic if she was sent home. She took a deep breath.

"I'm sorry, Mr. Boudreau," she said.

"It's Boo-Boo," he said, the lines of his thin face relaxing. "We shouldn't be fightin', Liz. We both want the same thing."

Yes, Liz thought. Control. "Yes, we do." The last word ended in a yawn. "Oh! I'm sorry." She found herself unable to stop yawning.

"I apologize. Y'all must be frazzled. Are we friends?" Boo-Boo asked, rising to help pull out her chair.

"Certainly," Liz said, rising with a smile for him. He was really quite nice. She'd fight the fight over dominance in the morning, when she had her wits about her once more.

Before dropping her off for the night, Boo produced one more surprise from his pocket.

"You're goin' to need this," he said, placing a cellular telephone the size of a pack of gum in her hand. "Courtesy of Uncle Sam. Yours prob'ly don't work here. You can call home on this, but mostly it's to keep in touch with me." He switched it on and showed her the controls. "My number's set on speed-dial one. G'night, ma'am."

Liz glanced at the clock on her nightstand and did some math. Still too early in London to call in her report. She got into her nightdress, clicked off the lamp, and slid into the blessed embrace of smooth, cool, clean sheets. Sleep ought to have overtaken her like a race car, but she found herself staring at the ceiling in the darkness. She groaned. She shouldn't have drunk that coffee, or she ought to have had a gallon more and just foregone sleep for the night.

Fee Kendale might have been a spoiled brat, but why would anyone seriously want to hurt her? The thought stayed with Liz all that night, and kept her from falling asleep, troubling her even more than the coffee did. What if magic *was* involved? When, in desperation to distract her brain, she turned on the room television, it was no help. Picking her way through the multitudinous channels available, she found herself watching a chat show where the host and the audience seemed more interested in taunting and shouting at the homosexual guests than in listening to what they had to say. When the host actually rose from his seat to punch one of his guests in the face, knocking him sprawling, she turned it off in disgust.

Hugging her pillow, she drifted off to a troubled sleep, haunted by images of shouting faces contorted in hate.

The dour-faced male announcer stared into the camera lens. "SATN-TV, 'The Voice of Reason in the Wilderness,' is now concluding its broadcast day. Thank you for watching. And now, the national anthem."

Over the familiar whine of the horns, the control room engineer, Ed Cielinski, began slamming tapes into the machines to cue up for the morning. The nighttime talk show looked like any one of three hundred others produced anywhere else in the country, but with one big difference. All the trappings were there, the host, the comfy chairs, the audience, but on stage there was also an altar in the shape of a pig. On its blood-red back was an upside-down pentacle, broken crosses and stars, a mangled crescent, plus black candles in holders. The aim of the show was to cause bloodthirsty controversy that almost always broke out in violence.

The police had finally dragged that night's combatants off the studio floor. A couple of them wanted to keep the fight going. The defender—designated

victim, if anyone had asked Ed for his opinion—
was being loaded onto a stretcher by paramedics
with his neck in a brace. The host of the live
broadcast, Nick Trenton, smug expression back firmly
in place, got up, wiped the blood off his chin and
straightened his tie. He strode out of the room. *All
in a day's work,* thought the engineer. Trenton would
never so much as glance backward at the problems
he caused. It was all good for the ratings, Ed
thought sourly.

Ed waited until the camera operators and lighting crew were gone, then turned out the spotlights.
The last one, at the rear of the stage, over the gigantic
enlargement of the rock group led by the lady with
green hair, faded slowly to black. *The next designated
victim,* Ed thought, not without a measure of sympathy. He slapped down the audio monitor switch as
his employer, Augustus Kingston, the owner and
station manager, walked into the room.

"Everything work okay?" he asked Cielinski.

"Yes, sir," said the engineer. "The frequency didn't
interfere with the picture a bit. Went out nice and
strong."

"How's reception on that special transmission line?"

"Nothing big. We haven't heard from our contact
out in New Orleans yet."

"That won't be for a day or two," the old man
said, rocking back on his heels in anticipation. "Let
'em get settled. Got to give it all a chance to build."
He pulled a cigar out of his pocket. The engineer
winced on behalf of his machines as his boss lit up
and blew a plume of cloyingly heavy smoke towards
the ceiling.

"Yes, sir, it's like casting your bread out on the
waters, Ed," he said, laughing heartily. "You get it all
back threefold. When we start casting that there bread

out there, we're going to collect plenty back again. Them godless, magic-loving pagans won't stand a chance, now, will they?"

The engineer gulped quietly to himself. "No, sir."

The old man stopped for a leisurely puff, and stared into the ember of his cigar with a pleased look on his creased face. "No. No, they won't. And the justice of it is, they'll do it to themselves."

Chapter 7

In the morning, Elizabeth waited with barely veiled impatience while Nigel Peters and Laura Manning went in to drag Fionna out of bed. Her old schoolmate had gone to sleep in her cosmetics, and the ruin of her mask made her look like the end of a horror picture. Boo-Boo appeared at the door in his ratty army coat, but he looked positively pristine compared with Fionna.

"Is she gonna make it?" Boo-Boo asked, with concern.

"With hydraulics or high explosives," Elizabeth said, stepping aside so he could see.

"Come on, ducks," Nigel said coaxingly, helping the makeup artist haul the somnolent singer back and forth from bathroom to bed, where they talked over her head as if she was a child. Fionna sat slack between them, her eyes half closed. "What do you think, Laura, the green sharkskin?"

"Hell, no, she'll sweat herself to death out there," Laura said, flipping through the hangers in the closet. "Have you stuck your nose out the door yet?"

"I'm dreading it," the manager admitted. "All right, the black gauze. It'll look great with your hair, Fionna, love. Lots of jewelry, now." He pointed at the box on the table.

"I'll get it," Elizabeth said, pleased to get her hands on Fionna's personal effects without anyone being the wiser. She turned over various necklaces and bracelets, trying each against the touchstone of her memory for protective characteristics. Not surprisingly, everything was a protective amulet of some kind. Fionna'd been doing a little reading up on her own. Again, not surprising, since as Phoebe she had taken a first-class degree. She understood research, and here was the fruit of it. Based on what was in the box Liz was beginning to feel that Fionna, at least, believed herself in real danger. Intuition was nothing Liz could put in her daily report to Mr. Ringwall, but it satisfied her that Fee was not merely crying wolf. Liz handed over several silver chains, all charmed for safety and peace, one at a time, and Laura arranged them around Fionna's neck. As for a colored piece to set it all off, a bulky carnelian necklace looked the best with the mystical outfit they were shoving Fionna into, but it was a fire magnet. Not the best omen, in Elizabeth's opinion, but it could channel outward as well as inward. She dropped a friendly cantrip of protection into the carved orange pendant just as the piece was snatched from her by Laura Manning.

"Just the thing, love," Nigel said as the necklace was fastened around Fionna's neck over the silver threads on the breast of the dull black tunic. He pulled her arm across his shoulder and stood, forcing her to her feet. She dangled loosely against him.

"All right, Fionna, up we get. We'll be meeting the public in twenty minutes."

The magic word "public" was just the kind of impetus Fionna needed. Elizabeth was amused to see the rag doll turned suddenly into a dynamic super-heroine on the short drive from the hotel to the broadcast facility. Patrick Jones and Lloyd Preston joined them in the limo. The hulking security man, dressed all in black like Frankenstein's monster, gave Elizabeth a slightly resentful look as he sat down beside Fionna in the rear of the car, but he didn't utter a word through the entire trip. Patrick sat close to Fionna on one side and drilled her on the upcom-ing interview while Laura sat on the other side and touched up the wild paint job on the star's face. Boo-Boo and Elizabeth sat jammed side by side at one end of the padded bench opposite the manager, who was sharing his seat with a box of equipment and tapes.

"You're meeting a woman called Verona Lambert," Patrick Jones said, reading out of a well-worn binder. "She's been at WBOY ten years, Fee. She's a real fan. I've got a sheaf of photos for you to sign for her and the crew. Be a good girl and do all of them, won't you?" He held out a large manila envelope.

"Right," Fionna said, holding her hand out. Patrick slapped a fine-point permanent marking pen in it. Fionna opened the envelope and slid out a stack of black-and-white enlargements of her clutching a microphone in taloned hands. The image of her face was a pale canvas for the dramatic makeup that brought out her eyes, lips and cheekbones in chia-roscuro. Liz nodded her head in approval. Just the kind of photo fans would love. Fionna signed her name through the bottom right corner of the photo over the back of the left hand and wrist, circling the capital F around a Claddagh hands-and-crowned-heart ring on the forefinger. "Verona Lambert. Have we got the other names?"

Patrick read them off from his list. Fionna personalized each picture in turn. Liz, reading them upside down, realized that Fionna was making each dedication a little different than the others. A real pro, she thought with surprise. She'd been judging too much by the appearance. Green Fire ran like a machine, and Fionna was truly part of it.

Elizabeth admired the staff. They were organized, genuinely concerned for Fionna's well-being, but very businesslike. Nigel had a cigarette for Fionna, but held it out of reach until she drank a repulsive, thick, pink shake he offered in his other hand.

"Brain food before you ruin your lungs, darling," he said, waving the glass under her nose. "Come on. You can't do an hour on an empty stomach. The cook in the Sonesta made it up just for you."

"Ugh, it's horrible," Fionna sputtered, after downing the shake in three or four gulps. She seized the cigarette, lit it from the flame Nigel held out to her, and drew smoke deep into her lungs. Liz scented fresh strawberry before it was drowned out by the stink of tobacco. "It's a sad thing when nicotine tastes better than something to eat. Thank God they let you smoke in this city. I thought it'd be another San Francisco." She blew a plume of smoke out of the corner of her mouth toward the ceiling. "Anything else I have to know, Pat?"

"That's all about the staff," said Patrick Jones, with his palms pressed together like an altar boy's. "Verona has the gen on the concert itself. All you have to do is talk about *you*. Now, remember, Fee, not a word about the attacks. They don't exist, right?"

Fionna took a deep breath, and clasped a hand

around the carnelian necklace and placed the other hand in Lloyd's. He clenched it possessively, and shot an expression of triumph toward Liz. She refused to react. Let him protect her on this plane. Liz's job was to deal with the Unseen, not the Seen. "Right. Let's go in there."

"So what brings you to N'Awlins, Ms. Kenmare?" Verona Lambert asked, her voice as smoky as the studio air. She was a chocolate-brown-skinned, plump woman with round cheeks, round eyes, and a huge pouf of straightened brown-black hair flattened over the top of her head by the earphone set she wore. The party was jammed into a small, dim room with pinholed acoustic tile on every surface but the floor. There were only three chairs, one for Verona, one beside her for Fionna, and one for the sallow-complected, thin, male producer/engineer who sat across the cluttered, beige console from them. Lloyd Preston inserted himself in between a couple of high consoles so he could stand next to Fionna. Occasionally she reached up to hold his hand. The rest of the party stood against the walls, not more than a couple of feet away. Square plastic cartridges stacked on a floor-to-ceiling rack jabbed Elizabeth in the back. The room was so close and hot she wondered if she might pass out. Her white, raw silk jacket was already sodden with sweat.

"Call me Fionna, me lovely. I think it's one of the finest places I've ever seen," Fionna said. Her accent made the word "foinest." She looked Verona straight in the eyes while she talked. If she wasn't sincere, she was one hell of a good actress. "Music's me life. I've got to love a place where it's on every street corner every night, where everybody plays or sings or listens to something every day. Music broadens your soul. I could click into this scene like I was born here."

"Do you find much in common here with your music?" Verona asked, with a lift of her brows. "N'Awlins is a kind of a mix of Acadian French style with Afro-Caribbean rhythms. Jazz is like nothing else in all the world, honey. I have all Green Fire's recordings, Fionna, and you'll forgive me for saying so, but they don't sound a thing alike to me."

"They all come from the same place," Fionna said, pounding her fist to her chest. "The heart. I've seen some people here, they've got nothing at all in all the world but their music. It's lovely. It's the same way I was as a child. I had nothing else, so I put my heart into the beauty I could hear."

That was rich, Elizabeth thought. For someone who'd gone through finishing school, Oxford University and at least fifty thousand pounds of Daddy's money, Fionna/Phoebe was very convincing as a North Dublin waif. She talked touchingly about her fictional childhood, her poverty, and the spirit that she felt that wouldn't let her stop until she could share her songs with the rest of the world.

The radio presenter took it all nonjudgmentally, though, and led Fionna through a good interview, bringing out interesting facets of her career and the founding of Green Fire. She'd certainly done her homework. At five minutes to the hour, Verona looked at Fionna confidingly.

"And now, I've got to ask you, darling, why all the magical themes in your music? Is it a sincere interest on your part, or just a little something you throw in to please the fans? Because, I warn you, N'Awlins is a very magical place. If you fool around with the spirits, they're goin' to gitcha."

"It's sincerely meant," Fionna said, her large eyes

wide with something akin to alarm. She certainly was very superstitious. Elizabeth thought her hands trembled. "I have a great respect for the powers that be."

"Wise words," said Verona, turning back to her console. "We've been talking to Fionna Kenmare. Remember, everyone, that's Green Fire at the Superdome at 7:30 on Saturday night. Hey, same time as the fireworks display over the river sponsored by WBOY. Tough choice, folks," she said, with a wry wink at Fionna. "Me, I'll be at the concert. I'll be back right after these words."

The engineer pointed to Verona, and hit a square button. Verona took off her headset. "Very nice, Ms. Kenmare. Thank you so very much for coming. I'm looking forward to the concert. Will any of us be able to sneak backstage and congratulate you afterwards?"

Fionna looked at Nigel Peters. "Should be, love," the manager said, noncommittally, shaking the announcer's hand and turning to the producer. "We'll see you're on the invitation list for the party to follow. Thanks for a good show."

Fionna rose and graciously offered Verona her hand. "Thanks, lovely. You made me feel very welcome. I hope the rest of the city's as warm as yourself."

"We're happy to see you, darling," Verona said, standing up and tossing her headset onto her desk. "And you!" She turned to Boo-Boo. "It's been a long time, you good-looking man. Where've you been?" She enveloped him in a huge hug.

"Oh, I've been around," Boo-Boo admitted.

"Do you know everyone in this city?" Elizabeth asked, with a wry grin, as they left the studio.

"Near abouts," said Boo-Boo.

Clinging to Lloyd, Fionna swirled ahead of them

in a cloud of gauzy black skirts, and looked plaintively over her shoulder at Nigel. "Can we get something to eat? I'm hollow."

Nigel looked at his watch. "Pat, Laura and I have got to get over to the Superdome, but there's no reason you can't find yourselves a meal, my dear. Perhaps Mr. Boudreau will oblige?"

"I'd be delighted to," Boo-Boo said graciously.

"You are supposed to be our native guide, aren't you?" Lloyd asked, striding along in Boo-Boo's wake after they'd left the limo at the curb near the Royal Sonesta. "So where can we get a bite to eat before we go over to the arena?"

Liz winced at the barely concealed sneer in Lloyd's voice, but Boo didn't seem to notice.

"There's a pretty good restaurant right in the hotel you're stayin' at. It would give the ladies a chance to freshen up before—"

"We're going to be living on hotel food through most of this tour," the security man interrupted. "I rather hoped you could do better than that."

"Well, we do have one or two pretty nice eatin' places here in the Quarter," Boo said with a shrug. "Let's see if I can't find somethin' that'll suit you."

He started off up the street with the others trailing along behind.

"Something a little different, I hope," Lloyd said, raising his voice to get in the last word. "Lord knows we have enough ordinary restaurants in England and Ireland."

"I think I know just the place," Boo called back over his shoulder.

"Not too far away, *I* hope," Liz said, stepping up beside him. "I still can't believe how hot it is down here."

In truth, she was having difficulty even thinking straight. Within half a dozen steps of their leaving the studio's air conditioning, she was drenched in sweat, and things seemed to weave and swim in the bright glare. It was like wearing a hot, wet, sweat suit in a steam bath . . . a very bright steam bath.

"Don't you worry none, darlin'," Boo reassured her. "We'll have you back inside in a jiffy. It's just around the corner up ahead."

"I feel I should apologize for Mr. Preston," Liz said, lowering her voice slightly. "He's being a bit of a prig. Not all of us are like that."

"We get people from all over down here." Boo smiled. "Both as visitors and them that settle down here. Near as I can tell, a certain percentage of people are light on manners, no matter where they come from."

In spite of her discomfort, Liz had to smile.

"I never thought of it that way, but you're right. I guess I just worry too much."

"No harm in worryin'," Boo said. "Just so long as it doesn't interfere with thinkin'."

Liz shot him a glance, but her partner's face was bland and guileless.

"That's it up ahead," he said, turning to the pair behind them. "It's new and folks say it's the latest thing. It's called Lucky Chang's."

He started to reach for the door, but Lloyd slid into the doorway ahead of him and barred their progress with his body.

"Okay, here's how it is," the security man said firmly, glaring down at them. "I know you're just trying to do your jobs, but the lady here would just as soon have a quiet meal without too many people hovering around her. She's going to have plenty of that once we reach the Superdome. Why don't you two find someplace else to have lunch, and we'll meet you back at the hotel."

"Now just a minute . . ." Liz began, but Boo laid a restraining hand on her arm.

"Works for me, he said. "You're sure you can find your way back to the hotel by yourselves?"

"Positive," Lloyd said, holding the door for Fionna. "If we get lost, we'll just take a cab."

"Okay. You two enjoy your meal now," Boo called, but the door was already shutting behind the pair.

"Well I never," Liz fumed. "I know we were just talking about manners, but that was rude no matter how you look at it."

"I'd have to say we're lookin' at it the same way, then," Boo said, taking her by the arm. "C'mon. Let's get you somethin' to eat. There's a place just across the street here I think you'll like."

Liz glanced at the white-fronted building Boo was steering her toward, then pulled up short as she caught sight of the sign.

"Antoine's?" she said. "I think I've heard of this place."

"It's been around for a while," Boo agreed, pointing at a sign that read SINCE 1840. New Orleans seemed to have the same gift of understatement as Scotland, where a "wee while" could be four hundred years.

"But isn't it kind of fancy?" Liz hesitated, glancing at Boo's somewhat bedraggled outfit.

"You forget, darlin'. The Quarter lives on tourist money. Not many places will turn business away just because they aren't dressed right."

With that, he led the way into the restaurant's cool interior.

Liz still felt slightly ill at ease as she surveyed the rows of tables with their spotless tablecloths and more than spotless waiters. It certainly looked like an upscale place.

"Boo-ray! What brings you out in the daylight?"

One of the waiters swept down on them, pumping Boo's hand vigorously with one hand while pounding him on the back with the other.

"Hey, Jimmy. Just showing the young lady here a bit of the Quarter," Boo said. "She wanted to see the most overrated restaurant we've got, so naturally I brought her here."

"I'm going to tell Pete you said that," the man said, hastily seating them at a window table. "You just sit here while I go tell him you're out here."

"Say, Jimmy. Before you do," Boo beckoned the man closer, "could you do me a little favor? Call Michelle across the street and tell her to give the couple that just came in special treatment. She can't miss them; the lady has bright green hair. Tell her particularly to pull the explanation sheet out of their menus."

Jimmy retreated, grinning.

"I take it you're known here," Liz said.

"I drop by once in a while," Boo said with a shrug. "Like I told you, most folks in the Quarter know each other."

"What was that bit with the 'special treatment' for Lloyd and Fionna?"

"Don't you want them to have a nice meal?" Boo's face was a picture of innocence.

"Don't be evasive, Boo," Liz insisted. "We're supposed to be working together, remember?"

"Well, I believe I mentioned that Lucky Chang's was different. Well, it's not the Chinese/Cajun menu that makes it different."

"Could you clarify that a bit? What is it about the place that requires an explanation sheet?"

"Mostly, it's the help. Did you get a look at them at all?"

"Just a glimpse, but they all seemed to be attractive young ladies."

"You're right. That's what they seem."

Liz frowned, then her face brightened with a mischievous smile.

"You mean . . ."

Boo nodded.

"That's right. The waitstaff may look female. In actuality, though, they're some of the most practiced cross-dressers and drag queens in the Quarter. I think it could get downright interestin' if your friend Lloyd makes an after-hours date with one of 'em."

They were still sharing the laugh when a black-haired cook dressed in a crisp, white apron emerged from the swinging doors and approached their table.

"Hey, Boo! Where y'at?"

"Pete, how many times have I got to tell you that you'll never get that 'yat' accent down well enough to convince anyone?"

He quickly introduced Liz, who was still chortling.

"So, what can I get you folks to eat?"

"Actually, we haven't seen a menu yet."

"Shucks, Liz," Boo put in. "Just tell Pete here what you feel like eatin', and if he can't cobble it together in that kitchen of his, he'll just order out for it."

Suddenly the tensions of the morning slid away from Liz, and she realized she was ravenously hungry.

"You know," she said, "I think what I'd really like is some of the hot Cajun cooking I keep hearing about."

"Darlin', Gen do that for you in a flash," Pete said, charmingly. "How does a bowl of gumbo sound?"

"Make that two," Boo said. "And be sure to make mine extra-extra spicy."

"Mine too!" Liz nodded. "Extra-extra!"

"Are you sure you want to do that?" Boo asked as the cook disappeared into his realm. "I though you British liked your food kinda bland."

"Don't believe everything you hear," Liz said with a smile. "Haven't you ever heard of the English Raj? We *invented* vindaloo curries. I believe there's more Indian restaurants than Continental in London today. And lately Thai food has been all the rage in England. We adore hot spices."

"Well, all right, ma'am."

True to her word, when the food arrived, she proclaimed it delicious and finished every drop, though in actuality she found it a little disappointing. There wasn't enough spice in the mix to raise a sweat. Still, she felt it would have hurt the cook's feelings to complain or add seasoning, as he had hovered over their table anxiously through the whole meal. Both he and Boo watched her as though they expected her to burst into flames. They looked almost sorry that she didn't seem discomfited. It would have been rude if she hadn't reacted, so she fanned her face with her hand.

"Oh, my," she said, echoing one of her elderly aunts who, it would have astonished both men to know, had lived in India with her army officer husband, and had come home from her years abroad with a book of curry recipes and a trunkful of chilies. Both men relaxed, satisfied, and Liz, with a secret smile, finished her lunch.

Walking back to the hotel, she found herself in a surprisingly pleasant mood. Lunch, with the jokes and the prank on Lloyd, had left her feeling well-fed and relaxed. Even the heat didn't seem as oppressive now. She mentioned as much to Boo, and enjoyed watching his ready laugh.

"It's the Big Easy," he said as he held the door into the hotel lobby. "That's why they call it 'the city that care forgot.' Once you get into the pace of things down here, you can just kind of float along and believe that whatever happens, it will all be all right."

"Speaking of that, " Liz said, looking around, "didn't Lloyd say they were going to meet us here after lunch?"

Boo-Boo shrugged. "Well, 'after lunch' isn't really a precise time down here. Hang on a second and I'll check with the desk to see if they left a message."

Despite the fact that she had just eaten, Liz found herself idly studying the posted menu for the hotel restaurant as she waited. It was extensive and delightfully varied. She guessed that Boo was right. Eating really *was* a major pastime down here, and the more you got into the pace of things . . .

"Sorry, darlin', but we've got problems," Boo declared, materializing at her elbow. "We've got to get over to the Superdome fast."

He had her out the front door and into a taxi before she could collect her wits.

"What is it?" she asked, following in his wake. "Was there a message?"

"They didn't bother to leave one for us," Boo said grimly, "but the desk clerk remembered the message that came in for Lloyd and Fionna. It seems that one of Fionna's costumes burst into flames. This time it was on stage in front of half the crew and the band."

Chapter 8

Liz and Boo pushed their way into the mob of people crowding the barrier set up by the firefighters across the rear entrance to the Superdome. Three fire trucks, surrounded by miles of unreeled hose, flashed their revolving lights weakly in the oppressive New Orleans sunshine. An equal number of chunky white vans bearing parabolic dishes on top announced the arrival of the media. Reporters were clustered to one side by a police officer, but it was clear the cordon wouldn't last long.

Liz and Boo showed their backstage passes to the sweating security guard at the door. Very reluctantly, he let them crawl underneath the barrier, while shouldering aside a couple of rabid fans with cameras who tried to follow. After the press of the crowd, the soaring, concrete room seemed cavernously empty, all the better to pick up the noises coming from far down the passage. The roar of voices behind them grew louder. Liz spun on her heel.

"Oh, no," Liz groaned, as the media came jogging

toward the entrance, turning the cameras their way. "We don't need this."

"Cheer up," Boo said, waving to the reporters over the security guards' heads. "You can tell your mama you were on American television."

"My super told me not to attract any attention!" Liz said.

"He's not here; how will he know?"

"They have cameras!" Liz said. "Our images will be on the evening news all around the world . . . never mind."

Boo seemed utterly unconcerned about security. He was even enjoying the attentions of the press. He waved to an attractive, blonde woman holding out a microphone. She shouted something at him, but he held his hand behind his ear, pretending he couldn't hear her. With a sigh Liz reached into her pocket for the strands of yarn she carried there, and twisted them together. The cantrip should fuzz her image sufficiently so it would be difficult to identify her. Ringwall still wouldn't be happy, but at least the damage was under control. Now to see what had caused all the to-do. She grabbed Boo's arm to turn him.

The steel-and-glass doors were pinned wide by dumpsters rolled up from the nearby loading dock. Boo hopped over lengths of hose flung everywhere in the corridor. Liz followed him, wishing she had worn lower-heeled shoes. A couple of people hung out of the dressing room doors, gawking at the two agents as they ran by. Everyone was yelling over the alarms, sirens, and crackling radios.

"Where'd it happen?" Liz called to Boo. He skipped nimbly over a twisting section of hose fifty feet ahead of her. Watching him, she stumbled on the same length and cursed her high-heeled shoes.

"Just follow the trail, I'd say," Boo said, stopping to wait for her. He grabbed her arm, and pointed ahead toward the double stage doors, braced open with crates. Half a dozen firefighters in yellow rubber coats, shouting to each other, rushed past them with extinguishers and axes. The two agents ran to catch up.

When she reached the stage, Liz stopped beside Boo to stare.

"What happened?" she asked. "With all the equipment they've brought in I thought the entire Superdome was coming down!"

After the round-shouldered cramping of the hotel and the restaurant in the Quarter, the chamber before Liz was vast. It engulfed the forty people on the raised stage at its heart like gnats in a multicolored bathtub. Yellow-skinned insects dragged long strands of hose behind them here and there through glistening puddles and heaps of overturned equipment. A bright yellow fire engine a third the size of the ones on the street sat beside the stage, its emergency lights rotating while men in coats and boots scrambled all over it. At the center of all the hubbub stood a single, tiny, forlorn, dripping figure. Two of the firefighters dragged a still writhing hose away from him. It was Thomas Fitzgibbon, the costumer, drenched to the skin. He saw the two agents and waved a hand weakly toward them, dribbling a stream of water from his sleeve.

"I can't explain it," the costumer said, when they reached him. He moved locks of his curly hair out of his eyes, and plucked at his wet shirt. He looked close to tears as he held out a scorched wisp of green cloth. "I brought Fee's dress out here on stage to see how it looked under the lights. The sleeves are gauze, like dragonfly wings. They would be so beautiful.

Then suddenly, poof! Flames everywhere! It happened so quickly I didn't have time to move. I thought I'd be burned to death." The thin man's eyes were huge with fear, but he appeared to be uninjured. "And then someone pulled the fire alarm."

"Was anyone hurt?" Boo asked, pulling a handkerchief out of his pocket and offering it to the man. Fitzgibbon looked at the grimy square and shuddered.

"No, but the dress is ruined. I can't stand it." He turned woefully to face Patrick Jones, the publicist, who was jogging toward them up the main aisle of the theater. Fionna, dogged by a grim Preston, strode behind him. Jones started to speak, but Preston pushed by him and shook a fist in Liz's face.

"What I want to know is, you think you call this taking care of the problem?"

"Shush, Lloyd," said Jones, patiently. "Can anyone tell us what happened? You, sir?" He snagged the arm of a passing firefighter, dressed in rubber coat and boots. "Are we in any more danger? Can we stay here?"

"The fire seemed to be localized right here," the man said. His dark-skinned face gleamed with sweat, and Liz empathized with him for having to wear a heavy costume like that in the middle of the hellish heat of the city, let alone a conflagration. "We're examining the rest of the scene right now."

"Well, can't you speed it up?" Jones asked. He looked peeved, but was trying to remain reasonable. "We've got a show to do."

"Sorry, sir. These things have got to be done in the right order," the firefighter said, patiently. "You don't want hot spots to break out. Burn the place right down."

"Oh, marvelous," Jones said, throwing his hands in the air. The fireman walked in an ever-increasing circle around the center of the stage, studying the floor, and occasionally stooping to touch the wooden boards. Jones watched him go with an expression of worry. Liz felt sorry for him. This would be a very public public-relations nightmare.

Other firefighters searched around in the outer reaches of the Superdome, clambering up into the tiers of multicolored seats. Liz spotted the ant-sized figures in their yellow protective gear, and marveled at how large the arena was. Without figures to compare for scale, it seemed no larger than a circus tent, but it was fully as big as a football stadium. Which, she recalled wryly, it was.

A few of the band members and some of the security staff were following the firefighters around, asking questions. The rest were frozen in a huddle on one side of the stage, staring at the sodden costumer.

Liz surveyed the scene, puzzled by the lack of evidence. When the accident, or attack, or whatever it was had occurred, there had been a blast of some kind. Fitzgibbon stood in the center of a ring of ash. It was marked by footprints of every size, left by firefighters, the members of the band, and now her and Boo. The pattern radiated outward from the costume itself in a complete circle, interrupted only where the costumer's body had blocked the burst. But it must have been a remarkably mild explosion. Fitzgibbon was unhurt, though badly frightened, and she couldn't say she blamed him.

"Who was near you when it caught fire?" Liz asked.

"No one!" Fitzgibbon exclaimed. He was still clutching the soggy remains of the dress. "I was standing here, holding up the gown for the lights. Robbie can back me up on that. Can't you, sweetheart?" he called to the special effects coordinator,

who was sitting on a folding chair at the stage rim
with her hands and knees together and ankles apart
like a little girl.

The special effects coordinator nodded her head
solemnly. She looked puzzled and worried.

"Take me through it," Liz said briskly to Fitzgibbon.
"Just what happened?"

The costumer threw up his hands. "Nothing! I
came out of the dressing room with the green number
for the ballad at the end of the first set. The crew
can tell you. Some of the spotlights were moving up
and down, and I saw some laser lights flashing.
Fionna's key light was pointed down onto the center of the stage. I went into the beam to see how
her costume would look. That's all. Then, *whoosh!*
Look at it! Those perfect, filmy sleeves, reduced to
ashes. I don't want everyone blaming me. I didn't do
anything!" His eyes filled with tears. "It was supposed
to match her hair."

"Now, now," Boo-Boo said soothingly, patting the
costumer on the back. "No one's callin' you names.
Could anyone have booby-trapped that dress?"

Fitzgibbon looked indignant. "Certainly not. I had
just finished tacking the hem. I had the whole thing
inside out on my cutting table. If there had been
any . . . infernal devices, I would have seen them.
There was nothing there!"

"I told you all this was real," Fionna spat, striding up with Nigel Peters trotting behind her. She
glared at the publicist. "Now do you fokkin' believe
me?" Jones held up his hands to fend off her fury.
"Things like this have been goin' on again and again.
I'm at me wits' end!" Fionna turned to Liz and Boo-
Boo. "Yer supposed to prevent this, right? Why didn't
yer fancy machines tell you this was happenin'? Didn't
you bug everythin' I own in the world?"

Liz marveled that Fionna's accent stayed intact even under stress. "You weren't injured, Fee—Fionna," she said, stumbling deliberately over the name. The look of suspicion in her old schoolmate's eyes verified that there would be no more hysterics, or Liz might let her secret out.

"This dress didn't exist until an hour ago, sweetheart," Peters said, soothingly. "Fitzy's only just finished it."

"I haven't even been here yet, and they're already trying to kill me!" Fionna shrilled. "And you've done nothing!"

"We couldn't prevent an attack until we knew where it was coming from," Liz said, looking at Boo-Boo for support. The American was on his knees, scooping ashes from the floor into his hand.

"And where is it coming from?" Fionna demanded.

"It's coming from . . . *beyond*," the costumer said, clutching himself. His eyes were wide with horror. "Oh, my God, what if all the green silk is cursed? Couldn't we, you know, call in a priest to bless it and make it benign? Otherwise, I refuse to work with it. Heaven knows what it'll do to my sewing machines."

"Will you calm down?" Peters snapped. "The fabric is not cursed. There's a perfectly sane explanation for what just happened. Right, Liz?"

"What are these things?" Boo-Boo asked, standing up with wires trailing from his hand.

"They're from the LEDs. They were arranged in mystical symbols sewn into the cloth. They light up on stage. There's no power source, though," the costumer said, suddenly looking worried. "We hook Fionna up with a battery pack before she goes on."

"We've done it a thousand times," Fionna said, her eyes wild. "There's no earthly reason why the dress should have gone up in flames. Someone's trying to

kill me!" She turned and, finding herself in Lloyd
Preston's arms, allowed herself to shiver. Robbie
Unterburger glared at her from the sidelines.

"Could the dress have been exposed to any flam-
mable substances? Or high temperatures?" Liz asked.
"Could the spotlight have set it off?"

"We're in that spotlight now," Robbie said, pointing
upward. Liz stared up into the blinding glare. It
focused into a single point, far in the back of the
amphitheater. "It's no more harsh than strong sunshine."

"It don't look like these two busybodies can do a
thing," Preston said, hulking over them all as usual.
Liz turned a high-power glare towards him, then
dismissed him. "I'll look this place over myself.
Fionna's security is my business." He stalked off to
confront one of the firefighters.

"What about those laser lights?" Boo-Boo asked.
"Could that ignite the fabric?"

"You couldn't even light a cigarette with them,"
Robbie said, scornfully. "There's stronger lasers in a
food store checkout. Besides, the laser never touched
this stage. I was testing it on the far wall."

"All right," Liz said. "I'd like to talk to everyone
who was here when it happened. One at a time,
please." She turned to the publicist, who looked as
if his ulcer was kicking up again. "Can we use one
of the dressing rooms?"

Everyone protested at once. "We've got work to
do, lady!" Robbie Unterburger said. "Tomorrow's the
show!"

"That's enough," Nigel Peters said, wearily. "There'll
be no show if there's any danger to Fionna, so we
have to let these people ask their questions, right?
A little cooperation, please? God, I could murder a
cup of tea."

"Could you make us all some tea?" Liz asked the costumer. "It'll give you a chance to calm down."

"I'm a highly paid professional, with respect throughout the entire music industry," Fitzgibbon protested, head high, but Liz thought he looked grateful for something ordinary to do. He threw up his hands. "All right. Tea."

"I'd rather have a whisky," Fionna said, crossly.

"You had four drinks at lunch," Liz said.

"Well, I need one now! And how the hell did you know that? Have you got a bug on me now?" Fionna demanded.

"She's already got one up her . . ." Robbie muttered to one of the other stagehands. Fionna couldn't hear her, but Liz could. Tactfully, she pretended she hadn't. She didn't want to revisit the matter anyhow. Fee would have had furious hysterics all over again if Liz had explained the psychic monitor she'd planted on her for security.

"Come on, sweetheart," Laura Manning, the makeup artist, said, putting an arm around Fionna's narrow shoulders and leading her away. "I've got a bottle in your dressing room. We can wait for the tea there." She glanced back at the two investigators. "That's where you'll find me. I've got things to arrange for tomorrow."

"We all have," Michael Scott complained, his blue eyes flashing with indignation. The other members of the band added their voices to his.

"This won't take but a short time," Boo-Boo promised him. "We just want to know where everybody was when the dress went up. We don't even have to go down to a dressing room. We can talk right here."

Eddie Vincent frowned. "I don't like this. You're accusing us? Us? We've been with Fionna for yonks, mate." He planted a finger in Boo-Boo's chest and poked it a few times for emphasis. "Now, she may not be the world's easiest broad to live with, but we back her up in more ways than one. Got it?"

"Everybody's gettin' so bothered," Boo-Boo said mildly, but Liz saw the glints in his eyes. He walked back to the instrument setup. Almost involuntarily, half the crowd of roadies and musicians followed him. He stopped beside the open square of keyboards. "You was here when Fitz came out? Rehearsing?"

"No, I was dancing on the ceiling with Fred Astaire," Eddie said, sneering. "'Course I was. Len saw me."

"Yeah," Len, one of the lighting crew, stepped forward. "I was fixing everyone's key lights."

"Good!" Boo-Boo beamed. "See how easy this is?"

Liz admired the way his easygoing manner helped to soothe the ruffled feathers of Fionna's entourage. After a surprisingly short time, their voices softened. Several people began to add their accounts, interrupting each other, helping to reconstruct the moment of the attack now nearly two hours past. Boo caught Liz's eye over the shoulders of the others, and she nodded back, understanding him. While he was charming everyone, Liz sauntered casually over to the keyboard setup, and sent a tiny tendril of Earth power through the floor where Eddie Vincent must have been standing.

Everyone's backs were turned when the glitter came to life on the dusty boards, showing pairs of footsteps overlaid on one another again and again, when Vincent was playing, turning from electric piano to organ to multi-synthesizer and back again. It looked like some bizarre Arthur Murray quick-step pattern. The air around them was empty of even a single spark of magic. Whatever had happened, the musician was innocent of the attack. Liz had just enough time to wipe the glamour away when Vincent broke out of the pack and came over to see what she was doing.

"Quite some instruments," she said, idly. She started to run a finger along the top of the synthesizer console. He reached over to slap her wrist. She snatched her hand away, staring at him in astonishment.

"Never touch my stuff again," he said, flatly. He aimed a finger at her nose. "Never handle anyone's instruments, do you hear? Anybody could tell you've never been within a mile of a band."

"Why would I need to?" Liz asked sweetly. "Anybody could hear you playing from a mile away. I'd never need a ticket." She was surprised at herself. Being peevish was not what the office expected of its agents. She ought to be acting like an adult in this crisis. "I'm sorry," she said. "We're all under a bit of a strain."

Vincent grunted wordlessly. Apology accepted. Liz turned and walked back to join Boo-Boo, who was standing with Voe Lockney. The drummer was explaining his drum set with enthusiasm, picking out rhythms with quick dabs of brush and stick.

"Anything?" Boo-Boo asked her out of the side of his mouth.

"Not a thing," she said.

"Do me now," Michael Scott said, coming over to loom over them. He was the tallest of the band members, and his blue eyes burned into Liz's like Green Fire's lasers. "I've plenty to get on with."

For a moment Liz was reduced to a quivering blob of adoring teenage fan. Here was the Guitarchangel, close enough to touch, and twice as handsome as any photo she had ever seen. Those sharp cheekbones, and that long, black hair! But her Departmental training shoved the adolescent firmly into a mental cupboard and locked the door.

"We are sorry for the inconvenience," she said, briskly.

"You sound like a sign on the London Underground," Scott said, the corner of his mouth twitching. Could that be the hint of a smile? "Get on with it. I was playing at that edge of the stage." He pointed. Liz and Boo turned to look. Liz noticed the blast pattern, much attenuated. It outlined a semicircle in ash where the guitarist had been standing when the dress went up. "I didn't see the fire start. I had my back to the center. I was starting my solo."

"Right," said Jones, joining in. "The lights are down at first. Fee comes on in the darkness. Her dress starts flashing the symbols, then all lights come up at once. The musicians whirl around to see her. The spotlights start wigwagging across the stage. Lasers! Smoke! It's smashing. You'll love it at the concert."

A brass fire hose nozzle slid noisily behind his feet, and Jones jumped.

"If we ever get to the damned concert," Robbie Unterburger complained.

Green Fire's dressing rooms were under the stage beyond a security door that was held ajar with a rubber wedge. Nearby was a reception room that must be used for parties and interviews. At the moment it was full of equipment in and out of battered, black travel cases. Most of the gear was unfamiliar to Liz. She assumed a good deal of it was special-effects equipment, under the direction of Roberta Unterburger. An angry young woman, that. Every time Fee reached out for Lloyd Preston, Robbie flared up as if she could light the show without benefit of laser beams. Liz was sorry for her.

Unrequited love might have been nice in poetry, but it was hell in practice. She wondered why the woman didn't quit her job, if she couldn't stand the realities of the situation. Then she thought about it—who wouldn't want to work for a world-famous rock band, no matter how hard it was on your heart? On Robbie's side, though, Kenneth Lewis kept staring at her the same way she did at Preston. He watched her when he thought she couldn't see, and turned his head away when she glanced his way. There was a neat little triangle going on, or quadrangle. All it needed was Fionna having unreturned feelings for Kenneth to really make a mess of the situation.

Fionna's dressing room was the largest and best appointed. The concrete floor had been carpeted over with a rich green plush, a compliment to her band and her hair. Instead of the acid fluorescent lights, she had floor lamps with restful low-watt bulbs. The singer herself was enthroned in a big armchair with Laura Manning on one side and Nigel Peters on the other offering her drinks and cigarettes. Someone had unpacked Fionna's possessions and arranged them around the room. Costumes of garish silks or black lace and tulle hung along the walls. The lighted mirror in the wall over the dressing table was supplemented by a double-ended magnifying mirror and a folding mirror, plus enough amulets arrayed along the rear of the table to open a shop. A couple of them did have the sniff of magic about them. They glowed feebly, to Liz's experienced eye, like a child's nightlights.

Enjoying an audience with Her Majesty was a plump man with a dapper summer-weight jacket slung over his shoulder by one finger.

"And there you are at last!" Fionna carolled. Her voice was a relaxed trill. The promised whiskey had obviously met a few friends on its way down her throat. "Meet Mr. Winslow. He's a true darling."

"Building management, ma'am, er . . . sir," the man in the white suit said, turning to offer a hand. "When I heard about this . . . regrettable accident I just had to come down and offer my support. Are you . . . with the show?" he asked, looking Boo-Boo's attire up and down.

"No, sir," Boo said. "I'm with the Department." He patted down several of his tattered pockets and came up with a shiny leather billfold. He flipped it open. "My credentials, sir."

Winslow's eyes widened as he examined the card and badge. "I see. I'm glad to see Miss Fionna has some . . . strong protectors. The fire marshall is upstairs now. They had to break in through the front doors, which will be replaced this afternoon, Mr. Peters," Winslow added, turning an eye to look over his shoulder.

"I'm glad to hear it," Peters said. "My people will offer every cooperation."

"Was there anyone strange in the building when the dress caught fire?" Boo-Boo asked the manager.

"God only knows. This place is the size of a palace, but everything was locked up. The rear doors were locked from the outside only. We had a grip stationed there to let our people in, but no one else. I suppose someone could have slipped in, and planted a booby trap."

"Which your Mr. Fitzgibbon . . . didn't see," Winslow pointed out. Peters looked disconcerted.

"Er, yes."

"I don't think it's too likely that what caused the trouble was in the dress itself," Boo-Boo said.

"It came from a distance, then?" Peters asked, uncomfortable. "Something was shot at him?" Fionna sat bolt upright in her chair with her lips pressed together. Liz wondered what Boo was thinking, but he gestured to her not to speak. He looked amiably at the building manager.

"Well, no. All that flash powder hovering in the air, and those laser lights, there *could* have been a little accident."

"Good!" Winslow exclaimed, then looked guilty. "That's good, isn't it?"

"Well, apart from Mr. Fitzgibbon having to make another dress."

Laura Manning waved the idea away. "Oh, don't worry about Tommy. He's probably in there at this moment inventing a new confection in silk and lace. He lives to suffer. Ask him. Why, he's even accused me of ruining his dresses with my nasty foundations and rouges. Greasepaint isn't up in that lofty sphere with *haute couture.*"

"Excuse me, Mr. Winslow?" A man in firefighter's rig with a clipboard appeared at the door. "Fire marshall. Everything seems to be under control. The building's all right. The crews are withdrawing. You've got a mess up there, Mr. Winslow. Sorry about that, sir."

Winslow was gracious. "You're doing your very worthy job, Marshall. My thanks. My maintenance people . . . will already be on the job, Miss Fionna." He offered her a courtly little bow.

In sharp contrast to the courtesy of the building manager, Lloyd Preston pushed his way in, a scowl on his face. He stood over Fionna, who reached out a thin and, Liz thought, dramatically trembling hand to him. "Everything's okay. We can get right back to work."

"But," Liz began to protest. Everyone in the room turned to look at her.

"But what?" Lloyd demanded. Fionna sat bolt upright in her armchair, ready to flee the scene at the sound of a threat.

"But," Boo said loudly, drowning her out, "we'll be keeping an eye on things." He nodded knowingly to Fionna, who shot them a look of relief. "We'll get right on it." He took Liz's arm and hustled her out of the dressing room.

Chapter 9

Liz pulled Boo to a halt just outside the door.

"What was all that about?" she demanded, in a fierce whisper. "Don't you want to keep the place under lock and key until we can have a thorough look around? This place is the size of a city!"

"There's no time," Boo said. "We don't want them cancelling the concert, which they will if they think there's some kind of assassin out there."

"There may *be* an assassin out there!"

"I know," Boo said, apologetically, "but it's the concert itself that'll bring him out in the open. If y'all whisk Miss Fionna away to the next stop on the tour, or cancel it altogether, it'll just start over again, and we'll never get a handle on it."

"No," Liz said, thinking hard. She hated to admit it, but he was right. "That's true. Very well, then. We'll need to question the grip if he let anyone in he shouldn't have. Someone carrying a device or the wherewithal to cause that kind of long-distance conflagration." Boo shook his head.

"We don't have to do that. He's clear. Of anyone toting magic, anyhow."

Liz gawked. "How do you know that? We didn't speak to him."

"Oh, well, there wasn't a sniff of magic in that whole corridor when we came in," Boo explained.

Enlightenment dawned as Liz recalled Boo's antics at the entrance to the Superdome. "Ah! So that was the meaning of that whole performance for the TV cameras. You were taking a reading."

"And settin' a detector," Boo said, with satisfaction. "Are you familiar with the Acardian Gate theory?" Liz nodded, wondering if he meant the original theory, or the update that had come down from the research boffins in the last six months. "Well, now, let's take a look at the rest of the Superdome. I want to see where they stove in the front doors, before they clean it up."

Now that Boo-Boo was out of sight of the others, Liz could tell he was impatient to get back to the arena. Liz made him wait before they went upstairs so she could set a protective cantrip over Fionna's dressing room. Not knowing where the attack might be coming from, if there was to be an attack, she drew power from the air around her and laid a spell on the door. As she gathered up the ball of energy, she could feel the tension permeating the Superdome. She disliked making personal magic in an unwarded space, but the cantrip itself was comforting, like a warm cat curled on one's lap. As old as time, the little spell couldn't stop anyone physically, but it would repel anyone of malign intent. It was layered with a fillip of her own invention that would alert her like a siren if something went wrong. She tied a knot in the energy and let it go, feeling it twang against the dressing room door. She hoped Fee wouldn't stir from there until she got back from their perimeter walk of the building.

Boo took Liz's arm and hurried her up the long ramps and escalators to the stadium level.

The fire department was withdrawing its equipment. The hoses which lay everywhere slithered underfoot as they were being rolled up. Liz saw Hugh Banks, the stage manager, trip over a coil that snaked around his foot. He got up, swearing, and went back to dressing down some of the stagehands.

Microphones were being brandished under the noses of the band members still on stage.

"Looks like a few of the reporters sneaked in," Boo said easily. "Can't blame 'em. Probably used police department credentials to get past the door."

"We need to get them out," Liz said, feeling frustrated that she couldn't manifest a huge broom and sweep them all towards the exit. "They couldn't have been here when the fire occurred, but we do not want them in the way."

It was time for Boo to look startled. "Why are you so sure none of them could be responsible?"

Liz tried not to look superior. "They'd have had to hide for hours. Can you imagine any of them waiting patiently in the wings before pouncing on their prey? Look at them!" The reporters were doing a fair impression of sharks shoving their way into a netful of bleeding tuna parts.

"They do kinda have that Christmas mornin' wrapper-tearin' thing goin' on," Boo said, with a grin.

Just in case Liz had misjudged one of them, the two agents did a quick walk-by of as many of the reporters as they could. None of them paid either Liz or Boo more than a cursory glance to make sure they weren't famous. Liz did a light magical frisking on them. None was imbued with more than a good luck charm's worth of magic, though there were many such charms, amulets and mascots tucked away in purses, pockets, and backpacks. Liz had never seen so much superstitious paraphernalia outside of the Avebury Stone Circle gift shop. New Orleans was steeped in awareness of the supernatural. What a place for Fionna to have planted herself! If there was a malign magical presence it might well be camouflaged by the locals.

Green Fire was living up to its name. The musicians were trying to be patient and gracious in the midst of the turmoil. They weren't succeeding. The reporters were relentless, trying to wrest any details they could about the attack. Eddie Vincent stood at the open side of his keyboards like a sentry, preventing entry to his sanctum sanctorum, and steering all questions toward the subject of the tour itself.

"Yeah, we're really happy to be here in New Orleans. I've always wanted to come here. The music's got its own soul, like. Fee has this vision of gathering up the spirit of the United States for the album we're cutting when we get back home . . . No, man, I don't know what happened. I was just setting up my boards. Sound good in here, don't they?" His long fingers danced up and down the keys, sending a weird, discordant wailing echoing through the auditorium. "Yeah, it's a thing I'm trying out for this gig. I think it's a new sound. Can't wait to see what they think of it in San Francisco." The music attracted the attention of the other reporters on stage. Like rats to the Pied Piper, they turned away from other victims and crowded in on Vincent, who played more eerie-sounding music to the rapt crowd.

Liz grinned. Vincent had a little benevolent magic of his own. Nigel Peters, Lloyd Preston and a cordon of security guards swooped in. They rounded up the protesting group of reporters and escorted them toward the door, talking all the while to distract them. Very quickly, the Superdome was cleared of members of the press. Green Fire seemed to breathe a collective sigh of relief. Liz followed Boo into the boxes surrounding the stage. The two of them split up and went in opposite directions.

The tiers of seats were raked steeply and the space between them was alarmingly narrow. Liz hated to admit it, but she was afraid of heights. Her heart pounded every time she stumbled, grabbing for the metal railing to keep herself from plummeting down the concrete stairs. There was no way for her to watch what was going on down on stage and walk at the same time. If she was to concentrate on magic-sniffing, it was better for her acrophobia not to be able to see how far up they were. She kept her gaze on the few feet of floor immediately in front of her, and listened.

She began to understand why Green Fire had chosen the Superdome as a concert venue. The acoustics were surprisingly good. Voices carried well into the bleachers from the stage. Over the racket created by grips dragging equipment to its places, the tuning of instruments, and the pounding of feet on the hollow platform, Liz eavesdropped on the crew and the band. They all sounded impatient and resentful of the long interruption of their jobs.

" . . . my opinion, Fitz won't admit he had a cigarette in his hand under . . ." a deep male voice rose out of the hubbub. " . . . set fire to it himself and . . ."

" . . . silk goes up in a puff . . ." another man's voice agreed.

" . . . filmy sleeves . . ." one of the stagehands drawled, scornfully.

" . . . really an attack on Fee?" piped a woman's voice. Liz recognized Laura Manning.

"No!" "Maybe." "Yes, and by whom?" echoed around the stage.

" . . . one of us?" asked Lockney's voice.

"No!" came the immediate protest, but other voices chimed in. "Maybe." "Could be." "Who?"

"Who knows?" Michael Scott's clear voice cut above the noise. "Let's get this done."

Who indeed? Liz wondered, as she reached the end of the tier. She had not sensed any magical evidence whatsoever in the circuit. She glanced across the open arena at the sea of multicolored seats, but she couldn't see Boo-Boo. If it wasn't an accident, perhaps the prank was the work of an earthbound stalker trying to make Fionna's life miserable. In that eventuality Liz would have to turn the case over to the FBI. Ringwall wouldn't like that, but he'd be relieved. Anything that smelled of the mystical worried the ministry. On the whole he would be happier if Liz could prove a negative instead of a positive. You open the floodgates, she thought wryly, and that let in all the bogeys down the coal cellar, the walking ghosts, and before you know it *Panorama* and *60 Minutes* are doing a special on you.

A dark-skinned man in a plain gray guard's uniform sprang up out of nowhere in front of her. Liz jumped in surprise and clutched for a handhold.

"Can I help you, ma'am?" he asked, his warm brown eyes serene but watchful. The temples of his black, curly hair were a distinguished gray. Liz showed him her credentials, which he examined with raised eyebrows. "Well, isn't that interesting. Welcome to America, ma'am."

"How is it going, Captain Evers?" Liz asked, reading his name tag.

"Under control, ma'am," the man said, taking a side glance down at the stage area. "We're clearing out the rest of the city folks. Pretty soon it'll just be us chickens in here. There's no damage we can find, no signs of a break-in. I guess they were right about that flash powder causing the fire in the first place . . ."

Liz found she was only half-listening to him. She was aware of a looming presence overhead, like a storm cloud. She glanced up at the large, square box hovering over the stage, a huge cube covered with lights, screens and speakers.

"What *is* that?" she asked, cutting Evers off in the middle of his explanation. His eyes followed hers upward.

"Oh, that's the Jumbotron, ma'am."

"What's it for?"

"She raises and lowers so you can watch the screens. They use her all the time during concerts and games, to show the scores, instant replays and so on."

"Good heavens," Liz said, gawking at its size. "What does that thing weigh?"

"Seventy-two tons, ma'am." Evers sounded proud.

Liz frowned. "Could it be detached?" she asked. "Is there any possible chance it could come down on anyone?"

Captain Evers looked very worried until Boo leaned around from behind her. "She's with me, Abelard."

The dark-skinned man's lined face relaxed into a wide grin.

"Boo-Boo, is that you?" Evers asked. He rocked back on his heels, and stuck out his hands to clasp the American agent's. "You young rascal, how you be?"

"Not as good as you look, old man," Boo said, grinning back. "Now, tell the lady what she wants to know."

Evers turned to Liz with an air of apology.

"Well, no, ma'am, the Jumbo can't come down; not without a lot of help. She's anchored to the steel girders holding up the roof. The roof's a soft plastic, not very heavy."

"How do they control it? Do you have to go up there?" Liz shuddered. Evers's eyes lightened mischievously.

"Oh, there's catwalks, ma'am," the captain said, his eyes crinkling. He seemed unable to resist teasing an obvious acrophobe. "Way high up. Yes, ma'am, you can climb up right inside the ceiling. But don't fall off those catwalks, or you'll come right through. Do you want to go up and see?" he offered, the impish grin returning. "It's just about two hundred sixty feet above the floor."

Liz, feeling green, shook her head weakly. She thought of the fall from such a height, and swayed slightly on her feet, holding onto the banister with a firm grip. "Not unless there's an alternative."

"Abelard!" Boo looked at the man with a wry smile.

"Well, you don't have to," the guard captain said, releasing his prisoner reluctantly. "They work her from the control room with a couple of buttons. It's as easy as raising your garage door."

Boo took her arm in a firm and reassuring grip as he helped her to the next level.

"Find anything?" he asked.

"Not a whisker," Liz said. "It's beginning to look as if it's a job for the Men in Black, not us."

Boo came up alongside her as she reached the top of the steep stairs. "I have to admit I'm kind of hoping not," he said.

"Me, too," Liz said. Though she would far rather not have to deal with a supernatural menace and it would be a relief if Fionna's troubles turned out to be a set of coincidences and accidents, the department needed all the credibility it could get, and this *was* her first solo mission. Negative results were no way to earn promotion.

They went out into the broad, tiled hallway. Names of corporations were engraved on plaques set into the metal doors on her left. Those must lead to the luxury skyboxes she saw from the stage level. Boo steered her toward a set of blank doors. Scraping sounds shook the floor, and sirens echoed through the corridors. Liz looked around in alarm.

"That's just the loading bay doors, opening to let the fire truck out," Boo explained. "Come on, let's take a look in the control room."

He rapped on the blind door, and a bearded man in T-shirt, jeans and headset let them in. Inside the cramped, glass-fronted room the crew was in a frenzy of activity. The technical director, Gary Lowe, stood shouting into his headset behind a man and a woman seated at the console. Behind him, the event director was talking simultaneously to Lowe and to the floor director down on the stage. Robbie Unterburger glanced up from her high-tech keyboard, and cocked her head to beckon them over. Her hands flitted from one control to another, tweaking levers, knobs and keys.

"This is a fantastic setup," Liz said, staring at the control panel as she tried to figure out what any of it did. "You aren't running all your machinery, are you?"

"No," Robbie said, tossing her straight, brown hair, "this is a dry run. I'm just following my cues this time. I'll test everything, and we'll have one live technical run-through just before showtime tomorrow. These are the triggers for the lasers, and here are the joysticks for each one. I can run them manually or program the whole thing to run by computer. They did *not* go off and set Fitzy on fire." Her dark brows drew down as she dared the agents to say otherwise. "This is the control for the smoke pots," she said, pointing to a bank of a dozen switches, "and here's the hologram projectors that show images on the clouds. It's fantastic." Robbie's eyes sparkled as she turned one of four small screens toward them so they could see the turning figures of constellations and mythical beasts that were cued up and ready to run. Liz found the change from sullen child to lively effects wizard a charming transformation. Liz caught Ken Lewis glancing at her out of the corner of his eye. He saw Liz looking at him and swiftly turned away. "The firing mechanism for sparklers and fireworks is disabled just now; we're not permitted to use it unless the fire engine is on standby. Pity. This is a great place for flash and bang. The bigger the better."

"Do you mind?" the technical director barked, cupping his hand over the microphone on his headset. "Excuse us, we're doing a show here. Sorry," he said to Liz and Boo. Boo put a finger to his lips and nodded to Liz. They retreated to the rear of the control room to watch the crew prepare. The female sound engineer shouted into the microphone set in the console in front of her. The lighting engineer gestured with both hands as he talked into his headset. Lowe gave Liz and Boo a brief glance, and then forgot about them as the disembodied baritone of stage manager Hugh Banks boomed out of the speakers overhead.

"All right, people! That's the last of the firemen and the cleanup squad out the door. Everyone's gone. Let's get to work."

Down below on the stage the miniature figures of the band took their places and lifted their instruments.

Michael Scott flicked his long fingers down and over
the strings of his guitar in the fanning gesture Liz
had seen in a dozen concert videos, drawing forth a
glissando like a harp. As always, the ripple of sound
made her quiver with delight. If this case wasn't so
serious she would be thrilled to be here with her idol.
Voe Lockney beat his sticks together over his head,
then attacked his drums with a frenzy. The other two
joined in. Liz could hear the music begin to echo and
thrum outside, but it was much muted here in the
booth. The sound engineer's hands flew over the
controls.

Fionna appeared at the edge of the stage in a
flame-red sheath dress that could have been painted
on her. Her eyes, cheeks, and lips were tinted the
same bright shade. What with her green hair close-
cropped against her skull Liz thought she looked like
a shapely match. Liz wondered why she hadn't
detected Fionna leaving her dressing room. She
counted back in time, and decided the cantrip alarm
must have gone off while Captain Evers was teasing
her about the Jumbotron.

The tiny, brightly colored figure stopped at the
edge of the stage, while a couple of men in security
uniforms ran around the open platform like quest-
ing hounds.

"All right," Lowe said, leaning forward with his
hands on the chairbacks. "Cue the spotlights, cue
Fionna, and . . . what the hell is the matter with her?"

The music died away, and all the band turned to
look at Fionna.

"Come on, down there!" Lowe growled. "What's
the hang-up now?"

"She wants them to check for bombs, sir," an
overhead speaker crackled. "She says she's afraid of
being attacked again."

"Bombs! Hell and damnation!" the technical director shouted, pounding on the engineers' seat backs. They sat rigidly, watching the screen. "We have a show to do! Get those men off the stage, or carry Fee over to her mark yourself. We haven't got any more time to waste." He flopped down into his seat, between Robbie and the sound engineer. "I wish that Fee *had* been in the damned costume when it went up, and then we'd have a reason for all this fuss! Let her writhe in agony! Let those rotten 'filmy sleeves' burn to ash! Now, let's get a move on! Get her on stage!"

Below them, a man in blue jeans and a headset went over to Fionna, and pulled her into place in the center of the stage. Fionna held out her hand in appeal. From the edge of the platform, the bulky form of Lloyd Preston came over to stand beside her. Next to Liz, Robbie let out an audible growl.

The band struck up again. Fionna grabbed her microphone in both hands, closed her eyes and emitted a piercing ululation that softened and resolved into a mellow warble that rose and fell like folds of silk. The technicians' shoulders relaxed visibly. Even Lowe stood back, arms crossed, to watch. Boo touched Liz's arm, and they slipped out of the room.

"No magic," Boo said, as they went through the next set of double doors on the level. This was the press box, another large area like the control room, with a broad, curved window looking down on the stage. Facing it were tiers of desks with microphones and places for computer terminals to be plugged in. Toward the rear of the chamber, television and radio transmission lines ran from a labeled console into the ceiling. Several video screens showed different camera angles of the stage, a necessary innovation to supplement the view, unless the reporters were carrying binoculars. At this distance the figures of the band were tiny, almost featureless.

Down on the stage, Fionna was making love to her microphone like a torch singer. She and the guitarist started to step toward one another, intent with passion. Liz felt a shiver of delight, waiting for them to close the distance and begin their duet.

"Nothin'," Boo-Boo said, bringing her back to the present with a disappointing snap. "Nothin' but what we brought ourselves. It's lookin' as if the cause was somethin' natural or physical. That'd be a job for the local police, not for us."

"My chief will be happy," Liz said, resignedly. "He'd always rather prove a negative. Less difficult to explain to Upstairs."

Boo-Boo grinned engagingly. "Y'all got one of them, too?"

"Don't we all?" Liz asked, smiling back.

She found in spite of her earlier misgivings she was beginning to like this American. No matter how unconventional his approach, nor that he looked like a bag of rags, he was a good investigator and an effective agent. She was convinced he was right. Nothing more here than an accident, and accumulated paranoia of a spoiled rich girl with powerful connections. Liz had no idea what would account for the Irish agent's difficulty. Possibly he had been drugged by someone who recognized him as MI-5. There were more strange chemicals floating around in the underworld than even most of the department was permitted to know. There'd be grumbling in Whitehall about her spending thousands of pounds to fly here to investigate, but at least Lord Kendale would be happy.

The music rose toward a crescendo. On the stage

Fionna stood in her place under the lights, trembling.
Her hands had fallen to her sides, but they were
slowly lifting with the music. Michael Scott stood
behind her, back bowed as he tore the notes out of
his guitar. Liz enjoyed the rich psychic waves this song
put out. It felt as though power was rising through
her. She stood almost on tiptoe waiting for Fionna
to shout out the last line, when the music would crash
around her like waves against a cliff.

And then, Liz felt it. Or smelled it. Or just knew,
in that way her grandmother always told her she
would. There was evil here. Powerful evil. But where
was it coming from?

"Do you feel that?" she started to ask Boo. Suddenly, there was a flash of light on the screens. Fionna
let out a shriek of agony, throwing her arms up against
the blaze.

Liz wasn't prepared for another attack so soon, but
her training kicked in without hesitation. Never mind
where the fire had come from, put it out! Liz summoned up every erg of magic she had, down to the
reserves, and threw it through the glass at Fionna with
both hands in a smothering spell that would have
extinguished a house fire. The force of the spell
knocked all the wind out of her for a moment. She
staggered backward, staring. The huge pane of glass
seemed to shiver and sing dangerously, threatening
to break. The little figures on the stage swayed and
ran towards one another. She had no time to consider the consequences when she was flung to the
floor by a blast that came from Boo's direction.

"Clear!" he yelled, too late. Automatically, the
analyzing part of Liz's brain recognized the effect as
a containment field to suppress any other occult
activity in the area. Liz was impressed. She didn't
know the Americans had been working on anything

so sophisticated. Boo glanced over at her. "Seems like we were wrong."

Liz scrambled to her feet and made for the door, the American half a step behind her.

"Rapid deployment, eh?" she asked, as they ran down the stairs toward the stage.

"Finest kind," Boo said.

"If you'd thrown that thing one second sooner you'd have blotted out my spell!"

"I saw what you was doin', ma'am," Boo said, peevishly. "I waited. Now, let's see what happened."

Liz shoved her way through the crowd of people that had gathered on the stage. The fire alarm was blaring overhead. Nigel Peters's voice cut through the noise.

"Someone shut that blasted thing off!" he raged. "We don't want everyone down on us again!"

At the center of the mob, Fionna had sunk into a heap on the floor. Lloyd huddled over her, frantically trying to bring her around. Nothing seemed to be wrong with Fionna apart from red, angry skin on her bare arms.

"A hell of a lot of help you were," Lloyd snarled at Liz.

All Fionna could say over and over as they bandaged her arms was, "Now you'll believe me."

And Liz had no choice. The stink of malignity rose from her skin like cheap perfume.

"You say the *hair* on her arms caught fire?" Liz asked, wondering if she had heard incorrectly. "Not the sleeves?"

"That's it," Laura Manning said, examining the skin carefully. "There were no sleeves. Left her smooth as a baby's bottom, apart from the burns, that is. Shh, honey. I've got some cream downstairs."

"We can't have any more delays," Patrick Jones cried, pacing up and down. "My God, if the reporters get hold of this. I'll kill myself."

"Oh, that'd be good press," Eddie Vincent growled. Nigel Peters tore his thinning hair.

Liz focused immediately on finding the source of the power. "Did anyone see where the fire came from?" she asked, but every face in the circle was blank. To them it was just another freak accident, one of many. Only Liz had felt the anger and hatred fill the arena just before the attack. It was fading quickly. They would have to work fast to find the source.

"It's symbolic that the fire was centered on Fionna's sleeves," she said under her breath to Boo-Boo, who knelt beside her near Fionna. "She didn't have any in this dress, but that's what everyone was talking about just before the blaze. That meant the energy *had* to have come from somewhere in here."

"How many people could hear the stage manager?" Boo asked. "Let's ask everyone again, one at a time. I can do that. I'll bring them back to what they were thinkin' of at the last moment before it happened."

"No, that's a waste of time," Liz said sharply. Fionna's eyes fluttered, and she sat up. Lloyd immediately pushed the agents away and cradled his girlfriend in his arms. "We have to examine the site at once, before the influence dissipates."

"I think," Boo said, in a low tone, "you're forgetting that this is my turf. You're my guest. I'm in charge here."

"Not this again," Liz hissed. "We asked for your help. It's my case."

"It's our country," Boo said loudly, his eyes glowing with the light of battle. "You can't operate here without our permission. You might as well pack it up and go home."

"Never! My government will never take a back seat to yours!"

"We tossed you out once. We can do it again!"

"Knock it off or leave!" Lloyd shouted. "Look at her. She's hurt! Let's go downstairs, love."

Liz looked down at Fionna, who was holding onto the bodyguard like a drowning swimmer to a float. She was ashamed of herself. It was the second time that day she'd caught herself behaving in a nonprofessional manner. *Two black marks, Miss Mayfield*, she thought, shaking her head. Lloyd helped Fionna to her feet. Fionna tottered toward the stairs to her dressing room, with Lloyd and Laura Manning in attendance. The crowd parted to let them pass. Liz and Boo-Boo followed behind.

"We've got to work together on this," Liz said, after a moment. The tension in Boo-Boo's shoulders relaxed. She knew the two of them were thinking the same things. Here was a case where she could produce proof of an actual magical attack. If they solved the mystery this could spell credibility for their departments, assuring the budget for next year, not to mention putting Lord Kendale in their debt. It would put the Department and OOPSI into the headlines. Horrified, Liz stopped her flight of fancy. If this made the headlines the furor would never die down. The general public was not ready. They already suspected the government of prying into their everyday affairs. If they knew about the departments devoted to the paranormal, there would be open rioting out of naked fear.

Boo-Boo *was* thinking the same thing. "We've got to solve this *and* keep it quiet," he said, guardedly. "Miss Fionna needs us, ma'am. *Both* of us."

"It won't be easy," Liz said. "To say we have

different styles is an absolute understatement, but I'll try if you will."

"It's a deal," Boo-Boo said, holding out his hand for hers. They shook on it.

"The first thing to do is talk to our crime victim," Liz said, briskly.

Instead of occupying her grand throne, Fionna was curled in Lloyd's arms on the couch at the side of her dressing room. She had her knees drawn up protectively, like a little girl.

"They're here," she whimpered. "They're listenin' to me. They're comin' for me."

"Who's they, honey?" Lloyd asked, rocking the trembling woman in his arms.

"Let me see the burns," Liz said, starting to sit down at Fionna's other side.

"Piss off," Lloyd snapped, glaring at Liz. "I don't want you within yards of her. This is all your fault."

"All our fault?" Liz asked, blinking at him. "Are you mad? How?"

"This has been going on all along," Lloyd said, his face stony. "She tried to tell you."

"We needed proof," Liz said.

"To hell with your proof," Lloyd said. "I'm calling this all off as of now. You're out."

"It's not so easy as that," Boo said.

"Oh, yes, it is!"

"Oh, no, it isn't!" Liz said. "You might have believed her, but what could you do to help?"

As they argued over her head, Fionna clutched herself in fear. She had felt herself hauled to her feet from the stage, and had obediently followed Laura and Lloyd downstairs, while angry voices rang in her ears. She didn't follow half of it, didn't want to. With her eyes closed, she felt her arms stretched out.

Something cool was swabbed along them, and the familiar feeling of gauze and sticky tape touched her skin. Fee was having a hard time keeping from raving out loud and crying for police protection or an exorcism. She might be Fionna Kenmare to millions of fans worldwide, but underneath the wild, Irish persona beat the upper-class English heart of Phoebe Kendale. Where Fionna delved into the supernatural with alacrity, Phoebe still thought it was a little naughty, something to taunt the Aged Parents with, who didn't like her choice of career or friends. She'd always known in her heart something bad would happen if she started to play with magic. Always. She'd been cautious. She'd followed every rite of protection she could find to counteract the dark forces just outside the light, just in case. Just to make sure. Never step on a crack. Never spill salt without tossing a pinch over her shoulder. Always wish on a star, a fallen eyelash, a candle flame. Don't let black or white cats cross one's path. But the evil had started to press too closely in the last few months. That was why she had come to New Orleans, in hopes of finding stronger magic than she had. But the bad ones had found her here, first. They were coming for her, just like before. She started to rock back and forth, worrying.

The strong arms surrounding her helped to push the bogeys away. All her friends were gathered around her. They wanted to help. They were the grownups, there to protect her from the darkness. She felt as if she was a little girl again, crying in the nursery when the lights went out. They'll make it better. But they couldn't help. They didn't understand. She had followed every one of the superstitions to the letter, even the ones that made her feel silly. It wasn't enough to keep her safe. She drew a ragged breath and burst into tears.

Oh, I want my mummy.

Fionna sobbed uncontrollably. The evil was here. It had followed her here. The emotional storm inside her rose to hysterical proportions. It was hard to breathe.

She felt herself being shaken. A calm voice, a familiar voice, cut through her misery.

"Fionna. Fionna."

Oh, it was that imperious prig, Elizabeth Mayfield. Forgot to set the tables again, or was it some equally tedious House task?

"Fionna."

Go away, she willed the calm, insistent voice. *Go away.* Elizabeth was just another manifestation of the evils that surrounded her, haunted her. She tried to shut them all out, using the ward chants she had learned from the books. *Go away, pesty voice.*

"Fionna."

She put her fingers into her ears. Two strong hands grabbed her sore wrists and pulled them away. She yelped, and went back to chanting.

"Fionna," the voice continued, in an urgent whisper, sinking lower and lower and becoming more and more intense until it burned into her very being. It was a mere breath upon her ears. "Phoebe Kendale, if you do not open your eyes right now and snap out of your sulk I will tell everyone here how you jumped naked off Magdalen Bridge into the Isis River at dawn on Midsummer Day five years ago."

Fionna's bloodshot green eyes flew open, glaring into Liz's serious blue ones. "You wouldn't! Of all the officious, interferin' candy-arsed bitches who ever walked the earth on hind legs . . ."

Liz stood up and nodded to Nigel Peters. "She'll be all right now," she said.

"My God, how did you do it?" Peters asked, staring

at his star in amazement. Fionna stopped raving and tensed up.

"Departmental secret," Liz said curtly. But she gave Fionna a look that said if she indulged herself in another screaming fit the secret would be out. The singer crossed her bandaged arms and stared her defiance. Liz shook her head. Fionna/Phoebe was as stubborn as the day they had met. She left the woman to the ministrations of Laura and Nigel, who began to argue about whether to put Fee to bed or to go on with the rehearsal.

"Let's get back to it," Voe Lockney said, fidgeting with his drumsticks. "We need the run-through."

"No," Lloyd said, cradling Fionna closely as if possession was nine-tenths of the law. Her eyes were closed again. "Call it off. Fee's frazzled. Let her rest this afternoon." The band and the crew immediately broke into protests.

"Oh, no," Michael Scott said, his blue eyes ablaze. "We'll be rusty enough. I have to hear the acoustics of this place."

"Is she going to fold in the show?" Voe Lockney asked, looking at Fionna with bewildered eyes.

"I don't see what all the fuss is about," Robbie Unterburger said, sourly. "I've had worse burns from flash powder."

At the sound of the word "burns," Fionna nestled closer into Lloyd's meaty arms. Robbie's lips pressed together as if seeing the couple like that hurt her. Eddie Vincent gave them a disapproving look.

"Godless," the keyboard player muttered. "Marry him already, woman!"

"The evil feeling has dissipated now," Liz said, as soon as she and Boo were out of earshot of the others. "Where did it go?"

"Where did it come from?" Boo asked. "We've

checked all over this place. The portals were cleared. Everyone was clean. We missed a leak somehow. It'd have to come in a vent, or on a breach in the walls to the outside. Malignity has to be invited into a neutral space. The only psychic doodads here belong to Miss Fionna. That kind of thing leaves a mark on people. No one has any deep-seated stains I can see."

"Too deep for you?" Liz asked.

Boo gave her a glance full of meaning. "Not for our detection methods, ma'am," Boo said mysteriously. "Can't say more'n that."

"This isn't like anything I've ever had to deal with before," Liz said, pushing departmental rivalry aside until later. "Is she really under attack from some kind of malign spirit that follows her around?"

"I dunno, ma'am," Boo said. "We need some special expertise here. I know people. We can have a couple dozen specialists here in an hour. There's a Santeria priestess I know. The local wiccans will want to be in on it, and there's the Evangelical healers. Maybe a shaman or two."

Liz only gawked. "Is there anyone in this town that you don't know?"

Chapter 10

The clean-shaven, heavyset man leaned into the SATN-TV camera lens. He was wearing a plain black tunic and breeches with white bands at his throat and wide white cuffs. The costume, coupled with the truncated-cone-shaped hat, evoked an image of a Puritan settler, but his speech had no relation to the founding fathers' simple message of religious freedom.

"Hate," he said, with all the flourishes and dramatic pauses of his profession, "liberates you. Hate sets you free. The ultimate freedom comes when you allow yourself to reach inside and draw out the burning fires within, to destroy your enemies and vanquish them into the netherworlds. Hate creates power."

Behind him was a clutch of stern-faced women dressed in a similar style, straight out of *The Crucible*. They were throwing handfuls of powder onto a fire that exploded in a flash and puffs of noxious, yellow smoke.

"Are you getting passed up for promotions because the boss likes a different candidate more than you?"

the man asked. "Then, curse your rival! Curse the boss, too! There's no reason for you to take ill-treatment like that without calling down eternal wrath upon those who do you wrong. Join our congregation! We'll be happy to offer a ritual for you. All you have to do is send us a donation of $100, and we'll invoke Satan in your name. Watch our show, and add your prayers that vengeance will be yours. Now, here's that address. Send $100 to SATN-TV . . . ."

The slim man in khaki trousers waited until the announcer had finished with his spiel. "Cut! Speaker Downey, come *on*. How come you're not going to show some skin? I thought Satan worshipers were, you know . . . naked girls on the altar?"

"How dare you?" the head Puritan said, coming toward the producer with a face like an angry thundercloud. "Private worship is not for public display!"

"We could guarantee you a hell—sorry, Speaker—a heckuva lot more viewers in the prime time slot if you would make your pitch, you know, a little more adult-friendly?"

"You mean, washed in sin!" Downey stormed.

"I mean, that's what people want to see," the producer said, imperturbably. "What you're doing now is strictly daytime—bored housewives and unemployed people with the tube on for background noise. The real money is in the evening, if you wanted to cater to the public a little, or after midnight for really hot stuff. Sheesh! Some of the evil you guys espouse is obviously sadomasochism! You ought to . . . let it show a little."

One of the women sidled up to him, seductive even in the heavy-skirted costume. "You're a follower?"

"I . . ." the producer began, uncomfortable even while he was starting to look interested.

"We prefer to keep our show in the light of day,"

Downey said, angrily. "Night is for the creatures of the dark, like . . . like that druid's wench!" He pointed at a poster of Fionna Kenmare and Green Fire that was being carried onto the set by a couple of grips. "The fire of our Master keeps us strong! Darkness surrounds her. Many of our viewers have called down curses upon her and her minions, but they bounce back at us. She is trifling with things beyond her ken! More power is needed to bring about her downfall!"

"Now, now," said Augustus Kingston, coming out of the shadows and throwing an arm over Speaker Downey's shoulders. Only the ember of his cigar end had given away his presence to the others. As he got closer the producer could smell the tobacco over the sulphur from the brimstone incense. "Don't you get all het up about Miss Kenmare. She's gonna get what's coming to her."

"She wastes the otherworldly power, brother," Downey said, shaking his head. "Her motives are suspect! What fool would use magic and not employ it for personal gain?"

"Well, you are so right, my friend," Kingston said, smoothly. "And if I have not said it lately, I, and all of my people here," he pointed the cigar at the producer, trailing along behind them like a worried watchdog, "appreciate your help in dealing with wrongheaded women like Miss Kenmare, there. Yes, she's got wards around her. There're some busybodies interfering with right-minded people like yourself who quite rightly want to see her blasted into the under-world, but in the end those won't be a barrier. No one can stand against the might of pure evil."

Downey's eyes gleamed from underneath the brim of his antique hat. "We will continue the fight, brother."

"We sure will. You all run along," Kingston said,

with an avuncular smile. "We've got to set up for the afternoon telethon now."

"They just stand there," the producer complained, watching the black-clad worshipers file out of the studio. "I could get more interest out of an oil painting."

"But they bring in the money from the grass-roots viewers," Kingston said, transfering his cigar to the other hand and taking the producer by the upper arm and leading him out into the noisy foyer, where a young, redheaded woman in a headset was punching the controls of a computerized switchboard set. "Look at that. The telephones are ringing off the hook. You just let them do their business, and concentrate on making it look as interesting as you know how. We've got our prime-time specials all locked up for this week. Might have a *special* special for you later on. Keep up the good work."

The producer looked doubtful. Kingston slapped him on the back and headed for the rear office.

The man was right, though. It would have helped a lot if they could have raised the kind of power Kingston dreamed of through normal operations, but they couldn't, not in a puny backwater like this, far off in the northwest states. But Kingston, and some of his acquaintances had a plan to put themselves on the supernatural map—and that goody-goody little singer was going to help them do it.

"SATN-TV, please hold," the operator said, poking the flashing button with the end of a pencil. "SATN-TV, please hold. SATN-TV, yes, Mr. Mooney! He's expecting your call. I'll put you right through, sir." She jabbed the HOLD button, and cleared her throat. "Mr. Kingston, Mr. Mooney on line three."

❖   ❖   ❖

Kingston sat down in a huge, black, leather swivel chair in his office and swung it away from the monitors trained on Studio One. "Eldredge, nice to hear from you."

"Is this going to happen, Augustus?" Eldredge Mooney asked. His voice was a low growl, like a bear awakened prematurely from hibernation. "People are beginning to ask me questions. They want to see results!"

Kingston kicked back and put one polished black shoe on his solid, non-sustainably harvested mahogany desk. "Yes, Eldredge, it's going right on schedule. We all ought to be getting one powerful charge in the batteries tomorrow night. I can't wait for the rest of the Council to see the setup. I'm looking forward to having you all here."

"This is the first major test of the system, you know."

"Of course I know it! It's an honor to be the one to push the button, so to speak, and I am sure it's going to be a big success. I was just watching some of our faithful who are providing the charge that primes the pump, so to speak. This technology's just plain brilliant. The machines have been ticking over just fine on the reactions we're getting to the nut fringe. The indicators say we're already showing about eight percent feed, and that's without any input from out of town. Technology's wonderful, Eldredge. I don't know why we didn't have access to something like this before. And what with the Internet channels coming in line, we'll be able to blow anything we feel like right out of the water, so to speak. And, since naturally that's what we have in mind here, it's going to work like a charm."

"It only works if you have direct access to the subject," Mooney objected.

Irritated, Kingston puffed on his cigar, surrounding himself with a fiendish aureole of smoke. It was clear that they were underestimating SATN and the planning skills of its chief of administration.

He had little direct contact with Mooney and the rest of the influential circle he represented. He'd met them on-line, in a private chat room on a black-magic website. Kingston had been amazed to discover that so many like-minded individuals turned out to live in his neck of the woods, although Mooney was the only one he had met in person so far. The others were holding back, waiting until he proved himself worthy of being one of them. Membership in the Elder Council of Deepest Evil, as they called it, was held out to him as a carrot—although a heavy stick was poised to fall on his back if he blew the chance they were giving him.

Kingston was doing his best to make sure he wouldn't. He wanted to be a part of their number in the worst way. His fondest daydreams, even as a child, involved world domination. As a grownup, he'd be content just to increase his dominion to absolute power over those under his control, and that was what the Council promised. These men were the real deal. The satanists, cursers, death-talkers, all the wrong-doers who made CNN were pigeons compared with his long-distance comrades. These evil worshipers had discovered the power of high tech. The one inescapable problem was power. They needed it. The easy way to raise it was from a strong emotional surge from as many people as possible all at once. Fionna Kenmare put on a mighty powerful show. He'd seen one himself. If at a climactic moment something happened to her, the power released would be tremendous. That was what Mooney and his friends wanted, and he was poised to give it to them.

"We've *got* direct access, Eldredge, I told you. We've got the perfect conduit to Fionna Kenmare. Our person on the scene guarantees that the link has been made. Has been for some time. We've been running little tests, and I've got to tell you, they've all worked."

"Wonderful," Mooney gloated. "We can claim that she's being attacked because she espouses magic, never knowing that those attacks were just trial runs, and have nothing to do with her own wretchedly limited beliefs. Can the conduit be associated with you in any way?"

"Our focus person picked the perfect accomplice, Eldredge. No one will ever be able to trace it back to us . . . or you. It's all so perfectly hands-off."

"This will mean big things for all of us, Augustus, especially you."

Kingston sat back and put his other foot up on the desk, and blew a long stream of smoke at the ceiling. He liked being appreciated. "That's the general idea, Eldredge."

"Well, I want an update later," Mooney said, trying not to sound as though he doubted Kingston's word. Kingston knew the Council didn't want him to walk away at this point. Not with so much at stake.

"You'll get it," Kingston said. "And, oh, Eldredge, keep CNN turned on tomorrow night. They've always got the most current coverage of *late-breaking events*. Nice hearing from you. Say hello to the missus for me."

Chapter 11

That evening Elizabeth circulated through the room, smiling and nodding to Beauray's arriving "specialists," all the time aware that she was experiencing another facet of the surprisingly complex world that existed within the bounds of the French Quarter. While she had seen examples of "gracious Southern living styles" in various old movies, and had experienced a minor taste of it in her own room, she nonetheless found it impressive.

For one thing, the surroundings were far more sumptuous than at any meeting she had ever attended outside of a great house or palace in the United Kingdom. Beauray had somehow gotten the use of a suite at the Royal Sonesta. (When she asked about how he could arrange it so quickly, Boo-Boo had simply shrugged and given what she was now beginning to recognize as his trademark answer: "I know someone on the staff.") It reminded her of the nicer kind of private London clubs, but decorated in lighter colors. The main area was roughly the size of a

volleyball court, and luxuriously furnished with
overstuffed sofas and chairs as well as small cocktail
tables draped with white brocade cloths. Heavy drapes
framed the large windows which looked out onto the
hotel's massive inner courtyard, and soft light was
provided by several bright crystal chandeliers. An
ebony baby grand piano stood underneath the window at the room's far end.

The others in attendance seemed to take it all in
stride, giving the room and its furnishings little notice
and even less comment, choosing instead to focus on
the well-stocked bar situated beneath a painting the
size of a bed. She was pleased to see the bar herself. Comments from other friends who had come to
American dos in the past had complained that Yan-
kees threw big parties, but neglected to provide alco-
holic refreshment in favor of soft drinks, as if all their
guests were still underage. Fionna/Phoebe's eyes
would probably have gleamed at the sight of the
warm, mahogany counter lined with bottles of every
size and shape, but she was locked up, shivering, in
her suite with Lloyd. Elizabeth was sorry she was so
frightened, but it kept her behaving. The issue was
not only what outside forces would inflict upon her,
but what Fionna could do to herself, given a free
hand. For once she would have to settle for room
service, and like it.

As they waited for the last few stragglers to arrive,
Elizabeth could not help but study those already
present with a mixture of curiosity and amusement.

In her own home offices of OOPSI they held
occasional staff meetings, and sometimes brought in
outside consultants. There, however, the consultants
were invariably either dusty academics or blustery
bureaucrats. The main challenge was staying awake
through the drawn-out lectures and discussions of

procedures. This gathering, appropriately enough for New Orleans, had more the appearance of a costume party.

Elizabeth accepted a sweet-smelling drink the uniformed bartender identified as a "Sazerac," and surveyed Boo's gathering allies.

"A few of my friends," Beauray had said. Elizabeth tried to imagine what life would be like with friends like these. If she went back through her entire life of memories and catalogued every strange character she had ever met or come into contact with, the list would not be half as large or varied as the group assembling in the room.

There were a large number of Blacks, both men and women, present, standing singly or sitting in small groups of two or three. One group was garbed in bright purple robes, while others were dressed in white and wore head scarves folded in elaborate patterns. From the night before she recalled the slight gentleman in blue jeans and a leather vest who carried an intricately carved wooden walking staff and wore a straw cowboy hat, ornately decorated with long feathers.

The Caucasians in the room presented no less variety in their dress. Two middle-aged gentlemen who stood talking quietly together wore conservative business suits that would have fit in anywhere in the Central Business District. Others more casual in their dress sprawled on the sofa, their beards and embroidered tunics making them look as if they had just wandered in from a medieval festival or stepped through a time warp from a Viking mead hall. One statuesque blonde woman in a floor-length black dress glittering with sequins seemed to have come directly from a Mardi Gras ball. Also scattered about were a few individuals whose olive complexion, long dark hair, and bead necklaces hinted of the Great Plains Native Americans.

The other noticeable thing was that, while they all might be friends of Beauray, there seemed to be little love lost between the various groups. Dark glares and muttered comments followed by unnecessarily loud laughter were increasingly frequent as more and more people arrived until Elizabeth began to worry that outright hostility would erupt if the meeting did not start soon.

As if reading her mind, Beauray stood up and moved to the center of the room, clearing his throat loudly. In response, the crowd ceased their conversations and focused their attention on him.

"I guess we might as well get started," he announced. "Even allowing for N'Awlins time and being fashionably late, I figure anyone who isn't here already has either decided not to attend or got caught up in something more pressing."

There was a low murmur as everyone craned their necks to survey the room, doubtlessly speculating on who hadn't shown up as opposed to who hadn't been invited.

"First, let me express my thanks and appreciation for those of you who have chosen to attend, and especially on such short notice. I'd have liked to give y'all more time, but there isn't any. Most of you know each other, at least on sight, and I don't suppose it's a big secret that not everyone in the room likes each other or agrees with some of the disciplines represented here. The fact that I would see fit to place you in this potentially awkward position should be an indication of how serious I feel the problem is, and how little time we have to try to come up with an answer."

That seemed to get everyone's attention, and they

leaned forward in their seats, focusing intently as Beauray continued.

"In a minute here I'll introduce my colleague from England, Miss Elizabeth Mayfield, but first let me give you the bare bones. There's an Irish rock singer, Fionna Kenmare, who's in town to give a concert at the Superdome tomorrow evenin'. There have been reports that she has been sufferin' from psychic or supernatural attacks, though there's some question as to whether or not they were simply publicity stunts. Anyway, Elizabeth and I are supposed to be checkin' it out, and protectin' her if the attacks are real. I don't know if y'all think it's good or bad news, but they are real." Some murmuring met this announcement. Boo-Boo raised his voice slightly. "We've seen it happen ourselves. The problem is, what we've seen so far doesn't match anything Ms. Mayfield or I have run into before, so I thought we'd bounce it off you folks to see if any of you have some knowledge or experience that might help us.

"First, though, I'll let Elizabeth tell you about what we've encountered so far. Elizabeth?"

Originally Elizabeth had resisted the idea of her handling this part of the briefing, fearing that her accent would hinder communications, but Beauray had insisted, and as she enumerated the details of the afternoon's events, she found herself warming to the subject and to her audience. It was rare that she could speak as freely as she did about apparently supernatural or unexplainable events and have it accepted and considered seriously rather than having to fight to overcome scepticism and disbelief. To her relief and delight she saw many of her listeners nod to themselves as she reached various points in her narratives where she described but did not identify by name the magical processes she and Beauray had used.

If only Mr. Ringwall could see her now!

When she finished, there was a period of silence as the assemblage reflected on what they had heard.

"You say this group is Irish and the first attacks happened in Ireland," one of the men in business suits said finally, in an easygoing but ponderous way of speaking. "Is there any chance she's gotten sideways to some spirit over there that's followed her here?"

"I thought about that," Beauray said, "but I haven't picked up any signs or feelings of an extra presence around the group or around the Superdome."

"Too bad!" quipped the black man in the straw cowboy hat. "Otherwise we might be able to convince it to stay. The Saints surely could use the help."

That brought a round of laughter from the whole room.

"How about a curse?" asked a stout black woman wearing a floor-length caftan and a plain, dark purple turban. "Maybe someone gave her somethin' that she's carrying around that draws trouble without her even knowin' about it."

"Naw," said one of the long-haired Caucasians, with a gesture of scorn. "I never heard of no curse that could make anyone or anything burst into flames. It could make 'em sick or real unlucky, but to have something catch fire like that in front of a bunch of witnesses? That'd take some *real* heavy mojo."

"And you don't think the spirits are capable of setting fire to a sinner?" asked an old, old teak-colored man in a neatly-pressed suit. Elizabeth noticed a well-worn bible on the table near his elbow.

"Now, now," Beauray said, holding his hands up peaceably. "No one here is calling Miss Fionna a sinner. At least, no more than usual." He managed to raise a chuckle from the warring groups. "Let's just put our heads together and see if we can come up with an explanation that rings true."

From there the talk broke down into a group discussion. Individuals began comparing notes, and various groups merged, then split and remerged with other groups as possibilities were posed and discarded. Boo was pleased to see that they could set aside their individual philosophical differences to concentrate on a problem. Even though only one person was in peril, and an out-of-towner at that, the greater matter concerned them all. He'd often thought that a council like this would be of great help to the Department, although the bean counters in Washington weren't too receptive to the idea. They wouldn't know how to catalog the expense. Too bad. This group was no weirder than any of the *other* think tanks going on in other places. Someone caught him by the arm.

"Hey, Beauray," said the tall Native American woman in the embroidered chambray blouse and silver-and-turquoise jewelry, "have there been any visible manifestations, apart from the fire and the scratches? Spirits? Faces?"

From there the discussion broke down into specific details. Elizabeth and Beauray were both cross-examined numerous times on what they had experienced and witnessed, as well as asked to give their own views on some of the theories being broached.

"Think someone's got a voodoo doll of this gal?" a voice rose above the crowd from a very stout woman in a flowered dress.

"They never *heard* of voodoo over there in Europe," another voice exclaimed, shouting down the first. It was a man, red-eyed with indignation. He felt in his pocket and came up with a yellowed scroll.

"Demons, though. She might have a demon following her. Look here, I got a list . . ."

"What you think you're doin'?" a woman with café-au-lait skin exclaimed with concern, rounding on him from a small group nearest the bar. She whisked a cloth bundle out of her purse and sprinkled a pinch of pale dust from it on the paper. "Even the names have power. You brought them in here!"

The man and woman immediately fell into an argument, paying no heed to the others around them. The rest regrouped and began to talk among themselves.

Elizabeth went from one cluster of people to another, listening and taking notes while she answered questions. Several forms of attack that Elizabeth had never even heard of before were all aired and reviewed by the gathered specialists with the seriousness of doctors consulting each other on a puzzling diagnosis. She made a mental note to ask Beauray about some of the terms they were using, but for the time being, the focus had to remain upon Fionna and her problem. Time *was* an issue.

After nearly two hours, the larger of the two men in conservative suits set his glass down on a table with a sigh. He raised his voice to get everyone's attention.

"I'm hittin' the same dilemma over and over again, my friends. For a force to be powerful enough to have the effect Beauray is talkin' about, there must be *some* trace or indication of its direction or source. It's a case of conservation of energy, y'understand? Big effects call for big energy, and I don't see where it's comin' in, here. Nor why."

"That's the problem, isn't it?" Elizabeth said. "In real life, even the wizard Merlin could not simply wiggle a finger and move a mountain. There's far more to the equation than that. Both Mr. Boudreau and I should be sensitive enough in our own ways to detect any energy source strong enough to produce those spectacular results, but neither of us could pick up the faintest whiff of anything even fractionally powerful enough."

"Well, let's call a halt to the proceedin's," Boo said, glumly. "I want to thank y'all for comin' today. I'd appreciate it if you'd try to think of anythin' we haven't covered. Y'all know how to reach me. And keep your eyes open for any display of energy that strikes you as new or unusual."

"We'll do what we can," the café-au-lait woman said. She rose from the wing chair, laid a sympathetic hand on Boo's arm, and shook hands with Elizabeth. Her grip was firm, dry and comforting.

"I'll tell everyone I know to intensify their personal alertness," said the other man in a business suit. "We'll pin this thing down, Beauray."

"Thanks, Bobby Lee," Boo said. "Thank y'all for comin'." The room cleared quickly, as the peace of the watering hole was broken, and lifelong rivals hurried to get out before the shadow of the others fell on them.

"I must say, that was a new experience for me," Elizabeth said after the last of their guests had left. "Your friends were really quite helpful."

"Not helpful enough," Beauray said, almost to himself.

"Excuse me?"

"Hmm? Oh. Sorry about that, Elizabeth. I'm just a bit disappointed is all. For all the drinkin' and talkin', we *still* don't have any clearer idea of what's goin' on than when we started. I guess we just have to stay on our toes and hope for the best."

❖   ❖   ❖

Lloyd Preston put his hand over the phone and turned to Fionna, who was sitting anxiously on the big bed on the upper floor of her suite.

"That was Kenny Lewis, wants to know when you're coming back to finish rehearsal."

"Not yet—not yet!" Fionna said, holding out her long-nailed hands. "I can't face them. It's been just too awful. I feel if I pull down one more disaster that it'll kill all of us!"

Lloyd spoke to the phone. "Maybe later, Ken boy. She needs a break. We're going to stay here for a while."

Fee's keen hearing picked up the tone of the grumble coming through the wire. She knew the others were upset with her, but she didn't know what else to do. Blast that Elizabeth Mayfield! She was always right—always had been. Fee started pacing around the sitting room, its dimensions suddenly too small. She flung herself into a chair and reached for a cigarette. Lloyd automatically dug into his pocket for the lighter before he even hung up the phone. She smiled up at him as she blew out a plume of smoke. He was *so* good to her.

"They're stopping for dinner, love," Lloyd said. "Mr. High-and-Michael wants you there for the evening run-through even if you're on your death bed."

Fee shuddered and let her head drop back against the cushy damask of the armchair. "I wish he wouldn't put it like that!"

She was too agitated to chant any of her spells of protection. How did she know they would do any good, anyhow? She had no way to tell. The books she'd bought from the occult antiquarian might be phonies. She hadn't read Latin at school, and had to rely on the translations. Liz seemed to be another deep believer, though, and she'd nosed around in the suite. Fee ought to be safe here. She wished she felt that way.

When the knock came at the door, Fee was unaware how long she'd been sitting and staring up at the ceiling. She shot a nervous look at Lloyd, who got up from the table where he'd been reading a book. He returned with a couple of large paper bags in his arms, and Robbie Unterburger trailing behind him.

"Hi, Fionna," Robbie said, timidly. Fee only raised an eyebrow at her.

"She brought us some dinner. Thank you, love. It was really thoughtful of you."

Robbie simpered as Lloyd set the bags down on the table and began to take clear plastic containers out of it. Something crisp-fried. Something stewed—two stewed somethings. A chunk of bread in a waxed paper bag. A mass of slightly wilted salad. The unfamiliar yet savory smells wafted toward Fee's nose, but couldn't work their magic on her. She was too tense to enjoy them. Unable to bear the sight of food, or Robbie, Fee looked away and stared at the curtains, conscious that the girl was staring at her.

"Thanks," she said. After a time, she heard the shuffle of footsteps. The girl was going away. Thank heaven.

Lloyd muttered something, and the hall door snicked shut. He came around Fee's chair and stared down at her.

"What's the matter with you? She just did you a favor!"

"I'm sorry," Fee said, with sincere contrition. "I'm just too worried."

"You could have sounded like you meant it when you said thanks," Lloyd said, his dark brows lowering to his nose.

"The girl's such a nosebleed," Fee said, more snappishly than she meant. "She's talented, but her personality . . ."

"She's nice enough," Lloyd said.

Fionna eyed him. "She'd be yours if you let her," she said, shrewdly.

Lloyd, just as shrewd, knew better than to walk into that kind of emotional mine field. He shrugged noncommittally. "Who, her? You're worth fifty of her."

Fionna hugged herself. Though it was good to have Lloyd say so, she felt uncertain whether she was worth all the trouble and the compliments. She had used to be so confident, back when she and Liz Mayfield were at school. She was a superstar now. She ought to feel on top of the world. What had happened to her?

Lloyd was about to administer another scolding, when they heard a gentle rap on the door. Fee looked at the clock on the mantlepiece.

"Oh, that's me appointment, darlin'. Will you let her in?"

The thin woman with a face like old, wrinkled leather in the hallway raised a bone rattle and shook it under Lloyd's face. She waited until he stepped aside to cross the threshold, then shook it all around the perimeter of the door. Fee stood up and watched her with fascination and alarm, as the woman rattled in every corner of the room. She stopped, and suddenly pointed at the containers on the table.

"Did you eat any of that?" she demanded.

"No!" Fee said, alarmed.

"Good," said the shamaness. "Fried food is bad for your aura." She turned to eye Lloyd up and down. "You can eat it. Won't do you no harm, and the donor is favorably disposed to you anyhow."

Fee smiled. The old woman had *his* number. She

was the real thing, just as Fee had been promised. There seemed to be nothing special about the healing priestess's outward appearance. Her yellow dress looked just like those of the other ladies out in the street. Hanging over her left wrist was an ordinary-looking leather handbag with a gold clasp. "What should I be eating?"

"When is your birthday?"

"January. January twenty-seventh."

"Fresh fruit and vegetables. Greens and bacon for security. Okra and black-eyed peas for luck. Alligator."

"Alligator?" Fee asked. "For courage?"

"No'm," said the shamaness, with a sly, dark-eyed look. "Tastes good. A little fatty, but you need some meat on them long bones of yours. Y'ought to try some jambalaya. Not that stuff," she said, with a dismissive wave at the table. "There's better in the Quarter. Ask Willie downstairs. He'll steer you to the good places."

Fee cleared her throat. "I didn't ask you here for restaurant reviews, er, Madam Charmay."

"I know," the old woman said. "This curse. It's still troubling you?" Fee nodded. "Whole cure takes maybe eight, maybe nine days. I've got to find me a black rooster and some other things. Won't cost you too much for the components, but you ought to be generous to the spirits all the same. You're lucky the full moon is coming, day after tomorrow. Otherwise it'd take a month and a week."

"I don't have eight or nine days! I've got to give a concert tomorrow."

"Oh," Madam Charmay said, cocking her head. "Then, you need the quick cure. All right. Stand you there. In the precise center. That's it."

For Fee to stand in the middle of the room, Lloyd

had to move the table. Fee stared up at the ceiling as the old woman walked in ever-tightening circles until she could feel the slight heat of the other's body. All the time Madam Charmay was chanting quietly to herself. Occasionally the rattles punctuated a sentence with their exclamation points. Fee concentrated, wishing she could feel something, anything, to prove that she was connected to the great beyond. But nothing stirred the atmosphere except the freezing blast of the air conditioning. There was another rap at the door, this one businesslike.

"Oh, for heaven's sake, this is getting to be like a drawing room comedy," Fee said, in exasperation. "Look, are you finished?"

"I am now, lady," Madam Charmay said, putting her rattles into her purse. "I can come again."

"Yes, please," Fee said, grabbing her small purse, little more than a wallet on a string. She riffled through the wad of American notes that she'd been given by Nigel and came up with three twenties, which she held out to Madam Charmay. The old woman regarded the money with distaste.

"No, do not give it to me. Give it to charity. This night. Without fail."

"I will," Fee said in surprise, ashamed of herself for not asking about the protocol of paying healers for their services. "Thank you so much."

"It is all in God's name," Madam Charmay said, with dignity. "I will go now."

Lloyd's face turned beet red when he opened the door and saw Liz and Boo-Boo in the hallway.

"May we see her?" Liz asked politely. She hadn't a hope of making this jealous man an ally, but at least she would keep from enraging him further. She had felt her ward alarms go off twice. There were, or had been, two strangers in the room. One of them was still there, yet Liz sensed no danger from the presence.

As if in answer to her unspoken question, a slender, little woman with a worn face and ineffable majesty was stepping daintily toward them. As she came through the door, she traded speaking looks with Boo-Boo. He raised his eyebrows, and the old woman shook her head very slightly. There was the ghost of magic in the room. Benevolent but very strong-minded. Concerned, Liz bustled toward Fionna, who was standing under the light fixture in the center of the room, eating jambalaya out of a carry-out container with a spoon.

"I don't care what the old darlin' said, this tastes wonderful," Fionna said indistinctly, around a large mouthful. "Oh, there you are, you two! I can't believe how hungry I am, and all. Have some." She held out the container. The food smelled good to Liz, but it looked awful. Thick pieces of sausage pushed up through the brownish gravy like monstrous fingers emerging from a swamp.

"Thank you, ma'am, but we've had our dinner," Boo said. "We came to see if you'll be all right to come down for the late rehearsal. Your people are kind of countin' on it."

"Oh, without a doubt!" Fee said, managing to trill the words without spraying food on anyone. She scooped up one last bite and held it up in the air before eating it. "We're going to do *such* a show tomorrow, me darlin's!" She licked the spoon tidily and set it into the empty lid. "Come on, then! Lloyd, me love, get us a taxi?" Liz noticed that she was already wearing her purse.

"Who was that woman we saw?" she asked Boo as they followed in Fionna's wake.

"Friend of mine from the Quarter, a Cajun healer. The real thing. Willie on the door told me Miss Fionna asked for a recommendation. I made sure they didn't send her no charlatans."

"Did she cure Fionna?" Liz asked, with interest.

"Naw. I can tell. There hasn't been time to really get to the roots of what's goin' on. She did the stuff she does for visitors. A little chantin', rattlin' to drive away the bad spirits. Short-term fix, but you can see it's cheered her up a lot. Half of healin's mental, y'know."

Liz sighed. "At least the show will go on."

Boo tilted his head and gave her a little smile. "Don't worry, ma'am. We'll catch whoever's behind this."

Chapter 12

At 10:00 P.M., the SATN-TV host pointed into the camera lens.

"Yes, ladies and gentlemen, you, yes, *you*! *You can* keep your children from falling under the influence of wrong-thinking people like this woman and her ilk." The camera pulled back from him to show the poster of Green Fire. In the amber spotlight, Fionna Kenmare's dark eye makeup looked sinister and terrifying, and the male musicians hovered like thugs. "Tonight we show you ways to combat the insidious influence of so-called *white* magic and rock music. We've got a lot of guests tonight I know you'll enjoy. Stay tuned!"

Augustus Kingston watched the screen with his eyes slitted like a pleased snake. This show was SATN's bread and butter. The average pollster from the FCC or either of the two big services would have been very surprised if they ever took a survey in this area of the country. Never mind your late night reruns of situation comedies. Never mind your home shopping networks. The big deal in this part of the woods was the *Hate Your Neighbor* show, hosted by Nick Trenton. In the last five years Trenton had shown a genius for raising hackles among his guests, half of whom had something to do with evildoing, and the other half who were the subject of their rants. It was a poor night when there wasn't one good fistfight. You could raise a contact high of black magic just sitting in the audience. The sponsors would see to it that it ran forever. They said that the evil that men did lived after them. Augustus Kingston could have thought of no better monument to himself than an everpouring fount of dark power that bore his name, although he intended to live a very long time and enjoy it.

That night's programming was setting up to be a good one. They had rounded up a handful of wiccans, a man and four women, and coaxed them to come on the show to promote their peaceful nature cult. They were on the set already, looking nervously at the black candles and the pig-shaped altar. What they didn't know was their fellow guests were unconstructed right-wing megaconservatives who didn't believe women should even be taught to read. Kingston turned down the audio monitor as he picked up the phone and punched the internal extension.

"Ed, how's that test running?"

"Pretty well, sir!" the engineer shouted over the noises in the control room. "I don't know what you've got at the other end, but the needles are showing almost fifteen percent feed coming in on the line. Wow, almost sixteen percent! . . . Sir, can I ask what kind of transmission this feed is?" he asked in a worried voice.

"No, Ed, I'd rather you didn't," Kingston said, in a paternal voice. He pulled a Cuban cigar out of the walnut humidor on his desk.

"Well, sir, if it's radioactive . . . I don't want to make a fuss, but my wife and I want to have kids one day."

"I promise you, son," Kingston concentrated on getting the end clipped off to his satisfaction. "This is nothing that would ever show up on a Geiger counter. You still don't want to stick your fingers in it, though."

"No, sir."

"Good boy. You got that transmission going in to the special power storage like I told you?"

"Yes, sir," Ed's voice said, resignedly.

"What's the reading?"

"Almost sixteen percent."

"Very nice. I'm proud of you, son. Keep me posted." Kingston glanced up at the clock as he depressed the plunger and dialed the operator. "Charlene, I'm expecting a long-distance call. Put it right through, won't you, honey? And don't listen in. If you do, you're fired."

The watcher's call came through on schedule, at a quarter to the hour. Kingston had never met the man on the scene. He had been hired by the friend of a friend of a friend. At least it sounded like a man. It could have been a woman with a deep voice. It was hard to tell, because the voice was distorted by one of those gizmos that they used on crime shows. Kingston didn't care, as long as the person made the scheme work. Everything he was hoping for depended on it.

"Mr. Kingston?" the voice buzzed in his ear.

"That's me," the station owner said. "How's it going at your end?"

"All the technology is in place. There was no problem hiding the mechanisms in among all the other electronics. What's two or three more boxes or cables?"

"Exactly," Kingston said. He felt pretty pleased. This friend of a friend had picked a smart one. "You need a feed from us this evening?"

"A short one, just to test the mechanism again," said the voice. "I need to rewire the transmission lines in the control room."

"Don't they already go there?" Kingston asked impatiently.

"They go to the switcher," the voice said. "I'm hooking it into my conduit's *chair*."

"Ahh," said Kingston. "I was wondering how you were making a direct connection. The Law of Contagion says they have to touch."

"The first connection was too general. It blew out. This one will be a lot better. I'm waiting until full dress rehearsal tomorrow afternoon for a full test. By then, it will be too late for the concert to be cancelled. After that, you can let the full power transfer rip. I promise you you'll get a return feed beyond your wildest hopes."

"Marvelous," Kingston gloated, foreseeing his own power rising like the sun. "The pipeline will bring in clouds of evil that will feed our evil, and make us immortal! . . . Er, you didn't hear me say that."

"No, sir."

"How many people you say are coming to that concert?"

"A maximum of ninety thousand tickets. They're not all sold yet."

"You know," Kingston said, easing back in his chair, "I consider every one of those empty seats a lost opportunity. Now, you're sure your conduit doesn't know what it is we're doing?"

"Not a clue." There was a hesitation. "Well, we've

got one possible hiccup. There's a couple of government agents on the job. They actually suspect magic," the voice dropped to a whisper, "and it looks like they *know* some, too."

"Really." Kingston's eyebrows went up, but he kept his voice from reflecting the dismay he felt. Chances were slim that these practitioners were his kind of people. "Don't worry. Give me a full description of them."

The voice ticked off the physical details of a prim, blond Englishwoman in a two-piece suit and a Southerner who wore ratty clothes that were half hippie, half ex-GI. Kingston took notes.

"Uh-huh. Uh-huh. Uh-huh," the owner said at last. "I'll take care of it. Get back to me tomorrow." He hung up the phone and sauntered into the control room.

The Trenton show was well under way. The male wiccan was trying to defend his congregants from the leering megarightists. The women had a few things to say for themselves, but kept getting shouted down by the audience. One of the opposition was out of his chair, hefting the overstuffed piece of furniture as if judging whether he could actually throw it. It looked as though the first fight was about to break out, when Trenton signalled for a station break. Kingston grinned. That'd keep the television audience glued to their seats. They'd have to stay tuned to see if punches flew.

After the police had cleared the combatants off the set, Trenton stepped into the audience. Time for the night's rail against Fionna Kenmare.

" . . . Do you really want a woman like this evil person influencing your children?" he asked them, his voice smooth and suave. He pointed at the poster of her on stage above the pig-shaped altar. In no time he had them worked into a frenzy. "She's horrible! She's a goody-goody! She believes in white magic!"

Some of the audience were out of their seats chanting, "No! No! No!" Kingston smiled.

The new transmitter-receiver near the switcher panel was sparking up. It looked like it had come straight out of Frankenstein's laboratory. The red digital indicator on the front read "16," ticking occasionally to "17." Kingston's mystery connection was right. The chosen conduit was one heck of a powerful transmitter. Good thing that neither the conduit or anyone else suspected what was going on. A lot of people's abilities were stifled when they became aware of what they were doing, or in this case, being led to do. It'd be one fine Saturday night.

Chapter 13

"Oh, well," Nigel Peters was saying gamely, "they say that a bad dress rehearsal presages a good opening night."

If that was the truth, then the Green Fire concert was going to surpass any performance in history by the Three Tenors, Barbara Streisand, the Boston Pops or Kylie Minogue. Anything balanced between going right and going wrong tilted and fell over into wrong. Lighting filaments popped and went black. Speakers refused to function, or wouldn't turn off when disconnected. People went for unexpected slides on patches of floor that were perfectly dry. Costumes tore, guitar strings sprang, and synthesizer keys were silent one moment and blaring out of tune the next. The front doors to the Superdome arena popped open by themselves and refused to stay locked. A guard had to be called in from his day off to keep the ticket-buying public out in the lobby. Liz knew that half of them blamed her and Boo's presence for the run of bad luck.

"Bloody government," more than one crew member had muttered as they went past her. It was difficult to hide out of sight on a round stage, but she was as self-effacing as she could be. She and Boo stood among the coils of cable behind one of the huge speakers. They weren't in anyone's way, and they still had the best possible view of the action, but she could feel the resentment aimed her way from every direction.

So far it had been a disaster. Green Fire hadn't made it all the way through the first song yet without at least one major blowup, and they'd been rehearsing for an hour. Liz put down part of the problem to sheer exhaustion. She knew she was reeling on her feet.

Last night's late rehearsal had been everything that anyone could have wished for. Boo's shamaness friend's temporary fix had turned the trick. Fionna had come in on a musical high that carried everyone else up into the heavens with her. She had been in her best voice, and knew how good she looked and sounded. All the special effects had gone off on cue, the lights were where they ought to have been, and the musicians played all their numbers without a single hitch. Even the fussy Guitarchangel hadn't been able to find anything to correct. He had just smiled his enigmatic, pre-Raphaelite smile as his long fingers wove music out of his instrument's strings. Liz and Boo had walked the entire perimeter of the Superdome without finding so much as a sniff of malign magic. They had all been in good spirits when they broke up. If they'd filmed that performance and showed it on those gigantic screens that hovered over the stage like doomsday, they'd have been better off than they were now.

In celebration, Fionna promised to buy everyone

a drink. The entire company had poured out into the French Quarter, chattering on about how well it had all gone. Buoyed up on the energy of success, Fee led her merry band from bar to bar in the French Quarter, until they simply ran out of places they hadn't been to yet. While out on the road they seldom got a chance to enjoy the city sights.

"Might as well hold concerts out on a desert oasis for all we see of one place or another," Eddie Vincent had complained, with a touch of bitterness. The others had agreed.

"Oi'd do anythin' to have an afternoon's shoppin' here," Fionna had said wistfully, as they passed by dozens of closed stores, "so this'll have to do me." Liz wasn't happy about such an unstructured outing, but she understood the poignant urge. And, as Beauray pointed out, there was nothing she could do to make Fionna go back to the hotel.

"It's best just to tag along and take it easy," Beauray said. "Who's going to attack her with so many people around?"

"Numbers could make an attack easier, not harder," Liz grumbled. But Boo-Boo was right: it was just best to follow along with the crowd. Liz couldn't defend against a negative. Until the mysterious malign force surfaced again, there was nothing she could do. She had kept on glancing into alleys and up onto the omnipresent balconies. Was everyone in New Orleans but her having a good time?

Wherever they had stopped, Nigel Peters had ordered drinks for everyone. Voe Lockney had fallen in love with Sazeracs. The band and crew put a serious dent in the Quarter's supply of good whiskey. They sang along with every song they knew, and applauded the performers with drunken abandon. Robbie Unterburger stared with mooncalf eyes at

Lloyd, who ignored her. Patrick Jones did humorous imitations of the people they saw walking in the street. Sooner or later, they wandered into the open-air coffee shop named the Café du Monde and ate square doughnuts frosted a quarter-inch deep in powdered sugar. Liz watched it all, staying awake on adrenaline, sugar, and the odd-tasting coffee Boo told her was flavored with chicory.

Dawn hadn't been far off their heels by the time everyone finally went to bed. By the time the technical run-through had gotten under way, noon had come and gone.

Chain-smoking unfiltered cigarettes, Nigel Peters had confided to the two agents that only with luck would they finish in time to take a decent dinner break and a rest before the concert itself. Everyone was on edge, but Fionna was in the worst mood possible. Her temper was beginning to affect everyone else.

"All right then," Michael announced in his clipped voice from the center of the stage. His forehead was creased as though he had a headache. He probably had. "We'll just take it from the top again. And we'll do so until we get it right. If we can get the programme moving, the rest will follow more easily. Understood?"

Mutters and groans met this announcement. Liz wondered if he'd ever been a schoolteacher. Fionna automatically trudged back to the short flight of steps at the rear of the stage. Later on, darkness would cover what was going on around her, but for now Liz could see everything. Laura Manning touched up Fee's wild makeup. Fitz, on his knees, fussed with the hem of the new green silk dress that was pinned to the shoulders of Fionna's black crop-top T-shirt. Because she would have to be sewn into the skin-tight sheath later, Fitz didn't want to have her wear it until then. Judging by the intricacy of the design and the handsome beadwork that outlined the LEDs, Thomas Fitzgibbon must have spent the rest of the night on his creation. He looked reluctant to get more than a few paces away from his creation, lest it burst into flames like the last one. His overprotectiveness was irritating Fionna. He kept getting in the way of her arm movements.

As her cue came, Fitz started to follow her on his knees, holding the hem of the dress up so it wouldn't catch on the floorboards. She swept her hand down and accidentally smacked him on the head. The two of them jumped at the contact. Fionna stopped to give him a glare that would have frozen mercury solid.

"All right, enough!" Fionna snapped out. "Go away. Now."

He halted, and retired to the edge of the stage, hands fretting with the tape measure slung around his neck. Laura Manning gave him a wry look, professional to professional.

"And, *mark*!" announced Hugh Banks, the stage manager, moving around the perimeter. "First sparklers start at six points around the stage. Six, isn't it, darling?" he asked, putting a hand to the headset he was wearing. He nodded. "And, *off*." The musicians carried on what they were doing.

Liz and Boo-Boo were on guard with every piece of magical paraphernalia at their disposal. Both of them had been reluctant to let the other know what he or she was carrying, but Liz had pointed out that they'd only get in one another's way if they started popping off spells at random. Not until she opened her own bag of tricks and dumped it out to the seams did he relax and let her examine his arsenal. She was impressed, though she didn't let her emotions show, and hoped he felt the same way. It wouldn't do for the British Empire, however reduced, to be superseded by its former colony in any way. She matched him defensive spell for defensive spell, truth-finders, serum for healing burns (always vital to have on hand when one did a lot of candle work), concealment spells to protect covert movement, and so on.

"Start again!" Fionna shouted, as the song they were playing fizzled noisily. "I can't stand these bleedin' crowds. Everyone who doesn't belong on stage, get off!"

In particular, she turned to glare at the two agents. Nigel Peters started toward them, but Boo had taken Liz's arm, and was already escorting her down the stairs. Liz backed off through what would be the mosh pit to the closest possible vantage point where she could see the expanse of the stage. Peters gave them a grateful glance. He looked haggard, as though he hadn't slept all night.

The looming Jumbotron hung further down from the ceiling than it had the night before. The barrels of stage lights and clusters of black-painted boxes were arrayed around the bottom of it. Liz guessed the mysterious boxes were part of the special effects equipment. Hanging from the lip of the Jumbotron on each side was an enormous poster of the band, concealing the lighting frame from the view of punters in the auditorium seating. Each enormous graphic showcased a different member in the center. Privately Liz thought the one featuring Fionna made her look like the bride of Frankenstein. Same open-mouthed, horror-struck expression. Liz grinned.

A dozen men and women in blue jeans moved purposefully throughout the room with blackened aluminum boxes hoisted on their shoulders. Liz didn't recognize any of the people, and pointed them out to her fellow agent.

"Television camera operators," Boo-Boo said.

Liz was appalled. "They aren't broadcasting this concert, are they? Not when we have so much else to deal with? It could be a disaster!"

Boo-Boo was happy to reassure her. "It's not being broadcast anywhere, although they're tapin' it for themselves. Those cameras have long zoom lenses. Mr. Peters said they want to cover the stage from a half-dozen points around the interior and show some of the good stuff on the Jumbotron screens. They don't want the folks in the cheap seats to miss the dramatic expressions, and all."

"What a good idea," Liz said, appreciatively. "Those screens are a real benefit when the length of a football field separates fans from the stage." She remembered that from the control room alone the band looked smaller than figures on a wedding cake, and wondered how concertgoers felt about it. Nonetheless, she still felt nervous about the Jumbotron. The gigantic box hung perfectly steady on its moorings, but she didn't trust it a bit. It hovered over them like the cloud of doom.

"Morning, Agent Boudreau," said a smooth voice from behind them. They turned to see Mr. Winslow, the building manager, dapper in his white suit. He came up to shake hands with Boo-Boo. "Just checking in . . . to see how things are going. Pretty well, eh?"

"Well . . ." Boo-Boo began.

Eddie Vincent brought his hands down flat on his keyboard, producing a discordant organ sting that blasted out of the speakers like the whistle at quitting time on a construction site. Everybody winced.

Mr. Winslow's face contracted into a mass of pained

pleats. "Well, I won't stay long. I don't want to be in the way."

"I'm sure the band won't mind," Boo-Boo said.

"Truth is," the manager said, with a wry grin as he retreated backwards toward the corridor, "this stuff hurts my ears. You young people . . . must like it, though."

Boo put a forefinger to his lips and tapped it conspiratorially. "Well, I'm sorry to mention it, Mr. Winslow, but the two of us is supposed to keep a pretty low profile, so I'm goin' to say excuse me for now."

"Oh! I understand," Mr. Winslow said, with the wide-eyed expression of someone pleased to have wandered into a real-life spy adventure. He shook hands with Boo again. "Nice to see you, Agent. And your . . . lovely assistant. Good afternoon, ma'am. We sure appreciate your helping out here." He gave Liz a half-bow.

"Assistant! *I'm* not . . ." Liz began, eager to correct his misapprehension, but Boo-Boo's hand closed over her wrist.

"Let him go, Liz," Boo said.

"But he thinks I'm your assistant! Why won't you let me—?" Mr. Winslow made a left turn out at the end of the corridor, heading for the long escalators that led to the lobby. She could just catch him.

"It doesn't really matter what he thinks, does it?" Boo asked, interrupting her.

Liz jerked her hand loose, but she was suspicious. She regarded Boo with narrowed eyes.

"All right, why did you want that man to get out of the way so quickly?"

"I don't know whether y'all noticed it," Beauray said, casually, "but Mr. Winslow has this little trick of waitin' in the middle of a sentence until you meet his eyes. That means if we have him standin' here havin' a nice conversation, we can't keep watchin' the set."

Liz's eyelids flew up in surprise. "Why, you're right. I apologize. But the next time I see him, I'm going to set him straight. I am not an *assistant*."

"I was tellin' the truth when I said we had to keep a low profile, wasn't I?" Boo asked, his blue eyes innocent.

"Yes, but . . ."

"Well, I'm helpin' you keep your cover," he said, in his easygoing way, as if that should settle everything. Liz glared at him. In any case there was no way to call Mr. Winslow back. Beauray had scored on her once more. She was not going to let that happen again.

The music had started again. Spotlights, faint in the brilliant noon sunshine, played around the interior of the stage. Michael came up the back stairs, and a pale golden light hit him, setting fire to the metal of his guitar strings, turned the flesh of his hands and face to incandescent ivory, and gilded his black hair. He looked so beautiful Liz forgot for a moment to breathe.

Lights came up on the other two musicians, setting halos playing in their long hair. Michael started forward, but the spot stayed where it was. Michael frowned down, then up.

"Hold it," he said. "Hold it!" The music died away. "What's wrong with the lights now?"

Just as everyone looked up into the flies, a gigantic flash of light burst overhead. Liz almost threw a spell to protect the people on the stage. Only well-honed reflexes kept her from crushing the components in her hand when she realized it was just a light popping. Sparks showered down onto the stage. The stage crew threw their hands up over their heads. Only Michael stood there in the rain of fire, looking authoritative and indignant. "Was that my key light?"

"Someone check!" shouted the stage manager, setting his staff into a flurry of motion.

Boo took a firm but not dangerous hold of Liz's wrist, and pried her fingers open. She stared at him in surprise as he picked up the fragile wax shell she had been clutching. "Y'can't use that in here, Liz," he said.

"And why not?" Liz asked. "It's perfectly safe. It's a fire-prevention cantrip."

"You'll have to forgive me sayin' so, but it don't have the range to cover the area of the stage."

"I could double the amount," Liz said, indignantly. "That would be more than plenty."

"Well, then it will be too heavy to have the range you want, no matter how loud you chant. What if you're not as close as you are right now?"

"And I suppose you have something better?" she asked, peevishly.

"Sure do," Boo said, companionably. "I checked with HQ this mornin'. They said I can give you these." He handed her a couple of sachets. Liz glanced at them dubiously. They smelled strongly of myrrh and purslane, a protective herb traditionally ruled by the element of water. She had to admit they were beautifully constructed, the edge of each fragile paper envelope sewn shut with corn silk. "You can have the formula later on. If these give satisfaction, that is."

"Oh, thank you," Liz said, trying not to sound sarcastic. *Helping the poor cousin,* she thought, furiously. Thought he knew it all. Their government could obviously pay for higher quality than her government. Another way of shamefully showing off.

"This isn't the spell you think it is," she said, now ashamed of the irregularly-shaped bubble containing a cluster of damp crystals like a handful of bath salts sealed in waxed paper.

"Well, actually, I think it is," Boo said, returning the components to her between cautious thumb and forefinger. "Our intelligence is pretty good."

"We've made improvements, and . . ." Liz stopped just short of telling him she was a hereditary witch and knew how to put together a workmanlike spell, dammit! With dismay she realized he probably knew all that, too. Annoyed at her own outburst, she reasserted her professionalism. There was a job to do. She'd give him a piece of her mind later. With grace, she accepted the spell components and his instruction on how to chant the incantation.

"*Bimity polop caruma?*"

"*Caruna,*" Boo corrected her. "It's an 'n.'" Liz nodded. It was ironic that though the Americans claimed to believe less in magic than the British, their department produced a better line of counterspell that they didn't believe would do anything to counteract the occurrence that they didn't believe could happen.

"Quiet!" shouted the stage manager. Liz looked up, startled, wondering if they'd been overheard. But they hadn't been the only ones making noise. Liz just became aware of the last faint echoes of a mechanical screech, as the huge box overhead swayed slightly. She felt giddy just looking up at the Jumbotron. She had enormous sympathy for the workers who had to climb the narrow iron catwalks twenty-six stories above the ground to maintain it.

Hugh Banks walked out to the center of the stage, accompanied by a representative from building maintenance, a heavyset man in khaki coveralls. They looked up at the grid. The burned-out spotlight was a black dot at the edge of the framework.

"One of those posters of yours was touchin' the light," the supervisor said, with an experienced nod. "Coulda started a fire. Lucky just the one light went out."

"We need that spot functioning again," the stage manager said, reading from a complex diagram. "Can you fix it?"

"We'll just have to replace that light filament," the supervisor said. "Have to raise the Jumbotron to do it. It can't be done while it's lowered."

"Wait until after the rehearsal," the stage manager said, with a sigh. "Five o'clock, all right?"

"No problem."

"This is supposed to be the *technical* rehearsal," Michael Scott said, peevishly. "What about the cues?"

The stage manager spoke into his headset again.

"We're on it," Ken Lewis's voice echoed over the public address system in the vast room. "I'll swap another spotlight as Michael's key light for the time being."

"Good?" Banks asked Michael. The guitarist nodded, not happily.

The group began again. And again. The third attempt was interrupted by the arrival of the backup singing trio and the hired percussionist, Lou Carey.

"Very sorry we're late," Carey said. He was a razor-thin black man with a razor-thin mustache under his narrow nose. "We got the time wrong."

"All right, then," the stage manager said. "Get in your places."

"Should we get our costumes?" one of the singers asked. A tiny girl with huge brown eyes, she had a thrilling contralto voice that resonated pleasantly even without amplification.

"You'll have to get dressed during the break," Michael said. "We're delayed enough as it is."

"Places for the fourth number, please!"

Michael started picking out a moody and frustrated melody. Liz recognized it as Green Fire's well-known rant against environmental destruction. It was powerful and disturbing. She knew every note, swaying slightly with the music.

The others joined in. The latecomers hurried toward their assigned spots, eager to catch up and join in. Eddie Vincent brought his hands down onto his synthesizer keyboard for a crashing crescendo that imitated a rising gale. Fionna's voice would rise out of the music like whitecaps on the crest of a foaming sea and tear the soul out of the audience.

Just then, the lights went down. Eyes accustomed to the glare of the spots and the brightness of noonday were temporarily blinded. In the momentary dimness, there was the sound of stumbling feet, a thud, a clattering. The wild music died away in a whine like deflating bagpipes. Liz felt a wrench in her chest from the unfulfilled promise of the song. Eddie Vincent's deep voice reeled out a string of profanities.

When the lights came up a moment later, a spotlight highlighted the unfortunate percussionist flat on the floor with his feet tangled in a mass of cables. Several of the stagehands leaped forward to help him up.

"He pulled the power cords out of my rig!" Eddie shouted.

"I didn't do it on purpose, man!" Carey said, his cheeks glowing with embarrassment. "I was nowhere near your stuff! Somebody pulled me—or something. The next thing I knew, I was on my face."

"Get out of here," Eddie said, angrily. "Move it. Nigel!"

"Eddie, he couldn't have done it on purpose," the manager said, striding up the stage steps. "We all saw it. He was going toward the opposite side of the stage. He must just have gotten lost in the dark."

"What dark? It's noon! He got lost walking across a wide-open stage?"

"I didn't get lost. Someone pulled me into the cables," Carey insisted. "Someone took hold of my arms and yanked me over that way. It just happened."

"Do you think I'm stupid?" Eddie snarled. "What kind of story is that?"

"I couldn't see, man! I'm sorry!"

Hulking roadies in T-shirts and jeans began to gather around the keyboards, looking menacing. Liz couldn't tell whether they were prepared to defend Eddie or the other man. She sensed a measure of ill will in the room, but not necessarily between the two groups of stagehands. The energy simply didn't feel normal. She was uneasy, but couldn't put a finger on just what was bothering her.

"Please, guys," Nigel said, holding his hands up for attention as he pushed in among them. "This gets us nowhere. We've got to get through this, or there'll be no time to rest before the concert. I don't know about you, but I could sleep for a year."

"Look," said Hugh, "he said he was sorry. Forget it, eh?"

Eddie lowered his thick eyebrows at the newcomer, but shook his head. He managed to find a smile somewhere among his dour looks. "All right, man. Just keep clear, all right?"

"No problem," said the musician, backing away with his hands up. The unlucky man was glad to escape and take his place among his fellow temps, two more guitarists, a violinist, a flautist, a harpist and a woman playing the uilleann pipe. The harpist, a very tall man named Carl Johnson, gave him a sympathetic look. Eddie went back to frowning over his instruments.

Fionna, having thrown off Fitz and his paroxysms of fashion, appeared in her second costume, a white dress that consisted almost entirely of long fringe over a flesh-colored sheath. It was fabulously effective, even sexy, but at the same time Liz thought it made Fee look like a white Afghan hound. She wasn't quick enough to suppress a snort of laughter. Unfortunately, the outburst came during one of the rare moments of silence. Everyone stopped what they were doing and looked at her. Liz felt her cheeks redden.

"And what the fokkin' hell do you think is funny?" Fee demanded.

"Sorry," Liz said.

"Pack up and move it the hell out of here!" Fionna shouted. "Go on with you!"

Boo pulled Liz further away from the stage and bent his head close to hers. "Don't stir her up. There's something wrong here."

"Can you feel it, too?"

"Yes, I can. Like sittin' on a powder keg, and everyone throwin' lit matches. It's makin' everybody touchy, but I can't find a source for it. Keep an eye peeled. I just feel somethin's goin' to happen. Don't know what, yet."

Fionna burst vehemently into song. The musicians caught up with her a line or so later, weaving their threads with the instrument of her voice. It was an angry song about injustice and killing the innocent. Unlike the quiet hurt the folk song had engendered the first night in O'Flaherty's, this one grabbed the listener by the ears and made him despise the abusers. Liz felt fury crackle in the air. The magic Green Fire were making was a dangerous kind. Fionna stalked from side to side of the stage, exhorting the invisible audience to join with her in hating the oppressors. She flung an arm around the microphone stand at the east side of the stage and screeched a verse into that one. The fringes whipped around the metal pole, but didn't drop back when she let go. As she took one whirling step away, the microphone followed her. It leaned dangerously for a split second, then crashed at her feet. Swearing a blue streak that could be heard from every speaker in the room, Fee stood and quivered with rage while the grips and Fitz jumped forward to help her free.

"Cut the damned fringe off the damned sleeves," Fionna's order echoed throughout the arena. Ears stunned by the level of the rock music, Liz couldn't hear Fitz's side of the discussion, but his pleading expression was eloquent. "I do not bloody care. I'm not a fokkin' snake charmer like St. Patrick!"

The costumer's face stiffened. Nigel Peters fairly leaped up the steps to make peace.

"Oh, no!" Fionna exclaimed, in answer to an unheard plea from her manager. "Do you think I want to have me own clothes making a fool of me?"

Nigel looked up toward the northwest and made a throat-cutting gesture at the booth. Fionna's microphone was turned off, rendering her inaudible to the rest of the people in the arena. She, Nigel and Fitz engaged in a three-sided pantomime row, only a few syllables loud enough to be understood. Nigel tapped his watch. As an argument, it was absolutely unassailable. There wasn't time to fuss. The show must go on. Sadly, Fitzgibbon produced his scissors and barbered the trim on the sleeves to three inches in length. A stagehand appeared with a broom. Fitz watched him sweep up the cuttings with the same dismayed expression a mother might watch her child's first haircut. Without looking back at him, Fionna returned to her spot at the east edge of the stage. The musicians struck up. Fionna grabbed the microphone and opened her mouth.

A mechanical shriek blasted out. Everyone jumped as steam started pouring upward from the pipes lined up in a long frame at the edge of the stage. Fantastic green figures swam upward along the insubstantial curtain. Snakes and birds twisted into Celtic knotwork, created with laser lights; Liz let out an admiring gasp, but it stopped everyone else dead.

"What in all the saints' names was that?" Fionna asked, recovering her wits.

"That effect isn't supposed to go until the sixth song!" came the despairing cry of the stage manager. "What's going on up there?" He seized the mouthpiece of his headset in one hand and started gesticulating with the other hand.

"Sorry," came Robbie's tremulous voice over the intercom. The steam ceased rising. "My hand slipped and pushed the cursor too far ahead on my instructions. It won't happen again."

"It had bloody not better," everyone on the stage muttered, almost in unison.

But it did. Little things continued to go awry. Effects happened late, or went off on the wrong part of the stage. Liz watched with the feeling that she was seeing a building being demolished a few tiles at a time with the debris falling on innocent passersby. The wonderful feeling that had pervaded the arena early that afternoon was gone without a trace, leaving behind it deep gloom. Much of it could be laid at Robbie Unterburger's feet.

"The girl is just plain off," Boo commented, not without sympathy, watching Fionna dodge tiny explosions that had been laid on the floor of the stage like an unlucky cowboy ordered to "dance" by a rival gunslinger. If Robbie wasn't clearly so apologetic, it would look like she was deliberately trying to make Fionna look bad.

"Do you think she senses the foreboding that's growing in here?" Liz asked. "She might be affected by it." The thought interested her greatly for a moment. "Is Robbie a sensitive? Could she be a possible recruit for either of our departments?"

Beauray's fair eyebrows rose high on his forehead. "Never thought of that, ma'am. She might be just what you say, but I'd doubt whether she'd be interested. You have to admit our wage structure don't sound as appealin' when you know what these people are paid."

Liz nodded. If it weren't for the call of patriotism she'd have been sorely tempted by the pay scales she saw listed on the FYI document in her briefing packet. She prided herself on her competence; she would probably do very well at one of these jobs— if it hadn't meant dealing with egos like her old school chum's.

The drummer struck a downbeat, and the rehearsal resumed. The band managed to get through a couple of numbers unhindered, for which everyone looked grateful. Protective spells at the ready, Liz maintained her vigilance, but she would have had to be lying to say she didn't enjoy having a rock concert virtually to herself. A small part of her missed the camaraderie of the crowds. In spite of the pushing and the occasionally impaired view, the people who attended an event like this one shared in a special kind of symbiotic energy. It came from the performers, but it was amplified a millionfold by the audience and given back again. At a really good concert, the transfer back and forth lifted the performance from enjoyable to stellar. Fionna and her players were certainly

capable of lighting that kind of fire in their fans. They
exalted, they comforted, they challenged, all at the
same time. Liz stood rocking to the beat, watching
Fee and Michael dance toward one another in the
center of the stage, then whirl outward again, like a
pair of electrons in a very active molecule. Michael,
all in black, dignified, powerful, stepped backwards
toward the north end of the stage, watching his fingers stirring the strings of his guitar. Fee, feminine,
excitable, vibrant, reached the south end and turned
in a wide circle. The flying fringes on her dress caught
the lights in slashing sprays of white. She halted,
standing straight as a candle. With the air of a priestess of a long-ago culture, she pointed down at a
crystal formation the size of a pumpkin. And waited.
She stopped singing.

"Hold it!" she shouted. "Right now!" As the music
died, Liz felt a sense of loss equal to that of someone snatching her teddy bear away. Fionna clapped
her hands to her hips and glared up at the control
room booth.

"When I am standing here and singing the cue
line," Fionna shouted in a rising tone that threatened
to end in a banshee shriek, "I expect to have the
green lasers meet at me feet and light up that bloody
crystal that is sitting right here. It is not a tiny little
rock. It is a monstrous, great chunk of rock. I should
think," her voice reaching to every corner of the
Superdome, "that even up there you might be able
to see it! Excu-use *me*!"

The technical director's soothing voice came over
the loudspeaker. "Sorry, Fee, darling. Robbie was just
a little behind on her cues. Other than that it was
perfect. Wasn't it, loves? Can we try it again? From
the last mark."

Moodily, Michael Scott took up his station at the

north end of the round stage, nodded his head at the other musicians. Voe Lockney beat his sticks together over his head. One, two, three, and the band began to play. Fionna, who had withdrawn with her arms crossed over her chest, listened, waiting. There was a feeling of anticipation, not happy. Liz would like to have enjoyed herself, reminded herself that this was a job, a still-unsolved mystery. The two dancers made their way toward one another, body language seducing, drawing inward toward one another and out again. Michael withdrew toward his dark fastness. Fionna stepped, whirled, and glided toward the gleaming crystal.

The laser beat her there. Green fire shot down from the overhead grid and sent knives of rainbow glory streaking outward to strike the farthest walls of the arena. Fionna stood bathed in the green light, rigid, with her hands by her sides.

"I have had more than enough," she screamed. "Is me whole performance to be made a mockery because one incompetent little bint can't keep her fokkin' mind on her bleedin' job?"

"Now, Fionna," Nigel said, hurrying toward her, in full placatory mode. Fionna was in no mood to listen. She shouldered past him and kept going, right off the stage, down the steps and out of the arena. Nigel trotted along behind, almost wringing his hands as he tried to reason with her. He might as well have tried dealing with a hurricane in full blow.

"I am goin' to tear her stupid head off her stupid shoulders and put it on me mantelpiece!" Fee raged, flinging her arms in grand gestures. "I am goin' to bake her in a pie and serve her to Shakespeare repertory audiences!" Even though she was wearing six-inch stiletto heels, anger helped her outpace everyone except Lloyd Preston. His long legs had no trouble closing the distance to bring him to her side, and he kept the rest of them at bay.

Liz and Boo hurried at their heels like a pair of terriers. In all their years of school, Liz had seen Fee Kendale go off like this only once. It had also been on the occasion of a matter of incompetence, but it showed how stretched the other woman's nerves were that she was reacting like a spoiled schoolgirl. The cacophony they made clattering through the hallway surprised a tour group on its way around the Superdome. A couple of the tourists recognized Fionna. One of them reached for a camera, but one glare from the ever-vigilant Lloyd distracted her from taking a picture until it was too late.

Not having had time to scope out the passage before Fionna set foot in it, Liz employed a little Earth power to sense around them, making certain there were no booby traps planted in their path. Luckily, the unseen enemy would have no reason to expect Fionna to come tearing out of the arena in that direction. Or would he?

Emotions were already high in the control room when Fionna burst in. The object of her fury cowered in the station behind the complex special effects board, eyeglasses gleaming owlishly in the fluorescent lights. Liz guessed from her red cheeks that Robbie had already been dressed down by Gary Lowe. Fionna marched up and glared down at her.

"Did you get up this mornin' and say, 'Today I think I'll screw up everythin' I touch'?" Fionna asked, in a tone so saccharine that it made Liz's teeth hurt. "Here we are, with only hours before the biggest crowd we've seen in a year comes marchin' in here, and you're behavin' as if you've only seen the equipment for the very first time!"

"I'm sorry," Robbie began, but she didn't stand a chance against the might of Hurricane Fee.

"There's a lot of people you're inconveniencing here, most of whom are pretendin' they're not as annoyed as they are. I've given you a lot of chances. You've broken the rhythm of the rehearsal. Do you know what that does to the band? To me? No, you haven't a clue, have you? How did you ever hold down a responsible job before this?"

Someone snickered.

"And the rest of you needn't think I'm forgettin' about you," Fionna said, spinning on her heel. She was right, Liz observed. Sheila Parker, at the sound desk, had a half smile curling up one side of her mouth that vanished when Fee glared at her. It was only human nature to be thankful at the discomfiture of others, as opposed to suffering it oneself. It was only a small step from there to enjoying the process. Fee was determined that no one was going to enjoy the lecture. "I know you're tryin', but it isn't enough. You're all professionals. We've got no time for screwin' up. There's a show in less than four hours! I'm countin' on you all. This is a grand opportunity for the lot of us. A whole new audience, seein' us live for the first time. Maybe for some this is the first concert that they've ever seen. Doesn't that mean a thing to you? We want this to be right. We want to *dazzle* them; make it an event they'll never forget."

Liz was as caught by surprise as the rest of them. It was such a reasonable argument, appealing to their pride, their better nature, not the flat-out dressing down that she would have assumed Phoebe Kendale would have handed out. She'd grown up. Fionna Kenmare sounded like the CEO of a multinational corporation. Liz realized, with surprise at herself, that that was exactly what her old school friend had become. Green Fire's music was sold in every country that had radio. Their revenue had to run to millions of pounds a year. Lord Kendale wasn't too pleased with his daughter's choice of causes to espouse, but he ought to be proud of the way she occupied the position she'd made for herself.

Fee was sweet and reasonable but stretched to the breaking point with everyone except the special effects coordinator, for whom Fee wouldn't soften under any circumstances. The star swiveled back again to glare at Robbie. "That is, if you can manage to do your job when it *really* matters."

"I know every cue in the concert," Robbie said, who had been pushed all the way through fright to defiance. Her voice shook, but she stood her ground. "I know them forwards and backwards."

"Yes, and so you've been telling me," Fionna said dismissively, lifting a hand to study the green polish on her nails. Robbie's complexion went from red to purple. It was an ugly contrast. "Too bad you've decided to do them backwards."

"I'm sorry I've been messing up. I'll make it right."

"You bloody well better!" Fionna said, dropping her hands onto the back of the other woman's chair and glaring at her. "Your job is to *add to* the spectacle, not be one. When you foul up you call attention to yourself. If that's what you want to do, join the circus. I hear they're always lookin' for another clown."

Robbie gasped. She looked around at the others watching her, hoping for a kind face. Her eyes brimming with hope, she met Lloyd's gaze. He locked eyes with her, but kept his face carefully expressionless. Liz could tell he didn't want to be part of this argument. No one sane would have. Robbie appealed silently to him, brows lifted.

"And you keep off Lloyd," Fee added, not missing

a thing. She interposed herself between the special effects engineer and her bodyguard. "He's here for me, not you."

That shot hit home. Robbie's face flushed even redder. The girl seemed really to have thought no one else had noticed. Liz felt very sorry for her.

"We get along," she said stoutly. "It's not against the law for him to be nice to me."

"So you don't deny you've been trying to steal him!"

Robbie saw the trap, but much too late. It was unwise of her to attempt to justify her feelings. If she'd been smart, she wouldn't have admitted to them at all. It gave Fionna another grievance she could level. Robbie shot out of her seat, standing as tall as she was able, but her voice betrayed how flustered she was.

"You're wrong! I don't have to steal him. I mean, I'm not trying to . . . There's nothing you can do if there's feelings involved! He only works for you. It's a financial arrangement. Not like . . ."

"You're trying to make out that there's more going on than there is, you silly creature," Fionna said, almost pityingly. "That in a minute I'm going to turn me back, and he's going to sweep you off your feet like Prince Charming and ride away in a Lear jet, leaving me to weep. Well, you're not a princess, missie. Nothing like."

"No! If anyone's the princess around here, it's you!" Robbie shouted. "You waltz around like the high priestess of something, but you jump if a shadow crosses your path. I'm trying to do my job!"

"You are trying?" Fionna exclaimed, her eyes widening as her brogue thickened. "You can't stay on cue! Your *job* is almost totally mechanized and you still screw it up! This is the *dress rehearsal*, damn yer sorry arse!" She flung a hand at the girl. "To hell with you. Those thousands of people are coming to hear my voice. Yer window dressin'. We'll do it without effects if we have to!"

Turning like a model on the runway, Fionna stalked magnificently out of the room, followed by Lloyd. Nigel offered an apologetic glance to the crew, but he couldn't look at Robbie.

With the agents and her bodyguard on her heels, Fionna strode back down the ramps to the arena door where the rest of the company was waiting for her. Their astonished expressions told her they had heard every word. The PA system had been switched on in the booth.

"Let's try it again," she said, calmly. She smiled at them, serene again but very, very firm. "Once, all the way through, no stops. All right?"

Everyone rushed to their places, unwilling to be the next to receive Fee's own brand of personal attention.

Liz shot a glance at Boo-Boo. His wary expression told her he felt the same magical buildup that she did. The pent-up energy that had been pressing at the edges of her magical conscious was reaching an overload. It could burst out at any moment.

She had no idea it would strike so soon. Fionna had no sooner stomped back onto the round stage when an explosion overhead made everyone's heart stop. The crew and band ran for cover, but they were in no danger from the debris. The snowstorm of colored dots fell in heaps directly on the cowering figure of Fionna. She shrieked and batted at the rain of trash.

"Who put confetti up there?" Hugh Banks demanded. "This isn't a parade!"

It wasn't confetti. The gigantic poster of Green Fire

attached to one side of the Jumbotron had shredded
itself into tiny bits. The huge faces on the three
remaining posters seemed to mock the crew.

"Ah, no," the stage manager moaned, clutching his
head. "It must be the one near the light that burned
out!"

The falling flakes of paper whirled and twinkled
under the beams of the intact spots. Liz was about
to thank heaven that this wasn't another fire attack,
when suddenly the ruins of the poster burst into
flames. Fionna screamed, but stood helpless in the
middle of the rising fire, like St. Joan at the stake.

"Somebody do something!" she cried.

This time, Boo-Boo was ready. He leaped forward,
hands moving in a blur, and lobbed a handful of blue
powder in the direction of the stage, chanting all the
while. Between one shrill outburst and another, the
powder spread out into a cloud that momentarily hid
the star from view. The mass settled a moment later,
revealing Fionna standing with her arms flung up to
protect her face. The colored dots lay in half-singed
piles around her feet. Her second cry for help died
away as she stared around her. Lloyd shoved his way
through the crowd and looked her over carefully.
Then he took her into his arms. Fionna collapsed
against him limply. She was too astonished to speak.
Thomas Fitzgibbon broke the silence.

"This wasn't . . . this wasn't the lasers this time, was
it?"

"What the hell did you do?" Michael Scott
demanded, rounding on Boo-Boo and Liz, as Nigel
Peters and Hugh Banks began shouting at everyone
else to clear the stage. The stagehands swooped in
with brooms.

"Just fire control," Boo-Boo said. "Government
issue." He showed the packet, which featured the

eagle of the United States holding a fire extinguisher in each outstretched claw.

"That wasn't just a chemical reaction," the guitarist said, with a wary eye. "What are you?"

"Government agent," Boo-Boo said simply, producing his ID. "It's not over yet, sir. Let's all just remain calm." But Michael and the others were anything but calm.

"I want to know what is going on!" the guitarist demanded. "Are you responsible for these outbursts?"

"I'm sorry, sir," Liz said, in an even voice. "I'm afraid we can't discuss details . . ."

"Don't 'sir' me," Michael said, raising his eyebrows alarmingly. "You've been underfoot for two days. I've heard Fionna's complaints for the last months now. We've all heard them. The things that are happening to her are real, aren't they?"

Liz was saved having to reply by Fionna herself. With a wild scream, Fee started turning around and around, slowly at first, but faster and faster until the white fringes on her dress stood straight out.

"Now, don't play around, love," Lloyd said.

"She's not doing it, Mr. Preston," Liz said, removing a white silk cloth from her handbag. "Look at her feet." They weren't moving. Fee appeared to be spinning on her own axis with no visible means of propulsion.

"Fee, honey, don't make a fool of yourself," Lloyd said. He put his arms around her to stop her, and got taken up in the vortex. "Hey!" He whirled around and around until his feet lifted off the floor. Fionna was going too fast for him to hang on. With a yell, the burly security man went flying. He landed several yards away, rolling over and over, missing Eddie Vincent's precious keyboards by a foot. Lloyd lay on his back, shaking his head to clear it. Liz clicked her tongue. Too impetuous. That was no way to pull her out of a spin.

Liz held out the white cloth in the air by its center, and began to chant, drawing power from the earth as she went. It would take a lot of Earth power to take Fee away from the Air element that had claimed her. With a swift glance at the people around her, she lowered her voice to a mutter for the last words of the spell. With the final word, she dropped the cloth to the ground. Fee stopped spinning so suddenly she staggered.

"Thank heavens," Fionna said, swallowing. "Now, I—"

But whatever had Fee in its grasp was not through with her yet. The spinning began again, faster than before. Alarmed, Liz picked up the cloth and dropped it again and again. No response. Fionna became a green and white blur that lifted into the air. In a moment she'd bump into the Jumbotron. The enormous magical power building in the Superdome was not to be quelled by a simple dampening spell.

The band and crew were taken completely by surprise. Even the imperturbable Michael stood gawking up at Fionna with his mouth hanging open. Even as she worked to quell it, Liz was dismayed. Spinning she could explain away. An exploding poster turning into party favors could be put down to natural causes. Even it bursting into flames had the potential to be excused under the circumstances. The manifestation of a flying dervish appearing in a public location was going to be *much* harder to excuse as not being supernatural.

Liz thought for a moment of making everyone clear the building. Unless they did, their secret was out. She and Beauray would have to employ their government-issue spell paraphernalia in full view of the public. But she mustn't wait. One look at Fionna's nauseous face told her that in a moment the star was going to be very sick, and she'd never forgive Liz if she spewed her guts out in front of a crowd of dozens. The agents couldn't wait, either. The huge reserve of power growing almost directly under their feet threatened to blow, and Fionna herself had lit the match.

Telling herself it couldn't be helped, Liz scrabbled deep in her bag for components to cast the biggest dissipation spell she had at her disposal. Clear the air, and perhaps they could get to the bottom of this whole disturbance. There was the candle and the lighter. Good. The incense was in a secret compartment of her powder compact, hidden from the view of casual observers. Where was the athame? Oh, *why* did just the thing one needed most always end up in the remotest corner of one's handbag? A sharp point pricked her finger. Ah, there it was. Heedless of the pain, Liz pulled out the pink aluminum knitting needle that served her as a working tool for invocation and dissipation. A standard athame was forbidden on commercial aircraft and tended to excite commentary on London streets. The needle was a reasonably good substitute. No one ever said boo to a knitter.

"Mr. Ringwall isn't going to like this," she said. Peevishly she thrust the candle at Boo-Boo, lit the wick and handed him a pinch of incense.

"My superiors won't like it much, either," Boo-Boo admitted. "But only if we don't succeed. It can't be helped. Ms. Fionna's goin' to rise right through the roof in a moment. C'mon, positive attitude, Liz!"

"It's all very well for you to say so," Liz grumbled. "You Americans like the spotlight." Liz held the knitting needle over her head in casting position, pointed toward Fionna. She hesitated, conscious of every eye on her. *Chin up, Mayfield,* she told herself. *No time for stage fright.* Straightening her back, she began the incantation.

"I call the whirling winds to cease, depart from her, from us, in peace," Liz said, putting as much force into her words as she could. Boo-Boo held up the candle. The wind whipping Fionna around flattened the flame, threatening to extinguish it. He shielded it with his hand while trying to keep the pinch of incense between his fingers from igniting too soon. "To calm the raging winds that spin . . . oh, drat, I can't think of the next line!"

"Go out from here as you came in." Boo really did know her grimoire, Liz realized. The Yanks certainly had their sources in her department.

Together they chanted the old spell. Liz tossed the incense into the flame, and put every erg of Earth power she had into concentrating on bringing Fee down.

With a *whoosh!* a cloud issued forth from the flame, enveloping the stage, people and all. She could feel Boo's influence alongside hers, aiding and strengthening. He really did know his stuff. Whatever they were fighting was stronger than she could have taken on alone. Melding their talents, they had enough power to do what had to be done.

Liz hoped the non-initiates hadn't heard precisely what they were saying. She'd have to put a forgetting on them later. It was a harmless technique that worked very specifically on the memory of words in certain combinations. A technique that OOPSI had originated that would be of great use to MI-5 and MI-6, except that they didn't believe in it. OOPSI barely believed in it themselves. On the other hand, a trained magical technician would be required, and one might not always be available in those pinches.

Liz had seen the budget, and knew there was no funding for training.

Fionna sank toward the floor. The spin slowed gradually until when her feet touched down she was facing the agents. Lloyd was there to catch her. He held her tight.

Liz glanced at the half-burned trash around their feet. There was some power left over after casting the spell, power that ought to be used up before it joined the well of fierce magic that underlay everything here. She muttered a cleaning cantrip that gathered all the papers together in a tidy heap on the side of the stage. So she might get in trouble with the unions. It was a small price to pay.

Lloyd came toward them, white-faced, clutching Fee around her waist.

"I've never seen anything like that in my life. You . . . she . . . you . . . I don't even know what happened!"

"We helped," Liz said simply. "That's our job."

"I didn't know the government could do anything like that!" he exclaimed. "I apologize for having doubted. I didn't know!"

"Quite all right," Liz said. "I hope you'll continue to accept our assistance."

"In a minute! Cor, with you there's nothing that can touch her!"

Liz smiled. She liked the newly-cooperative Lloyd. He was a professional, after all, and his main job was to keep Fee safe. It had to be frustrating to him that he couldn't. He was genuinely glad to discover that Liz and Boo-Boo would be of some use after all.

Liz had been so intent on her work that she never thought what would be the immediate reaction from the rest of Fee's people. She glanced around. Everyone seemed frozen in place, staring at Fionna and the heap of confetti. As her eye fell on a handful of the roadies, they flinched and started running for the door. Liz sighed.

The drummer came up to them with his eyes wide.

"That was *awesome*, man," Voe said, impressed, "but your lyrics suck!"

"We've got to follow it just the way we learned it," Boo-Boo said, apologetically.

"Bummer."

The others ranged from fearful to openly admiring. Liz was pleased and embarrassed by the fact that the Guitarchangel was one of the latter. He wanted to know all about it.

"Would you like to sit down some time and have a talk?" he asked eagerly. "About the parts you *can* talk about, that is." From his careful phrasing Liz understood that he did know something about real magic. He regarded her with shining eyes.

"I would love to," she said, feeling as though she could purr, in spite of the danger of the situation, "but right now we must concentrate on Fionna. Now that we know who is at the bottom of these attacks, I think we can work with her and solve the problem."

"Who?" Fionna demanded.

"It's Ms. Robbie," Boo-Boo said. "She's the source of the disruption. She doesn't mean to be, but she is. Liz and I intend to go up and have a little talk with her."

"That bitch?" Nigel Peters asked, in surprise, walking up onto the stage. "I fired her."

Liz and Boo-Boo shared a brief, horrified glance. "That was *not* a good idea," Boo-Boo said. The two agents hurried out, heading for the control room.

Nigel Peters looked around at the circle of shocked faces, then at the ruin of the burned poster on the ground. "Say, what just went on down here?"

❖   ❖   ❖

"*What* happened?" Nigel asked, jogging to keep up with the two agents.

"You must be the only one who didn't see it," Boo-Boo said, over his shoulder, his pleasant face perfectly serious for once. "In a way, you're the one who lit the match. Y'all have just been treated to an exhibition of a sorta grownup poltergeist. Ms. Robbie's too afraid of Ms. Fionna to snap back at her in person the way she'd like to, so she's been manifesting it in a different way."

"Let's just hope she won't go up like a rocket now that there's nothing left for her to lose," Liz said. Fear was closing in like a cold hand clenching her stomach.

Her dread was justified. The special effects station was empty.

"Where is she?" Liz asked. The technical director, Gary Lowe, had half a dozen people with clipboards around him. He glanced up, then back at his notes. He had to try to rearrange the show without special effects, with only three hours to go.

Sheila Parker detached herself from the group to come over to them, looking apologetic for her previous smirk.

"Gone," Sheila said.

"When?" Liz demanded.

"Almost right away. After Fionna left, Nigel stayed here," she said, with a guilty glance at the manager. "He pulled Robbie over into a corner so the rest of us couldn't hear, but we all knew what was coming. She was pale as a ghost. The conversation started out quiet, anyhow. Then the two of them started screaming at each other. Gary said something like, hey look down there! We all started watching the stuff going on on stage. I kind of got distracted," Sheila added, embarrassed, "but I heard Nigel say, you're fired. Robbie was crying. As soon as he stamped out of here, she took off. Was any of that stuff real?" Sheila asked, with interest, looking from her to Boo-Boo. "We were trying to guess how it was done. It was really cool."

"This is a disaster," Liz said, turning to the others. "If she had stayed we could have contained her. Now she's on the loose."

"Sorry," Nigel said. "I didn't know. I believe, you know that, but Robbie Unterburger, of all people! Who'd figure a sad creature like her for a sorceress or a telekinetic? She was screwing up so much I thought it'd be less trouble if she was gone."

The agents looked at one another.

"We'd better find her," Boo-Boo said. Leaving Nigel Peters fretting, they made for the exit.

Chapter 14

"Where are you going?" Lowe asked Ken Lewis. The lighting director had risen from his station and was heading for the door of the control room. "We've got to keep on with this miserable rehearsal."

"I've got to make a call," Ken said, very casually. He didn't even bother to take his headset off, just unplugged it from the console. "Family emergency."

Lowe narrowed an eye at him. "You'd better not be calling the press," he said.

Ken held up his hand in a Boy Scout pledge. "I solemnly swear this is not going to be a call to a reporter or anyone who will call one."

"All right, then," Lowe said, not mollified. "Hurry up and get back—"

Ken didn't wait to hear the rest of Lowe's speech. Keeping an eye on the tiny screen of his cell telephone, he walked until he got an indication for a clear signal. Hitting the memory redial, he fidgeted uncomfortably until the call was answered on the other end.

"SATN-TV," the voice of the receptionist said brightly.

"I've got to talk with Mr. Kingston," Ken said. He drummed his fingers on the wall, then glanced around to make sure no one was overhearing him. "Mr. Kingston, we have a problem."

Augustus Kingston listened intently. His mystery employee had been channeling the energy SATN was sending via satellite transmission lines through their conduit to see the results. They'd been spectacular, but not exactly what they wanted. "I was just trying a few little tricks during the rehearsal, to make sure it would all work tonight, and the girl went out of control. She was too nervous, and there were other things going on . . ."

"Cut to the chase, young man or young woman, whatever you are. Let's hear the worst."

Ken chose his words carefully. He didn't want to explain the love triangle. He knew that the boss he'd never met wouldn't care about the emotional entanglement or the jealousy.

In retrospect, once he'd become aware of those issues, maybe he should have realized Robbie Unterburger hadn't been the best choice for the job. It had been just too tempting to take advantage of such a natural magical channel. She'd responded so well when not under personal attack, but the moment she drew attention to herself, she became flustered, and hit out with everything she had, including SATN's precious power storage. Ken had been lazy, and he was paying for it.

" . . . Between one thing and another, it was more than I should have made her handle before the big moment."

"Well, what's done is done," Kingston said,

calmly. "There's not much time left. My, er, friend assured me you could handle the job. There's a lot riding on it. Bring that girl back and make this work."

"She's split," Ken said, sullenly. "She's vanished into the city."

"You find her and bring her back. I thought you had a leash on her."

"I do," Ken said, sullenly. He wasn't used to having his competence questioned, but he had to admit Kingston had reason to be upset. "I have a tracer that picks up the energy she emits. It's an electronic dowser." He took the device out of his pocket. It looked high tech except for the Y-shaped piece of wood attached to the top. He'd made it himself. New technology, not like his dad's old means of water-witching with a plain hazel switch.

"Well, I don't care if it's a sign that says 'You are here.' Use it. A lot depends on this working out right. Go on! Go get her!"

"What about those agents?" Ken asked.

"That matter's taken care of," Kingston said. "Didn't I tell you? Now, call me when everything's back in place." There was a click at the far end as the other man hung up.

Irritated, Ken switched off his phone. He looked back toward the control room, then past it to the door of the press box where the transmission lines into which he'd tapped ran into the building. His connections were still open. He ought to close them, or the evil power transmitted from SATN that acted as a catalyst for Robbie's outbursts would continue to leak into the arena like gas. Little might be left over for the concert itself. The event was still hours away. Torn, he wondered whether he should go back or head out after Robbie. Suddenly, he heard the control room door open, and footsteps clap on the concrete walkway.

" . . . Better see where Ken is," said the technical director's voice.

Ken started running for the escalators.

"Hey, Ben," Boo-Boo hailed a gray-haired black man in a guard's uniform standing at the guard station on the ground level. "You see a little thing go by, brown hair and glasses? She woulda been in a little bit of a hurry."

"Yeah, I saw her, Boo-ray," Ben said. He exchanged complicated handshakes with the FBI agent. "She flew out of here in a big hurry. Came out of the main door and practically jumped down the escalators."

"She get a taxi?"

"Nah, she just went right straight out of here on foot," Ben said, pointing. "Crossed Poydras without lookin', and kept on moving. Looked like she was preoccupied, I'd say."

"Thanks, Ben. I'll be seeing you." Boo-Boo looked worried as he took Liz's elbow and hurried her out the door.

"What's wrong?" Liz asked.

"She's on foot. I'm guessin' she's gonna try to get back to the French Quarter," Boo-Boo said. "She doesn't know where she's goin'. It's that way, but that's not the best neighborhood. It's got some lonely stretches, where nobody sees nothin', if you understand me. Most people don't go walkin' through it alone. A stranger, walkin' fast, not payin' attention to her surroundin's, is just askin' for problems."

Liz's eyes widened. "We'd better catch up with her."

Two shadows peeled themselves away from the side of the Superdome, and fell into step a dozen yards behind Boo and Liz.

Liz held out the psychic detector that she carried with her in her purse disguised as a box of breath mints. The faint traces of energy that she could find on the sidewalk opposite the Superdome verified the security guard's statement that Robbie had come this way, broadcasting a blue streak, so to speak. The girl had been moving fast, but still left behind a distinct trail. Liz shook her head at her own blindness.

"How could we have missed seeing the obvious? Robbie has had a longstanding grudge against Fionna, and she must have been with the company while it was in Dublin, the scene of our other agent's attack."

"One or two things are still botherin' me," Boo-Boo said, after exchanging a word with an old man eating a late lunch on a park bench. "Robbie Unterburger doesn't strike me as the kind of person who would take out the kind of revenge on a rival that she's been wreaking. In fact, she seemed kind of freaked out by the effects. And yet, there don't seem to be any doubt that she's the source."

"Could we be witnessing the birth of a rogue talent?" Liz asked. She'd read of such things in the departmental archives. Mass destruction often accompanied the emergence. Not that the reports lent any credence to the occurrences, citing instead natural catastrophes such as lightning storms and earthquakes.

"That'd be one good thing that came out of this situation," Boo-Boo said. "That is, if we can catch up with her before she hurts herself or someone else too much just to be able to walk away. We could get her some trainin', anyhow."

"It's not personal," Liz said. Beauray glanced back at her with his brows drawn up in a question. "I have the strongest feeling that Robbie still doesn't really want to hurt Fee. With the amount of power she's slinging, she could have killed Fee any time. That gigantic poster might have come down in a single piece, but she caused it to explode into little paper flakes. She doesn't mean any harm. She's venting frustration, or so it seems to me. She just can't control herself."

"That amount of power in an untrained practitioner just didn't seem natural," Boo said. "I've been thinkin' about it myself. We woulda detected it if that girl was buildin' it all up inside herself. You get some spillover even in experienced people. It's almost as if she was channelin' it from somewhere. I'm more curious about that. Where's it comin' from?"

"We won't know until we catch up with her," Liz said, grimly. "So far, she's managed to blend in far too well. She could stay hidden until it is too late."

"Not really," Boo said, encouragingly. "This is the Vieux Carré. It's a community. We're aware of strangers. Someone will know where she went."

In reference to strangers, Liz had taken note of a couple of large, muscular men walking behind them on the other side of the street. Wearing the usual working uniform of button-down shirts and twill pants, they could have been a couple of bouncers on their way to work, or a pair of musicians going anywhere, but she noticed that they kept pace with her and Beauray, although taking care to remain at least a dozen yards behind them. They turned when she turned, crossing the nearly deserted street in the middle of the block to follow them along a narrow street that ran parallel to Rampart. Once they crossed Canal into a rundown street that led between a huge yellow brick building with boarded up windows and an empty lot, it became an undeniable fact that the two men were following them with a purpose in mind. A glance at her companion told her that he had noticed them, too. His hands, deep in the pockets of his ratty coat, were working.

Liz paused very casually to dig into her handbag, coming up with a handkerchief under which she concealed one of her government-issue containers. As though she was freshening up her lipstick, she unscrewed the small vial and dribbled a little of the powder into her palm. The men had no choice but to saunter slower, and pretend to study the elderly brick building. As they came within a few yards, Liz put her handkerchief to her nose and blew a few grains of the dust toward them. The grains, part of a sensing cantrip she had learned in her first year at the department, revealed no magic in particular about their pursuers. Ordinary common-or-garden thugs. Well, she'd heard there was street crime in New Orleans. She should be prepared. And she was not alone. That was good. She started walking again, faster. The two men behind them picked up the pace, too.

As they neared the center of the lonely street, she readied the chamomile-and-gunpowder mixture that would stun or knock out an attacker.

What she couldn't have foreseen was that there were four of them. The other two heavies were waiting at the head of the narrow street where it came to a dead end. As Liz and Boo-Boo came within a few paces of the cross street ahead, they stepped out from the brick doorway where they had been concealed.

The surprise nearly spoiled her aim, but Liz reminded herself the British Secret Service was made of tougher stuff than street muggers. With amazing clarity of mind that surprised even her, she turned and lobbed the sandy mixture at the large man farther to the right. A flash of light erupted from Boo-Boo's hands, hitting the left-hand pursuer square in the chest. Both ruffians went flying several feet.

"Have you got any more of those?" Liz asked. He grabbed her arm and started to hustle her back the way they had come.

"'Fraid not, Liz," Boo said.

"Pity." They started running.

The second pair, seeing their quarry escaping, put on a burst of speed and ran after them. The first two had not been knocked completely unconscious. Liz dodged around the first one, who lay partly across the cracked sidewalk. He made a grab for her ankles. In evading his grasp, she nearly tripped over the second thug, who was on his hands and knees, shaking his head like a stunned steer. He wrapped an arm around her leg and hung on. Liz let out a squawk. Time to see if those unarmed combat lessons she had paid for had done her any good.

Boo-Boo, who had made it nearly all the way back to Canal, turned at the strangled sound. Liz was now surrounded by all four of the ruffians. One of them had snatched her purse and held it away from her, while two of the others grabbed her arms. The third one hovered over her menacingly, drawing back a fist. Boo-Boo ran back to help her, but arrived just half a second too late. In the blink of an eye, Liz squirmed loose from one man, kneed another soundly in the crotch, and was chanting with intent as her free hand worked in a hazy pattern Boo-Boo recognized as a confusion spell. She was pretty good, now that he had to admit it. The trouble was that her attention was divided between more than one person. Even if she succeeded in clouding the mind of one man, the other two would still be threats.

He circled the tableau, wondering where to jump in. Liz'd done an admirable job of getting herself out of a jam, but she wasn't free yet. The three men feinted toward her, trying to catch her off balance by drawing her attention. She hadn't much time before she had to cast her spell or let it fade. The fourth man had gotten over the radiating pain and was climbing up from the ground, angrier than ever. Though he would have been curious to see how his efficient British counterpart would handle the situation, it was time to intervene.

Boo pulled a bag of dust out of his pocket. With only a cursory glance to make sure it was the right one, he slammed it down on the ground in the midst of the group. Billows of noxious green rose around the group. They wailed miserably, clawing at their faces and one another. Boo-Boo felt a twinge of guilt. He hated to use that stuff because of what it did to people—the residual effect gave them nightmares for days, sometimes as much as years after exposure—but it was really effective. It was comprised largely of graveyard dust and bile, but it had half a hundred other ingredients. One man cried out in alarm and struck out with a fist, smacking his nearest comrade in the ear. The man he struck responded with a wild yell and began flailing with both arms, dropping Liz's purse. Things were getting just a little too dangerous in there.

Pulling the lapel of his ragged jacket over his mouth and nose, Boo-Boo reached into the roiling green smoke and pulled Liz free. He helped her over to lean against the wall of the derelict department store while she coughed the powder out of her lungs.

Chanting the counterspell in a whisper so it would only affect her, he kept an eye on the four men while she recovered her sanity.

"What *was* that?" Liz demanded, coughing.

"Fear dust," Boo-Boo said. "Local product. Effective, isn't it?"

"Very." Liz watched the men screaming and struggling, fighting against invisible opponents and hitting the others in their frenzy. "Will they recover?"

"Sooner or later," Boo-Boo said. "They're fightin' with their inner demons just now. I'll give 'em a moment before I stop the effect and ask 'em questions. It's amazin' how cooperative they get when the terror stops. They see nightmares, monsters, all kinds of terrible things. I hate to use it, but it works."

"You're right," Liz said, shuddering. "It does."

"What did you see?"

"Mr. Ringwall."

Boo-Boo grinned. "Hey, now, hold on. I know those two." He pointed at the two men who had been waiting concealed at the head of the street, a white man with a handlebar mustache and a shaved head, and a black man with a grizzled beard clipped to a point. "One of them works as a bouncer for one of the jazz clubs on Bourbon. The other is security in the state museum buildings. They're not the kind who normally go in for muggin'."

Over Liz's protests, Boo-Boo pulled them out of the miasma and counterspelled them. The first pair, startled at the sudden movement, cowered, throwing up their hands. The eyes of the other two stopped whirling. The men shook themselves like large dogs coming out of a lake. The bearded man's mouth dropped open.

"Beauray! Hey, man, what happened?"

"Oh, just a little thing, Samson. Whatcha doin' hangin' out in this neighborhood?" Boo asked. "Gets kinda dangerous in the evenin' around here."

Samson and his companion looked sheepishly at their feet. "Sorry, man. Din't know it was you. Sorry, ma'am. If you're a friend of Boo's, we're pleased to meet you. I'm Samson. This is Tiger."

"Eliz—er, Liz," she said, holding out her hand to them. Her fingers were swallowed up in their vast handshakes.

"You gonna tell me why you're standin' on street corners scarin' strangers?" Boo-Boo asked, in his easy way, but there was steel in his bright blue eyes.

"*They* hired us," Tiger said, in a basso growl. "Said there was some bad-ass who needed a little kickin' around. Thought it was a good cause. We had no idea they were puttin' a mark on *you*. *I* woulda known better than to try. You want us to mess 'em up a little?"

"No, thanks. I'd rather talk to 'em," Boo-Boo said. "I need to know why they hired you." But when he turned to the others to undo his whammy they shied away from his moving hands. Before he or Liz could do anything, they ran away down the street, shrieking as if the fiends of hell were after them, which, for all he knew, they might be. "Left it a little too long," he said apologetically to Liz. The spell would work itself out in a few hours. "You fellas have any idea what was goin' on?"

"Not a clue," Samson said apologetically. "They're from out of town, that's all we knew. We thought there was some big problem they needed help with. They sounded like nice fellas. They had some money. We had some spare time. We sure are sorry, ma'am. Can we do anything to help?"

The sudden surge of courtesy did little to calm Liz's temper. So much time had been wasted! She produced the picture of Robbie she had taken from Nigel Peters.

"We're looking for this young woman. We were in pursuit of her from the Superdome when you interfered with us. Any assistance you can offer would be greatly appreciated." She knew her voice sounded cold, but the men didn't seem to mind. They looked at one another, and nodded.

"This girl's not much to look at," Tiger said. "But we'll keep an eye out. If she comes into the bar tonight, I'll let you know."

"I'm on night shift," Samson said. "If she comes through Jackson Square, I'll see her."

"Don't make a fuss," Boo said, genially. "We just want to know who she's drinkin' with. We feel kinda protective of her, you understand?"

And the men seemed to.

"We'll spread the word," Samson promised. "You can count on that."

"Thanks," Boo said. He felt around in his coat pockets for a grubby notebook and pencil, tore out a page and handed half to each man. "Here's my cell phone number. And if you see those guys again . . ."

"You want us to mess 'em up a little?" Tiger asked, hopefully.

"Not right away," Boo said. "We need to know who hired 'em."

Tiger crossed his huge arms. "We'll find out for you. Least we can do."

"In the meanwhile," Liz said, "we'd better resume our search for Robbie. Time is running out."

Chapter 15

Ken Lewis followed the pointing fork attached to the top of his direction finder as he trudged slowly along Bourbon Street. This stupid city smelled. He was tired of the pervading odors of mold and spice and old paint. The river behind him was a power presence in its own right he couldn't ignore, and far too big for him to deal with. His feet were so hot and sore he wanted to go soak them in the Mississippi and tell Mr. Kingston to hell with him and his project. Trouble was, he knew it would be to Hell with *him* if he failed. Kingston wasn't the only person who had a vested interest in its success. Ken was part of only a distant outer circle of the Council, but he, too, had hopes of ascendance one day. If he didn't make this work, he was cooked.

He'd run up and down half the crumbling streets in that section of the French Quarter, only to find every track he followed belonged to a total stranger, and some pretty weird strangers at that. Who the hell knew there were so many people in this city giving off magical vibes? Voodoo priests, shamans, witches, clairvoyants—the place was full of practitioners and talents. Why did he have to lose a sensitive in the middle of all this? Why couldn't Green Fire have had its all-important concert in, say, Cleveland, Ohio?

He'd had a heck of a time extracting himself from the last place, the sitting room in a private home on a little side street. The green-robed woman with the long henna-dyed hair had closed her door behind him and didn't want him to go. Only by promising to come back after dark did he persuade her to open the door. He had no intention of keeping that promise. If he managed to pull this job out of the toilet, he intended to spend the hours after midnight getting very drunk in a hotel room. He was still sneezing sandalwood incense out of his nostrils.

This Halloween town had some advantages. The sight of a man walking down the street with a dowsing rod should have had people following him, or calling the cops. Here, nobody stopped him or asked what he was doing. That one big, old, black man in the pressed shirt and trousers back there around the corner had shown some knowledge, and wanted to talk about the device. Ken put him off, too. He ought to send his father down here for a vacation. These were his kind of people: total weirdos.

He turned off the main street just west of the river and headed inland again towards Bourbon Street. It was a long shot, trying an area so far from the Superdome, but he'd covered nearly every street from Poydras to the Quarter without finding a trace of Robbie. He had no choice but to keep trying. She was the linchpin in the whole system. He couldn't run it without her. How he'd get her into the Superdome again later was a problem he'd figure out when he had her back.

The little hazel fork rotated on its spindle and pointed toward the storefronts on his right. By the strength of the reaction, Ken was pretty sure he had found the right trace at last. It took a little backtracking to figure out which doorway was the right one. He was in luck. It was a bar. He'd found her.

He peered into the dim room, lit only by a television set and some track lights over the mirror behind the varnished serving counter. Sure enough, the slender figure of the special effects engineer was hunched up on a stool with her elbows on the bar all the way in the back.

Ken switched off the electronic dowser and put it into his pocket. It had worked like a charm. Well, the rest of his act had better work, or he might be finished. He sidled up and sat down next to his quarry.

She'd been drowning her troubles. Pretty understandable, considering she'd been humiliated in front of everyone in the building. A tall, stemmed glass stood in front of her, half-emptied, but it couldn't have been the first one. Drying rings of neon-colored liquid glistened on the honey-colored wood in the muted light.

"Hi, Robbie," he said, gently. The television audio warred with some good jazz music coming from an overhead speaker. "Where'd you go so suddenly?"

Robbie Unterburger started, but she didn't look at him right away. The bartender, a white woman in her early fifties, appeared only a few feet away. She gave him a wary glance. Ken guessed she wondered if he was the cause of her customer's misery, and if she'd have to throw him out. He smiled at her, and she returned it, friendly but businesslike. Carefully, but not ostentatiously, she drew a Louisville slugger baseball bat out from underneath the bar so he could see it, nodded meaningfully at him, then put it back again. Ken gulped. Message received.

"I'll have whatever she's having."

"All right, sir," the bartender said, in a musical voice. "One Hurricane, coming up."

Unhesitatingly, she moved to an array of bottles on the back counter, and started to mix the drink. Ken noticed she kept a close eye on him, either directly or in the mirror on the wall. Long experience enabled her to prepare his order and serve it without looking at it, but not missing an ingredient or spilling a drop. The tall glass she set down in front of him was filled to the brim with Day-Glo red liquid and had a toothpick with a cherry and a slice of orange in it. Ken blanched, but he put ten dollars down on the bar and pushed it toward the server. He hated sweet drinks. The bartender left him his change, still wearing a warning expression. Robbie was watching him now, so he took a good sip, and smiled at her.

"Are you okay?" he asked. "You took off out of there so quickly."

"I got fired, remember?" Robbie said, bitterly. She drained her glass and held up her finger for another one. With a glance at Ken to make sure he was watching, the bartender poured another Hurricane and set it down in front of the young woman. "What did I have to stay around for?"

Ken almost said, "to see the fireworks." He patted her on the shoulder.

"You didn't have to take off like that. Nigel's not such a bad guy. He knows you're a stranger in this city. He was going to arrange for you to get home again. He was going to exchange your ticket."

"He was?" Robbie asked, amazed.

"Yeah! Swear to God," Ken said, hoping she

wouldn't notice that he stuck his hand into his pocket so he could cross his fingers. No sense in giving the Other Side anything it could use against him. He might practice black magic, but he was honest about it.

"Oh, Ken," Robbie said. Her hazel eyes, slightly rimmed with red, fixed on him. They filled with tears. "You're so nice."

"I'm your friend," he said. Robbie drained her glass in a few gulps. This time Ken signaled for the next one. "Come on, everybody gets fired a few times in their life. There's more bothering you than that. You want to tell me about it?"

"It's nothing," Robbie said, hunching over her drink.

"It's Preston, isn't it?" Ken said gently, patting her wrist in a fatherly way. Robbie nodded. "Oh, come on, you could do better than him."

"No, I couldn't," Robbie muttered. "He's the one I want. No offense, Ken, because you're really a great guy." She regarded him blearily. "And you're good-looking, too. But Lloyd's the sexiest man I've ever seen. I feel so . . . It's like lightning running through . . ." She began again, blushing more than ever. "When I'm near him, I just want to throw myself at him. But I can't."

"And he'd like you, too, if it wasn't for . . . *Fionna*." Ken put all the scorn he could into the name, and was pleased to see the young woman straighten her spine and glare at nothing.

"Oh, yes," she said, decidedly. "I wish the bitch would fall on her face."

"Maybe she will. Have another drink?" Ken said. They had the back corner of the bar to themselves. The bartender had other customers to look after, and no one could hear them over the combined noise from the speakers. "C'mon, you can tell me all about it."

The French Quarter seemed more crowded that late Saturday afternoon than London during the legendary January sales. Boo and Liz struggled through knots of happy people with stacks of beer cups, and skirted by acrobats performing in the middle of pavements, psychic palm or tarot readers speaking intently to their clients at little tables under beach umbrellas, and artists painting or sketching in chairs set against walls or fences where their wares were displayed. Countless tourists clogged the streets, drinking, taking pictures of one another, diving into bars and shops, and emerging with plastic cups full of beer and armloads of sparkling plastic beads. As the sun tipped westward, the neon on the buildings looked more garish and threatening.

Everywhere, Boo reached out to tap a local man or woman on the arm and chatted for a moment before bringing out the photo of Robbie. No one could remember having seen her. All of them promised they'd keep watch, but they didn't hold out a lot of hope. Liz's heart sank at the enormity of their task. It wasn't going to be as easy to find an ordinary-looking woman in blue jeans and a T-shirt on her own as it had been to locate Fee with her short green hair and personal entourage. Even *that* search hadn't been simple. If it hadn't been for Boo-Boo and his connections . . . which weren't doing them a lot of good just then. His friends were observant, but they'd have to be superheroes to pick out one non-descript stranger in this scrimmage.

They came away from speaking with a very limber Jamaican man in Jackson Square who was trying to fit himself inside a small glass box.

"We coulda just missed her, or she's on the move," Boo-Boo said, putting the photo into his pocket as they left the square. "Robbie's a stranger in town. I'd say she could be anywhere, but there aren't too many places that she'd feel comfortable about goin' to if she was in trouble."

"The hotel," Liz said, as a thought struck her. "Perhaps she just went back there. She might want to go directly to the airport or the bus station. We should find out if she's taken her luggage."

Boo raised his fair eyebrows. "Maybe that ought to've been our first stop. I wasn't even thinkin' when we came running' out of the Superdome." He looked so chagrined that Liz felt sorry for him.

"To tell you the truth," Liz said, "neither was I. That can't be helped now." Boo-Boo recovered quickly, and gave her his brilliant smile. They were equals again. Partners. A small benefit to come out of this awful mission. Only, he had to remember that *she was in charge*.

The tall, blond manager of the Royal Sonesta Hotel came bustling out to greet the two agents waiting at the lobby desk at the summons of one of the uniformed clerks.

"Does one of our guests need help?" he asked in a discreet undertone as soon as he reached them. "Does . . . she need help?"

"Not she," Liz said, "but one of her employees. Ms. Unterburger. Roberta Unterburger."

The manager and the attractive clerk behind the desk frowned.

"I'm not certain I recall her," the clerk said.

"She's kind of an everyday-looking person," Boo explained, producing the photograph. "It's important that we find her pretty quickly."

"She might be ill," Liz explained, hoping they wouldn't ask for details.

"Well, we'll be happy to call a doctor if she needs one," the manager said, friendly and ready to help.

"It's a serious condition," Liz said hastily, thinking of the poor doctor who might encounter a wild magical talent without warning.

"We have some fine medical facilities in this town," the manager said. "Why, Tulane Univ—"

"Can we check her room?" Boo-Boo asked. "As I recall, she's sharin' room 2153 with another woman who works for Ms. Kenmare. She might have come in without anyone noticin' her. She's kind of a shy young lady."

"Certainly," the manager said. He disappeared into his office and emerged with a set of passkeys. "Just in case she's collapsed."

Liz shot a look at her associate. They couldn't be that lucky to find Robbie present and unconscious.

They stopped a maid in the hallway to ask if anyone was in room 2153. The woman shook her head. The manager knocked on the door. When no one answered, he used his passkey to open the room. Liz was relieved to see the ordinary clutter of two women sharing temporary living quarters. Heaps of garments stood on the bed and the dresser. The luggage piled in the closet seemed of sufficient quantity for two. Liz checked the name tags. Some of them belonged to Robbie. Liz opened them, and found them empty. Thank heavens, the girl hadn't packed up her bags and disappeared out of town. Not yet.

The manager was watching with keen interest as the two agents inspected the room. Liz finally had to admit there wasn't a single clue that would tell them where Robbie would go if she felt troubled.

"I think we've learned what we can," she said. "Thank you for your assistance."

"Always happy to be of service to our guests," the manager said, with a bow, but Liz knew he was thinking of Fionna.

"We need to get Ms. Robbie to a specialist. Just let us know if she comes back here." Boo grabbed a pad of paper and a pen from the nightstand, and scribbled his cell telephone number on it. He handed the slip to the manager. "We shouldn't let her leave on her own. It could be very serious. If you'll just have her call us the moment she shows up."

"I'd be happy to," the manager said, tucking the piece of paper into his breast pocket. "You can count on us."

"I never doubted it," Boo said.

Boo left the same message and his telephone number with the doorman.

"That's about all we can do here," he told Liz. "Should we keep on searchin'?"

"The concert isn't long from now," Liz pointed out, checking her watch. "We'd better go back to the Superdome. We know the target is Fee. We ought to be there to protect her."

"And hope there aren't any fresh booby traps waitin' for us when we get there," Boo said, raising a hand for a taxi.

Feeling considerably more comfortable under the influence of alcohol and Ken's friendly overtures, Robbie reeled off into a catalogue of adolescent complaints about Fionna. Her looks, her habits, her money and fame were all reprehensible and unfair. How dare she be tall and beautiful and rich and talented? What right did she have to get all those clothes handed to her as though she was some kind of princess or something? What could fate have been thinking, sending all those millions of people to swoon at her feet? Especially a man like Lloyd, who ought to see past the makeup and the phony exterior? Didn't he know that that green hair was dyed?

Ken nodded and smiled at the right places, all the while keeping one eye on the clock. He had to get her back into the Superdome, reconnect with the machinery somehow and get it turned on and running, and avoid getting thrown out until he caused the chaos he had been hired to cause. Mr. Kingston had a lot at stake, and he wasn't going to take any excuses if Ken failed. He ought to get her moving soon. *Not yet,* he thought, *but soon.* She was still too skittish to react the way he wanted her to. In the meantime, he needed to keep her talking.

"If Fionna was out of the way, then he'd notice you. You're . . ." Ken swallowed, trying to think of a compliment. He had never really studied her before as a person. He hadn't thought much about her except how easily she responded to suggestion and magical manipulation. Robbie didn't inspire poetry, or even much thought beyond plain existence. She wasn't exactly pretty. Her voice was unremarkable. She didn't exude sexuality or sensuousness like Fionna did. " . . . You're smart. You do everything right. I've noticed that about you. You study your cues, and your timing is usually exactly right on. You've got a great memory. That's really special."

"Yeah," Robbie said, her voice breaking. "I'm efficient. Big deal. Except I left all my stuff hooked up when I left. The board is still hot, and all the switches are armed. Can you believe it? Normally I turn everything off. I'm so stupid! It's like Dublin all over again, when that poor man got knocked out during that rehearsal." Her shoulders heaved. Ken was afraid she was going to cry. The last thing he needed was an emotional outburst, and he didn't want her mouthing off about that nosy guy in Dublin. That had been a mistake. If it was ever connected to him, he was in big trouble. You never knew who was listening to you. Robbie started to cry, her shoulders heaving in deep sobs. He had to control her. He put his hand onto her wrist and squeezed sympathetically.

A tingle crossed between them, like a spark of static electricity.

Ken jumped up with surprise, then sat down again, trying not to show his eagerness. Robbie was still chock full of magical energy coming off the transmitter from the SATN-TV satellite feed. The Law of Contagion was still in force! She'd made the connection, and she was still channeling power. Maybe he could make the situation work *without* having to go back to the Superdome.

He glanced out the door to make sure the two agents weren't in sight. They could queer the whole thing if they turned up unexpectedly. Mr. Kingston had promised to do something about them, but he hadn't said what or when. In the meantime, the bar was wide open to the public. Anyone who came in could see them. Did he have any of the materials he needed for an obfuscation charm? He started feeling in his pockets. He couldn't improvise. Ken knew he wasn't much of a natural magician. He thought of himself more as a technical operator.

Robbie was talking, and looking at him as if she expected a response to what she was saying. Ken nodded whenever Robbie paused for breath. He'd only hope Ms. Mayfield and her grubby friend would keep chasing their tails until he'd managed to do what he needed to.

"Under the circumstances, I understand how you

left everything running," Ken said, inwardly exalting. "It was pretty intense back there. It won't do any harm. If no one touches anything, it will all still be intact later. Come on, cheer up. Hmm?" He gave her a hopeful smile and chucked her under the chin. The tap was still open on the power feed from SATN. By 7:30 tonight, the full force of their stored-up energy would be coming down those transmission lines and trickling into the chair at Robbie's station, ready to spread out into the full arena. He eyed the girl speculatively. He had an idea. It was *possible*. It could *work*. He toyed with his glass, wondering how to begin.

Robbie watched his fingers. Her eyes looked solemn as an owl's behind her thick glasses.

"You have really long fingernails," she announced. "I think that's kind of creepy in a guy. It makes me think of that scene from *Rosemary's Baby*. Those scratches on her back." She hiccuped. "I'm sorry. I must be getting really drunk. I would never say something like that normally."

"It's all right," Ken said, somewhat put out by the comparison. The blather that those two agents had been making about Robbie being a sensitive was more true than they'd ever know. He wondered if she could smell the brimstone incense he burned at home, and whether it was affecting her perceptions. "You know, you're a really nice person, Robbie."

She hiccuped. "Creak, creak, creak," Robbie said suddenly, tilting her head and staring at the ceiling. "Do you hear that? It sounds like a rocking chair." Ken glanced up. He didn't hear anything. Whatever she was tuned into, it made him uncomfortable. Hastily, he brought the subject back on track.

"You know," he said, "Lloyd's such a perfectionist.

If Fee made a total fool of herself, like screwing up the concert, he'd reject her."

"You think so?" Robbie asked.

"I'm sure of it," he said almost casually, making a spinning gesture. "Throw her out flat on her tush. If she was out of the way, he'd go crazy for you."

A crafty expression appeared on her face. He made a note of it as he reached into his pocket for a small package he kept there. When the bartender brought the next installment of drinks, Ken slipped a tablet of LSD into Robbie's.

"Come on," he said. "Let's drink to watching Fionna fall on her face."

Chapter 16

"Where the hell have you two been?" Fee snarled as Liz and Boo-Boo came into the dressing room. "There's only minutes left before the concert starts!"

"We know it," that annoying Elizabeth Mayfield said, in that maddeningly calm voice of hers. How could she and Fee have been such close friends once? "We're here now."

Fionna paced up and down, smoking cigarette after cigarette. The tight, green dress caused the wires sewn into it to rub against her skin. The itch made her frantic. She wanted to tear the dress off and run naked out of the place. *Hmmm,* she thought, *that might make good headlines.* Then she dismissed the idea. The last thing she wanted to do right now was draw extra attention to herself. The monsters could come out of nowhere and get her. What a comedown! New Orleans ought to have been the saving of her. Instead, she was more uncertain of herself than ever. New evils were popping up all over, ones she'd never heard of before, and people were walking out on her all over the place. Even her assigned minders had gone on a tour of the town!

She took a long drag at her cigarette and breathed out twin plumes of smoke at the agents like a dragon in pre-toast mode. "You're supposed to be protecting me!"

"We were looking for Ms. Robbie," Boo-Boo said, calmly, "but we're here now. You look very nice, ma'am. The dress matches your hair just exactly."

Seeing nothing but a blandly pleasant face, Fionna threw up her hands and started pacing again. Lloyd came to loom over them, expressionless as a golem. The security man was clad in black turtleneck and slacks, topped off with a charcoal jacket that set off his broad shoulders and concealed who knew what else. He looked devastatingly effective, very masculine and completely dishy. Elizabeth understood what attracted Fee to the man.

"Has everything been going all right?" Liz asked Lloyd.

He nodded. Liz admired his ability to be a total professional when the occasion called for it. Now that he had accepted the situation, he was willing to be cooperative. "Show's ready to go. I haven't let her out of my sight, not even in the toilets. Did you find the silly woman?"

"No," Liz sighed. "We lost the trail."

Lloyd frowned. "Shouldn't you still be looking?"

Liz shook her head. "Our place is with Fee. If there's going to be another attack, we need to be right here with her, not out looking for Robbie." Lloyd nodded curtly. He didn't fuss over what couldn't be helped.

"That makes sense." He flipped open a radio and spoke into it. "No sign of her, Mr. Lemoine."

The mild voice of the Superdome master control

operator came from the small speaker. "I'll let Security know, Mr. Preston. Everybody's on alert."

Lloyd flipped the unit shut. "If she shows her face, she's ours."

Fionna lit another cigarette off the first one, dropped the stub and ground it into the tiles with a silver-lame-stacked-heel shoe.

"I hate the waitin'," she said. "I've always hated it."

Fitz stood by the wall of the dressing room with sewing supplies at the ready in case Fionna's dress needed last minute repairs. He regarded Boo-Boo and Liz with an open-eyed stare of wonder blended copiously with fear. Liz gave him a smile meant to be reassuring. His hand groped in a pocket. Liz, with every sense tuned to its highest chord, sensed a small touch of magic within the cloth, probably a good luck charm for protection against the unknown.

They might need that little bit of good luck to help get them through the night. She herself had grounded firmly in Earth power and filled up her personal batteries as far as they would go before entering the Superdome. She wished that they'd been able to find Robbie. So many questions were left unanswered. Was she working for anyone else, and if so, who? What was her motive? Why attack Fionna, whose music espoused largely benevolent causes?

Nigel Peters came into the dressing room, looking haggard. He headed directly for Fionna and took the cigarette out of her fingers.

"Give me that!" she wailed. "I need it."

"Don't constrict your voice with smoke, darling," he said. "Here." He handed her a drink instead. Fionna gulped it greedily. Laura Manning stepped forward and deftly made up Fee's mouth again with bright orange paint. Fionna didn't even notice her. She was too preoccupied.

"What'ch you starin' at, Ms. Mayfield?" she demanded, brogue on full red alert.

"I . . ." Liz stopped herself from sounding too familiar with all these people here. "What's the matter? I know you've done hundreds of these shows. This isn't even your largest crowd. You couldn't possibly have stage fright."

"It's not that." Even under the heavy makeup, Fionna looked white-eyed. She refused to make eye contact with Liz.

"Don't be a fool," Liz said briskly, stepping right in front of her to get her attention. "You've proved that there really is bad magic attacking you. It's real."

"Oh, that really helps!" Fionna exploded, glaring at Liz. But the attack of bad temper did help her. It helped her forget how frightened she was for a moment. Curse Elizabeth Mayfield and her Yank scarecrow. They were right much too often.

The scarecrow had something to say as well.

"It's better to be afraid of real things, Ms. Kenmare," he said, aiming those blue, blue eyes at her. "You can do something about 'em. Meantime, you just give 'em the best show you know how. You'll be fine once you're out there."

"And what the hell do you know about show business?" Fionna demanded, shooting looks of hate at both agents.

"Apart from small parts in school dramas, nothing," Liz said, cheerfully. "But you're an old pro, Ms. Kenmare. These are your fans. They love you. All you need to do is go out there and . . . er, wow them. There's nothing new for you in that."

"This," Fionna said tightly, "is the first time in two years we've done a show without any effects."

"I see," Liz said. And she did. Fionna herself was on show, as she hadn't been for ages. Once upon a time, Phoebe Kendale had been a part of those same small school productions as Liz. Those were as bare bones as any skeleton, but she'd shone as a natural performer, drawing every eye. Once she'd gone into music, Green Fire had been a small group that played coffee houses and small venues. In part, it had to have been her charisma that rocketed them into the view of some unknown talent-seeker. Since they had made the big time Fee had hidden behind all the fancy touches available to her. *She's forgotten that her talent means something,* Liz thought sympathetically. She considered reassuring Fee, but realized how stupid it would sound coming from a secret service agent who supposedly had never met the star in all her life. And Fee probably wouldn't be grateful for it anyhow.

Lloyd was underimpressed. "This is what they pay you for, from my tax dollars? Pep talks?"

"If that's what's needed," Liz said. "And now, if you'll forgive me, I have to concentrate."

She withdrew to the side of the dressing room to ready the arsenal in her handbag. Everything had been replenished from the suitcases in her hotel room and augmented by materiel from Boo-Boo's bottomless pockets. She flicked through them, fifteen, sixteen, seventeen, eighteen packets, plus whatever charms she knew that didn't require a physical component. The most important tools she had were likely to be the litany of her memorized spells of protection. She started muttering them to herself, readying a framework to weave around Fionna. It was a shame they hadn't found the girl. It was a shame they hadn't had time to go over the facility again before the concert began. All they could do was concentrate on the focus of every attack so far.

Fee went back to pacing. It was hard because the damned floor was parquet wood. Every little crack broke her mother's back. She was afraid of causing bad luck to her mother, or anyone else! That kind of thing rebounded upon one. Instead of wanting to run out into the street, she wanted to find a tiny, enclosed place and hide in it until this was all over. Ten minutes. Eight minutes. Six minutes.

Liz watched Fee twisting her feet to fit inside the narrow boards, and guessed what was going through her mind. Little acts like that didn't do much good, not when there was so much power floating around. Fee had a right to be nervous. The heady feeling she had sensed earlier was greater than before, growing as the Superdome filled with people excited about the upcoming concert.

The assistant floor director appeared at the door of the dressing room. "Ready for you in five, Ms. Kenmare. Will you come upstairs with us now?"

"This is it, darlings," Nigel Peters said. He came up to clasp Fee's hands and lead her toward the door. Fitz caught up the train of her green dress and followed like a royal courtier. The others fell into step behind them.

The tunnel at the top was dark. The only light was provided by tiny laser flashlights directed at the floor by stagehands invisible on either side of them. Liz could feel those thousands of people out there all waiting excitedly for the moment when the show would begin. The crew was taut with anticipation, too. The red dots shook as they guided the group safely to the curtained enclosure behind the north end of the stage behind the huge speakers. The rest of the band, musicians and singers waited there, concealed in the dimness. Spotlights went on, shakily, Liz thought. Hugh Banks was invisible in his circle of video monitors just behind the stage, but she could hear his calm voice counting out, "Ready in three, two, *one*."

The unseen crowd erupted in a thunderous roar as Michael, looking like an angel in shining white silk, led the band out onto the stage. As they appeared, each man and woman was encased in a spotlight's beam, transforming them from people to tall, white church tapers. He raised a hand as the others took their places, and brought it down across his guitar strings in a deafening *thrummm*. One, two, three beat Voe's drumsticks, and the music leaped to life. It filled Liz's ears, and caused her ribcage to hum.

She hung back with Fionna, standing on the first step, eye level with the bottom of the stage. She had the impression of a mosaic of faintly gleaming dots in the middle distance. Faces. Thousands of faces. All these people had come to see Green Fire, to see Fionna. Every seat was packed. So was every square inch of floor right up to the foot of the stage. The tunnel behind them was an artificial lifeline to the empty spaces behind the scenes. She could well understand why Fionna might want to flee, but why she couldn't. The very force of their anticipation took hold of her, pulling her, making her want to go forward into the spotlight. She could go out there, in a pale, slinky blue dress, burst into song, and make them love her! Her, Elizabeth Mayfield!

Oh, yes, of course, she corrected herself wryly. What would *she* sing? "Happy Birthday"? "God Save the Queen"?

She became aware that Fee was clutching her left forearm. Lloyd loomed over both of them from behind her.

"Stay where I can see ye, all roit?" Fee asked, in a breathy whisper. Just for a moment, Liz's old school friend peered out from behind the bright face paint.

"We'll be with you the whole time," Liz assured her. She drew a circle over the other woman's head, dropping the net of protection over her and closed her hands to seal the spell. Fee nodded once, then she was gone. Glowing Celtic knotwork appeared in midair, the product of Tommy Fitzgibbon's careful tailoring, then another candle appeared on the stage, a green one. Fionna's key light flashed on, revealing her to the audience. The shouts and cheers grew louder.

Borne forward on the crowd's acclaim, Fionna Kenmare sailed straight out to the center of the stage, where a dozen lights hit her all at once. She threw her head back, and with a wild scream, leaped straight into her song, landing between one note and another. Liz held her breath. She was *fantastic*. They were *all* fantastic. Rehearsal had been a much-diluted image of what was to come. No matter how scared Fee had been, she would give them a terrific show.

A hand encircled her elbow, startling her out of her reverie. She glanced to her left. Boo-Boo stood there, a grin on his face. He brought his mouth very close to her ear, to be heard over the incredible din.

"Wish we could just stand here and enjoy it," he said.

Ah, yes, Liz thought, with regret. They were on guard, and their unknown perpetrator was still on the loose. Boo nodded forward. After exchanging glances with the stage manager, the two agents slipped into their watching post, in among the gigantic speakers. Lloyd was already on stage, an ominously large presence in self-effacing charcoal among the thick cables that snaked up a decorative pillar to a platform containing now-to-be-unused special effects materials. His head turned as the agents appeared. He regarded them for a moment, then the head swiveled back to continue the ongoing surveillance of the arena.

Invisible to the crowd, Liz and Boo stood in reflected darkness while the show went on only feet away from them. The arguments and disagreements that occurred during rehearsal had dissipated, and were forgotten. No disharmony existed in the circle of the stage. No mental or emotional space separated the hired musicians and backup singers from the band itself. They were all one in an uplifting tornado of sound. The natural magic arising from Green Fire's fierce music was benevolent. They loved their fans, and their fans loved them. The stage was surrounded by a sea of tossing hands as the patrons in the seats on the arena floor got up to dance.

Fionna circulated about the big stage, one hand clutching the microphone, the other beckoning, exhorting the audience to get into the spirit of song with her. Vibrated nearly off her feet by the rhythm pounding out of the towering speakers, Liz almost wished she'd worn earplugs, but then she'd have missed the way that the whole sound came together. The contact high of magic was heady. She drew on it, keeping her protective spell strong.

As Fee rounded the west side, heading for the rear, her eyes were scanning. Liz wondered what she was worrying about. Had she spotted Robbie in the crowd? When they settled on Liz and Boo-Boo in the shadows, her shoulders relaxed visibly. Elizabeth relaxed, too. Fee just wanted to make sure they were keeping their promise to stay with her. Across the way, Lloyd shifted. Jealous again, Liz thought, though the man's face was the blank mask he assumed on duty. Liz felt a certain amount of sympathy for him. He couldn't protect her from this kind of danger, and he hated that.

Michael stepped forward, coming up beside Fionna. The two of them circled, challenging one another line by line with the melody. Liz watched his fingers fly with fascination, then gave herself a mental slap on the wrist. She was not to fall into a trance, no matter how wonderful it was to have the Guitarchangel playing only steps away. Her job was to protect Fionna.

Which was not too difficult at present. Robbie had not turned up again, according to Hugh Banks, the floor director, who was hovering around behind the scenes, whispering orders into his headset. Liz was concerned with the steady buildup of magical energy in the hall, but perhaps the threat would not be realized, since the antagonist who might have misdirected it was gone.

She had been trying all this time to work out the ramifications of a magical onslaught against someone like Fionna Kenmare. What purpose could it possibly serve? She was famous, but there were hundreds of music stars with household name recognition. It had to be because of the magic. She was associated with it. No one would blink an eye if tomorrow he or she read a headline that said there had been a magical blowout at a Green Fire concert. But what was the international connection? No foreign presence had been remarked upon at the site of the previous attack in Dublin. Only an insider could have recognized the undercover agent for what he was.

The biggest puzzle was why Robbie?—and, more to the point, how? How had she channeled her natural though untrained knack for magic into a formidable, focused weapon without it showing up on the radar of either Boo-Boo's department or Liz's own? The incantations involved must be new, powerful and far-reaching, the product of some heavy-duty research. That made Liz nervous. The department had a watchlist of hundreds of fringe groups that called themselves Satanists or black magicians. It would be horrifying to find one that had actually found a means to attain massive quantities of power. She sighed. She didn't relish bringing up such a suggestion in her next report to Mr. Ringwall. He was having enough difficulty accepting the notion that magic or other inexplicable causes were actually to blame. Her reports were probably the talk of Whitehall right now.

Colored spots and lasers arced over and around the stage, creating patterns of light and shadow through which Fee and Michael moved as though they were the Fair Folk dancing in the woods. The lighting effects that had been arranged to take the place of the pyrotechnics looked amazingly good considering Liz knew they had been put together in haste. Michael slipped past them, his long black hair plastered to his head. Time for his first costume change. Fionna, accompanied by the traditional Irish instruments and the backup guitarists, was giving the audience a ballad of frustrated love. Her voice soared to the dome.

Liz touched Boo-Boo on the arm. When she caught his eye, she tilted her head toward backstage. He nodded. She wanted to check around. He crossed his arms, and continued a dispassionate scanning of the stage and the audience.

Liz moved into the dark space. The stagehands were busy with a piece of the set, a tiered dais that went in the middle of the stage for one of the numbers. Hugh Banks was still there, shouting into his headset mike, but now he was red-faced with frustration. Something was not going well.

Michael shot back through the tunnel, now clad

in black leather pants and gleaming black silk shirt, hair flowing and dry again. He clapped Liz on the shoulder with an encouraging pat. The roadie nearest the entrance handed back his guitar. Michael stepped onto the stage. His key light hit him within a few paces, but it was late. Liz winced, knowing how picky the guitarist was about timing.

As soon as he appeared, Fionna backed away from center stage, ready to change into her white silk dress. Her light didn't turn off quickly enough. Fee gave a snort of frustration as she came off stage into the capable hands of Fitz and Laura.

"They love you, me darling," Laura shouted at her. "It's going marvelously." Liz followed them downstairs to the dressing room, where the costume change was accomplished within moments. Fee stood and stared at nothing while they ripped the green silk off and zipped her into the peach-nude sheath. She gulped a tepid mineral water and strode upstairs, fringes flashing in every direction. Her retinue followed in silence, not wanting to break her concentration.

The crowd roared with delight as Fee reappeared, all in white under the lights. She twirled, letting them see the new dress. Did Liz imagine the tiny stumble? That uneasiness Liz had sensed while observing the stage manager continued to build, small mistake piling upon small problem. Liz felt rather than heard when Voe slipped a beat, throwing everyone else off just slightly. Eddie's fingers fumbled a note, flattening a chord. The audience didn't seem to care. The rapport had been established. The magical give-and-take between them and the performers that Liz so loved was beginning. Energy was building like the Pyramids.

"Ready to cue the cascade of rainbow light," Banks said to his headset. "This replaces the Roman candles over the conclusion of this number. Yes, maybe. We'll go to a short instrumental break after this, give Fee a chance to breathe. Somebody make sure she has something to drink on hand when she comes off. God knows she'll need it. She must be sweating buckets. Ready? And . . . cue!"

In the bar, Robbie was getting nicely suggestible. "Why, if Fee wasn't in the picture," Ken said, "you could just lift your little finger, and Lloyd would come running right to you." Involuntarily, Robbie's little finger raised itself off the surface of the bar. "Yeah, you could give him a little wink, and the guy would be on his knees." Wink. Ken grinned. He could go on like this all night.

That magical electricity Robbie was generating had aroused Ken's hopes. If his supposition was correct, his idea could fulfill the conditions of his assignment and save his butt.

"Hey," he said casually. "It's seven-thirty. Time for the concert to begin. Boy, if we were back in the Superdome, the first number would be beginning right now. Michael likes everything to start right on the dot."

Robbie seemed to understand some kind of response was called for, and stirred herself out of her drug-and-alcohol-induced haze to make it. "He's very prompt."

"That's right," Ken said. "You'd be heating up your stuff right now, wouldn't you?"

"It's already ready," Robbie said, and giggled at the rhyme. "Already ready. To go. Everything. Lasers. Lights. Rockets."

"Lots of rockets," Ken agreed, keeping his voice low and smooth, like a snake creeping up on an innocent prey. "I know you've got all your cues on computer, but you don't really need the list, do you?"

"I"—*hic!*—"memorize everything," Robbie said, unsteadily. "Otherwise, I couldn't take my eyes off the screen. Got to do my job. My job!" Tears started leaking from her eyes. "All gone."

"No, baby, no," Ken said lightly, mentally crossing his fingers. "You've still got your job. You've got to do the special effects for the concert. Everybody's counting on you. Look out the window. Down below, there are eighty thousand people in the dark waiting for the show to start. Are you ready? Cue the first effect. Wait for Gary to tell you to go on three, two . . ."

"No," Robbie interrupted him, growing agitated. "Nigel fired me. He doesn't want me to do it."

"Sure he does, baby."

"No! He threw me out. Hates me. Hates me!" She was crying, digging at her eyes with the side of her fist like a little girl. Her nose turned red.

Ken was keenly aware that the bartender was keeping an eye on them. She had noticed Robbie's distress and was starting to walk toward them with intent. Gulping at the thought of the baseball bat under the bar, he pulled a handful of money out of his pocket and slapped it on the bar. Very gently, he helped Robbie to stand up.

"Let's go for a walk," he suggested. He put his arm around Robbie and helped her off the bar stool. Casually, he strolled with her out into the neon-glazed night, with one final glance over his shoulder to make sure the bartender wasn't picking up the phone to call the police.

"Okay," Ken said, steering her out onto Toulouse. "I know a good place to go."

"Okay," said Robbie, biddably, her sorrows forgotten. The drugs were taking effect at last. Ken held out his free arm and gestured toward the sky.

"Now, the lights are coming up. Michael's already out on the stage with the band. You're sitting behind your console. Your hand moves toward the control board. . . ."

Upstairs, in the empty press room beside the control room, a finger of green-tinged power crept out of the metal box containing the transmission lines, down the cables snaking from it to the room next door. Everybody in the control room was too busy to notice the tongue of flame dancing along the black cables. It rippled over to the special effects station, which hummed into life.

"Tone down the mikes on Voe's drums, Sheila," Gary Lowe, seated at the lighting station, was saying. He slid several pots and hovered his finger over a button. "We want to hear Dijan's bodhran here. Bring up Carl's harp. Lovely. And . . . cue the cascade."

The green fire blazed into life. The readout on the laptop computer beside the special effects station began to scroll down its long list.

Liz squirmed back into her place next to Boo-Boo. The American seemed troubled.

"Do you hear that?" he asked, pointing vaguely up toward the ceiling. "It ain't exactly music."

Liz listened intently. A chord had added itself to the topmost registers of the music, a disturbing harmonic that set her teeth on edge. Fee and Michael both heard it, glanced at each other, wondering what it was. Michael gestured at the techies with a flattening hand, ordering them to do something about it. They all shrugged. Alarmed, both singers glanced backward to where Liz and Boo were concealed. Boo-Boo waved his hand, showing them there was nothing to worry about.

"What is it?"

"Dunno. Bad mojo on the way. Any minute now, I'm guessin'."

"Then why did you tell them to go on?"

Boo-Boo's blue eyes glinted at her. "It'd be worse if they stop."

Hastily, Liz started chanting the protection cantrip over and over. She hadn't begun a moment too soon. The cascade of colored lights had just ended, changing Fionna's white dress to every color of the rainbow. Without warning, there was an explosion at the south end of the stage. Brilliant pillars of white and gold roared up practically under Fionna's nose. The Roman candles were launching! With shrill whistles, fingers of flame shot up halfway to the ceiling. They burst into sparks that showered down on the wildly yelling crowd. Tiny red embers fell over Fionna's head, but bounced harmlessly off the bubble provided by the spell.

No one noticed the effect but Lloyd, who glanced toward the agents and gave them a surreptitious thumbs-up. He approved.

Fee looked nervous for a moment, then took the reappearance of the pyrotechnics in her stride. She stretched out an arm toward the fire as though she was invoking power from it. As the rockets launched, she matched them scream for scream. The crowd loved it.

"I thought they were doing this without effects," Liz said, watching the rockets zip around the huge arena. Mentally, she ticked off the sequence of events as they each appeared on schedule: rockets, lasers, smoke, more lasers, light show. It was as though Robbie had never left.

"Maybe the guys found another special effects technician here in town," Laura Manning speculated, huddling in behind them to watch Fionna dance.

"After all, she left her cue sheet program and all the equipment. Good thing, too. Gary Lowe's had just one headache after another. It's bad enough that the lighting director took off, too."

"What?" the agents asked in unison, turning toward her.

The makeup artist looked from one surprised face to the other.

"Nigel didn't tell you? Yeah, right after he canned Robbie Unterburger, Kenny Lewis disappeared. Went out to make a phone call, Sheila said, and has never been seen again. I thought he had feelings for Robbie, but she couldn't see he was alive with the eye magnet over there," Laura nodded in Lloyd's direction. "Poor Gary's running the lights himself."

Boo and Liz exchanged glances.

"I thought that young lady wasn't doin' all this on her own," Boo said, his mouth set in a grim line. "It just seemed out of character. Now, *him* I could believe."

"We'd better check upstairs and make sure," Liz said.

Hugh Banks thought it was an odd question, but he grabbed his headset mike and inquired. His face was troubled when he looked up. "You're right. No one's at Robbie's desk. The whole thing is working by itself. Is it a ghost in the machine?"

"Could she have mechanized it to work off the cues?" Liz asked. "She had everything listed on a laptop computer."

"Possibly, but why didn't she tell us she was doing that?" Banks asked. He turned to the manager, who looked shocked.

"Can they turn it off?" Boo asked. Banks muttered to his microphone again. His usually ruddy face turned pale.

"No."

"It's going by remote control," Liz said, feeling icy fingers gripping her stomach. "She's making it all happen by remote control."

"But nothing bad has happened yet," Nigel Peters said, hopefully.

"I wouldn't take no bets on it stayin' that way," Boo-Boo said. Liz agreed with him. "Can't do anythin' now but stay on guard, and hope we can handle what he throws at us."

Nigel tore at his thin hair. "This is all my fault. I should have kept the silly girl where she was."

"Should we stop the show?" Banks asked. Boo-Boo shook his head.

"Just do your job, and let Ms. Fionna do hers."

The star was responding magnificently to having the fireworks and lasers running, however unexpectedly. Privately, Liz thought she must be vastly relieved. No need to show her bare face, so to speak.

The exciting rock number was ending. After a halt of a few beats, the tempo changed to the challenging rhythm of Green Fire's diatribe against hostile occupation of one country by another. The plaintive wail of the uilleann pipe began to snake in and out of the melody.

The music itself began to sound sinister to Liz. During rehearsal she had put it off to the subject matter of the song. It was a violent protest against partisan hatred, a touchy subject to one of her nationality, yet there was more to it than the theme itself. Something was wrong in the fundamental *sound* of it. A destructive force seemed to be taking hold within the Superdome, but how was it happening? The girl was not there, had never entered the building at all. Every security guard there had her picture and was on the lookout. Ken Lewis hadn't been seen either. Neither one was on site, yet it was undeniable that the feeling of the concert had changed. No matter how benevolent the meaning of the lyrics, it was being perverted somehow into bad magic. The figure of a rampant lion etched in green lasers leaped up out of the steam and roared at the crowd.

"Cor! Effects are getting better all the time!" Laura Manning said, wonderingly. "I didn't know they could do anything like that."

"They're not," Liz said. Cupping her hands around an imaginary bubble of air, she strengthened the ring of protective energy around Fionna. Who was at that moment launching herself forward, toward the front of the stage, step by step, following the lyrics of the song. Liz felt as though she wanted to race out there and pull her back.

It was too late. One more lunging step, and Fee kept moving, right off the end of the stage. Instead of falling into the crowd, she was hoisted up into the air by invisible hands. Her singing turned into more of a scream than usual. The dangling white fringes of her dress went into frenzied shimmying as Fee kicked at the air. Rockets began to blast off again, practically going up her skirts.

The question of *how* Roberta Unterburger was doing this, with or without Ken Lewis, would have to wait. Other things, like saving Fionna and the band, were more important. The singer was floating higher and higher, until Liz feared she would crash into the Jumbotron. Four gigantic images of her frantic face were being projected on the screens, thanks to the roving cameras in the crowd.

Liz sent an alarmed glance toward Boo-Boo. She couldn't stop the protection charm. He nodded and stepped forward with his arms outstretched.

"Spirits of the air, release. Let your hold on this

one cease," he recited. He tossed out a pinch of the
feathers he always carried in his pockets. They were
caught up in the maelstrom that engulfed the singer
and whisked out of sight in a twinkling. "To earth
softly let her feet return . . ."

"Oh, my God, she'll crash and burn!" Laura Manning cried, wringing her hands.

"Do y'all mind?" Boo-Boo asked mildly, with a look
of reproof at the makeup artist. "I'm chantin'
here . . . and let her then in peace sojourn!" Boo-Boo
threw a handful of energy up towards Fionna. Sparks
engulfed the woman in white and settled around her
waist like a celestial belt. The crowd *oohed*, thinking it was part of the special effects.

"Technically this here spell doesn't work, y'know,"
Boo said to Liz, hauling an invisible cable down
hand over hand. Fionna dropped toward him with
a shrill cry that echoed out of every speaker in the
hall. Boo resumed pulling, but more gently. "But in
point of fact it does, in the hands of real magical
folks like ourselves. It's about as close to telekinesis as departmental regulations go. I'll show you how
if you like."

"I'd enjoy that," Liz said, watching with admiration. "Can I help?"

"Just hang on in there protectin'," he said.

Liz redoubled her chants. When Fionna looked
about frantically for them, Liz caught her eye and
mouthed, "Keep singing!" Fionna responded like a
champion, putting everything she had into her lyrics. Liz felt a rush of affection for her old school
chum. She was showing the stuff St. Hilda's girls were
made of.

The pipes hissed, producing a huge cloud of steam.
A dragon etched in laser fire stretched up from it and
spread gigantic wings that extended beyond the wisps

of steam. Uh-oh, thought Liz. The energy here was beginning to take on a life of its own.

The line-drawing dragon nipped at Fionna's heels. Descending toward the floor through Beauray's efforts, she was being drawn right into its jaws, bubble and all. It shot out a line drawing of red fire that licked around her legs, causing the fringe on her dress to singe. She kicked at the dragon. Her foot disrupted some of the lines, kicking up sparks. The dragon roared an angry protest. It leaped up, reared back its head, and closed its jaws around her. The protective shell cast by Liz reacted to the attack, blazing up like a light bulb. The dragon burst noisily into a thousand flecks of fire. Tiny flames hissed down onto the stage. The audience, thinking it was all part of the show, screamed with delight. Liz sighed, relieved. Her spell had held. Fionna was safe. Soon, this would be all over, and the concert could proceed uninterrupted.

Fionna kept singing gamely while Beauray continued to haul her down from the air. When she was only a few feet from the floor, there came an audible *snap!* Fee squawked as the invisible cord broke. She shot up, stopping herself from banging into the Jumbotron with her outstretched hands.

"For pity's sake," she shouted, shoving herself away from the multiple grimacing images of herself and the band. "Get me down from here! I'm not a bleedin' kite!"

"Well, I'll be," said Boo, shaking his head. "It's not strong enough. Whatever that Robbie is pumpin', it is some powerful mojo."

"Do somethin', you sufferin' fools!" Fionna shouted, her accent thickening. "I can't do me dance steps up here!"

The band stopped playing to stare at their lead

singer hovering over their heads. When the music
died away, the crowd let out cries of protest. In the
upper stands a few people started to chant.

"No! No! No! No!"

"Oh, no, we can't have that," Liz said in alarm.
"They'll start a riot." She leaned out of the shelter
of the speakers, heedless of whether the audience
could see her. "Start playing!" she ordered the band.
Voe and Eddie looked at each other uncertainly, but
Michael strode forward into the center of the round
stage, and struck a forceful chord on his guitar.

Bless him, Liz thought.

Automatically, the other musicians followed suit and
began to play. Fionna, still hovering above them,
started singing again. As the positive side of the
energy began to reassert itself, Fionna dropped
slightly, lowering to within twenty feet of the stage.
The audience, or most of it, cheered.

Not all the protesters stopped complaining. In the
area around the apron of the stage, some of the fans
began to fight. A skinny man in a T-shirt yelled as
he was hoisted up and tossed onto a crowd of
bystanders. They threw him off and went to beat up
the people who had flung him at them. Up in the
stands, more fights were breaking out.

Fed by the anger building in the arena, monsters
leaped forth from the steam pipes. Each new creation
was larger and more fearsome-looking than before.
Each pulled angrily at its roots, achieving a little more
distance from the curtain of vapor. It looked like soon
they would be able to sustain their reality without
touching it. The crowd's own energy was making the
threat worse. These new creatures were drawn in
multiple colors, disgusting hues of sickly green, blood
red, decay brown. Fans near the stage retreated,
shrieking, as the beasts struck out at them. The

creatures were still insubstantial, but that could change any moment.

"What's going on?" Lloyd demanded, appearing at their shoulder. "Make it stop! Get her down from there!"

"We are trying to," Liz said. "Robbie is employing an astonishing amount of psychic energy."

"What? I thought she couldn't do anything if she wasn't here."

"Somehow they're using a kind of remote control," Boo-Boo said, regarding the security man with reproachful eyes.

"Man!" Lloyd said, crushing his huge hands together. "If I'd known that foolish little bird was capable of causing trouble like this . . . !"

"She's not to blame, Lloyd." Liz took a chance using his first name, since he'd never given them permission. "She's being used. Ken Lewis is behind this."

That put an entirely different complexion on the situation. Lloyd's face darkened with angry blood.

"I'd strangle that bloke if I had him here. Have you called the cops?"

"And tell them what?" Liz asked, reasonably.

"Dammit," Lloyd raged. "Do something! Fee's afraid of heights!"

He stormed off to his post and began to talk into his cell phone. Liz understood his frustration. She felt it herself.

"Try something else to get Fionna down," she asked Boo. "In the meantime, I'll try to put a lid on this outburst."

Everyone was getting too excited. The protection spell would have to look after itself for the moment.

Calm, she thought, opening her arms wide and leaning back with her eyes closed. Summoning the first lessons she'd learned in the use of power, she called upon the element of Earth to spread out among the crowd. *Calm. Serenity. Pleasure.* She felt herself floating above all the people, settling down like a hen on the world's largest nestful of eggs. Everyone must calm down. This kind of outburst was unseemly even for a rock concert. *Everyone had to get hold of their emotions and calm down. We are not barbarians here. We are adults at a public entertainment.*

It was no easy thing soothing 80,000 people. She tapped all the way down into the bottom of her reservoir of magic to touch the outermost rows of the audience. It was a technique she'd learned from her old grandmother, to scotch negativism at its source by appealing to the need for order within, something within each human being. She urged her mood of calm on the thousands of people, chivvying them to release their harmful emotions in a positive way. For just a moment, everybody's shoulders heaved up, then relaxed as they let out a huge, collective sigh.

As if to field-test her enchantment, a new laser-born monster, more horrible than before, with glowing red eyes and huge tusks rose up out of the steam pipes, its claws reaching for fans in the first sixteen rows. Liz was rewarded when, instead of screaming in fear, the audience erupted with glee at the exquisite complexity of the special effects, applauded appreciatively, then settled down into a quieter enjoyment of the music.

"Good God," said Boo-Boo. "Some of 'em are even foldin' their hands."

"I had some good training," Liz said, with satisfaction, "as a room monitor at a girl's school."

"That's mighty impressive," Boo admitted. "But they're tied to your emotional state now. If you get frightened or excited, sure enough, the crowd will do the same. We'd have a bloodbath."

Liz shook her head. "I am capable of retaining my cool," she said. "I *am* an Englishwoman."

She viewed the scene with deliberate detachment. The visions in the laser works had ceased to be bloodthirsty monsters with scales and huge fangs. Instead, green-edged horses, rabbits and other natural animals sprang about on the misty gray wall, as though the programmer had tapped into a benevolent nature show. Dragons appeared, too, but they were friendly dragons, with softer muzzles and not so many spines on their tails. The crowd reacted with polite applause and shouts of "Hurray!"

"Ain't that a little bit of overkill?" Boo-Boo asked, beginning to ready his next incantation.

Liz shook her head. "I've only grabbed hold of the edge of this blanket of energy. It could still explode into . . ."

"Explode" was the operative word for what came next. From the frameworks on either side of the stage that held the Roman candles, huge cylinders launched toward the ceiling. Popping in time with the music, they burst overhead into stars of color that filled the whole room. The crowd burst out in cheers of delight. Clouds of gold spangles expanded under the light plastic ceiling like dandelions opening on time-lapse photography. Fionna dodged this way and that, trying to avoid the onslaught. Liz stopped meditating on peace to renew her protection spell around her old school friend. The sparks might scare her now, but they couldn't hurt her.

"I don't remember seeing this kind of sophisticated fireworks on Robbie's list," she said, puzzled. "It looks like Guy Fawkes Day up there."

"Y'mean like the Fourth of July," Boo-Boo

corrected her. "You're in the U.S. of A. right now, ma'am."

"Don't argue," Liz gritted through clenched teeth. The crowd was loving what they saw as unique special effects, but they were getting more excited the longer the display went on. Fights were breaking out again, and she heard some angry shouts. "The power is growing. Help me dampen it down."

Her American counterpart was already chanting. A feedback loop of some kind was at work here in the arena, transforming the positive energy flowing out from the fans into negative power. That influence had to be coming into the building from somewhere or someone. She wished she could pull away to search for the source, but that was impossible. Until the concert ended, she had to maintain her post and keep the audience in order. If she left now, noisy chaos would follow within moments. It wouldn't matter if she found what she was looking for, apprehended the perpetrators, and managed to solve the mystery that had led across two continents and at least three countries. She'd be too busy explaining to HQ why she allowed a riot to begin when she could have stopped it.

Calm, she instructed herself. Mustn't let maybes and coulds interfere with the here and now. Most of the audience was responding well to her determined serenity.

But such high-minded platitudes didn't help when the level of power was rising higher all the time. Liz threw her entire soul into keeping the peace. The laser pictures displayed a placid beauty now. Landscapes. Waterfalls. Eagles soaring above the clouds. A dove with a budding branch in its beak. Perhaps, Liz was forced to admit, not a *perfect* fit with the wild, acid-rock song Fionna and the others were performing. She heard some unhappy voices not far away to her left, criticizing the mix. Liz worried that someone might begin to panic and set the whole thing off all over again. Her shoulders sagged. She was getting very tired.

Beauray moved behind her and put his hands over the hollows just underneath her collarbone. Before she could ask what he was doing, she felt a rush of energy flow through her. He was very good at multitasking, being able to continue his own spell-working and at the same time feeding her more Earth power. Liz perked up as she felt her psychic batteries recharging. And only just in time. More fireworks filled the air, exploding in multiple colors. The next *boom!* shook the building. She sent out a burst that pacified the pockets of unrest beginning to break out in the east quadrant. The audience let out a collective "Ahh" of pleasure.

Nigel wailed behind them. "But we don't have any chrysanthemum skyrockets! The fire marshall wouldn't approve them! Or those spinning Catherine wheels! Where are they coming from?"

It was just bad luck that Michael was passing close enough to the rear speakers for Nigel's frantic voice to be picked up on his guitar mike and carried throughout the auditorium speakers. The band paused for half a beat, not knowing what to do. The audience heard and felt the hesitation, and shuffled uncomfortably. The rowdy ones picked up on the uncertainty, threatening to start rioting again. Liz felt control slip. She dug deep into the new power reserves, refreshing the protection spell around Fionna and keeping the peace.

On stage, Michael gave the musicians a stern look. They were to carry on and pretend nothing was wrong. Even though their lead singer was hanging in midair kicking like a hooked salmon. Even though they were surrounded by rockets as though they were on a battlefield under attack. The Guitarchangel whipped the band into a musical frenzy, using gestures and shouts. He strode around the stage, urging the audience to clap along with the beat.

As he passed Liz his next circuit around, he hissed, "Do something!"

"We're trying!" she growled back, frustrated, not wanting to interrupt her multiple chants for long.

Boo's cell phone rang, somewhere deep in his pockets. Liz shot him an exasperated look.

"You'd better answer it," she shouted. Boo scrabbled for the little box. He popped it open.

"This is Tiger," the tinny voice in his ear said. "I think I've seen your lady, man. She walked by with some guy a little while ago. I couldn't get to the phone until now."

"Which way they goin'?"

"Toward Decatur."

Boo reached into Liz's shoulder bag and felt for the little cell phone. He turned it on and tucked it into her neck.

"I know where she's gone," he shouted. "Keep things together here."

Leaving Liz chanting, Boo-Boo trotted out of the Superdome arena, out the back door onto Giraud Street.

A taxi swung into the curb at his wave. Boo-Boo clambered into the back seat. The young black man behind the wheel twisted around to exchange hand slaps with him.

"Hey, Boo-Boo, where y'at? Where you want to go?"

"The Quarter," Boo-Boo said, settling back against the seat. "Run the lights. I'll make it right later."

Chapter 17

Ken Lewis held Robbie cuddled against his chest on the grass in the shelter of the gazebo overlooking the riverfront, hoping passersby would take them for a pair of overamorous lovers in the dark enjoying the fireworks display along with the thousands of other people hanging out along the Moon Walk. At least, he was enjoying it. He doubted whether Robbie was truly aware of them in any intellectual way. She'd had quite of few hits of LSD and one or two of Rohypnol. The "date rape" drug made her easier to manage. She reacted to exterior stimuli, including his voice, without conscious will power. It was too bad he'd had to drug her so heavily, but he couldn't let that strong moral backbone of hers interfere with his last chance to make his plan work. No matter how he played up the provocation she had been suffering, she didn't really want to hurt anyone, not even Fionna. Who ever heard of somebody with the perfect opportunity to take revenge on a hated rival without consequences who *didn't* take it?

On the way to the park he had picked up a bottle of tequila and a couple of glasses, and he had more acid in his pocket, all the better to make sure she didn't regain control of her faculties before the show was over. He splashed some of the booze into her glass and held it up to her lips.

"Had too much," she said, her voice slurred. Tequila dribbled out of the corners of her mouth.

"No, you haven't," Ken said, wiping up the spill with the cuff of his shirt. "The night's just beginning."

"Oh, all right," Robbie said. She swallowed and made a face as the liquor burned its way down to her stomach. "Oooh."

"Now, concentrate," Ken said. He squeezed Robbie's face between thumb and forefinger and held her head up, making her look at the pulsing waves of white-hot light shooting up into the night. "Follow the sequence exactly. Can't you hear the director? He wants the flames to rise higher. Higher. Higher! Yes!"

Robbie's chin sagged slackly against his palm, but her muddy-colored eyes were fixed on the starbursts filling the air over the river.

"Like that?"

"Wonderful, baby. You're the best. Keep it up. More. Yes, more!"

He caught the indulgent smile of an older couple sitting close by on the grass. So what if they thought he was talking about sex. This was better than sex. This was better than *anything*.

Ken kept up the description of what he wanted to go on in the arena. Robbie acted as if she could see what he was talking about, responding to cues as he gave them. It was like leading her in a guided meditation minute by minute through the concert, except with added explosions and starbursts and a special surprise ending. Inside her head, the stage was laid out before her. Her slide pots and push buttons were underneath her hands. When she operated her controls, the special effects came to life in her mind. Yes, if he could keep her going like that, he could bring her to cause a disaster when the audience was the most worked-up and the power was at its highest level.

He'd forgotten about the fireworks display. Pure serendipity. To Ken, it was just Satan's way of telling him he was in the right place at the right time.

He found it hard to believe that he could be working magic without any physical contact. He felt naked without the familiar technology surrounding him. But doing sorcery by remote control was definitely the way of the future. The satellite feed from SATN-TV had helped to prime the pump, and now the pump was running full strength. By the time he lowered the boom on the concert center, he'd be able to send Mr. Kingston a bolus of magical energy not just threefold, but three thousandfold. It ought to blow the roof right off SATN. Ken watched the fireworks, feeling smug. He ought to hit Kingston up for a bonus on top of his fee. It would have been worth it just for locating Robbie in the first place.

What a conduit she was. He could feel the edge of the power as it poured through her body. She almost crackled with it, but at the same time was totally unaware of it. She didn't know any more than the paper a message was written on knew its contents. Roberta Unterburger, special effects engineer, was a special effect in herself. The perfect dupe. He and she had sat there in the midst of Green Fire's company for months waiting, while Ken had plotted and planned for just exactly this moment. No one had suspected a thing. Now it didn't matter if they knew the whole story. Nothing they could do would stop the destruction of Fionna Kenmare, and everyone in the Superdome with her. There'd be headlines all over the world tomorrow morning, but only three people would ever know who was responsible: him, Mr. Kingston, and Mr. Mooney.

Ken could even monitor the havoc he was causing. It was a shame he couldn't watch, but now and again he could hear through the earphone on his headset. The audio only seemed to arise in momentary bursts, maybe coinciding with bursts from Robbie exerting her psychic gift and causing something to happen, but Ken felt as if he was sitting at his console in the control room in the Superdome, listening to the chatter. The disconnected cord hung down on his chest, but thanks to Robbie's gift, through the Law of Contagion the headset was still a part of what it had touched. As much as he was having fun giving Robbie ideas, he really enjoyed those little glimpses into the pandemonium at the concert. The crew was going nuts. In the background he could hear the roar of the crowd. They sounded scared. No one understood what was happening, not even those nosy secret agents. The effect was better than he could have hoped.

"Okay, you see those red fireballs?" he asked, lying back on the grass and pointing to the sky. Robbie nodded obediently. "Let's make 'em chase the band around. Give 'em a little hotfoot. It won't hurt 'em," he assured her as she started to writhe uncomfortably. "You have my solemn word on it." She relaxed.

"Okay," Robbie said. "If you're sure."

Ken grinned wickedly above her head, out of her line of sight. He enjoyed feeding her suggestions. "I'm sure, baby. Go for it."

He heard a blaze of static in the earpiece. It

cleared to reveal the businesslike mutter of the technical director's voice giving instructions to the crew. Then—

"What the hell . . . ?" Lowe demanded. The connection cut off. Too bad, Ken grinned. They were making headlines. He'd have to read all about it in the morning.

Robbie started to sag backward against his chest.

"Oh, no, baby, we're not done yet." He helped her sit up. She swayed to the music in her head while he poured her another drink which he laced with another dose of acid.

"Don' wanna . . ." she said, as he held the cup to her lips.

"Come on, baby, you're doing really well. Everyone loves you."

"Not Lloyd." Robbie's face contorted. Tears filled her eyes.

"Yeah," Ken said. "Him, too! He loves the way you're making this all work. Come on. Make a big purple monster just for Lloyd. When he sees what you can do, he'll forget all about Fionna."

"Forget . . . her," Robbie said. She squeezed her eyes closed, concentrating. Her hands played up and down on her invisible controls.

"Is it a really big, purple monster?" he asked encouragingly. "With lots of teeth and scales and long, ba-aad claws?"

"Yes," Robbie said.

He leaned back on the grass and whistled. "Baby, you are the best."

The taxi dropped Beauray at the end of Toulouse where the railroad tracks crossed it. As the car bumped the last hundred feet and came to a halt, Boo-Boo worried that Lewis had poor Robbie hidden away someplace he'd never find her. Once the sky-rockets had started to go off inside the Superdome he hadn't really needed the phone call from Tiger to tell them where Lewis and Robbie had gone. He remembered about the fireworks festival that was being sponsored by WBOY.

His greatest concern was that they might not be on the Moon Walk itself. The riverfront was lined with old warehouses that had plenty of windows open to the northeast from which she could see the fireworks but not be easily seen by anyone else, like him. He didn't have much time. Night had already fallen, and the embankment park was hundreds of yards long. If he didn't spot his quarry pretty quickly he would have to ask the local police to help him search the surrounding buildings. Fortunately, most of the police were friends of his; he wouldn't have to make the request official.

Whistling and a loud *boom*! heralded the eruption of a gigantic globe of colored sparks that pattered lightly down into the Mississippi to the accompaniment of cheers from the thousands of bystanders crowded on the brick-and-concrete walk to watch. Boo-Boo pulled out his little phone and hit the speed dial.

"Liz? Did y'all just get a purple chrysanthemum in there?"

"Yes, Beauray, we did," the British woman replied very slowly and deliberately. She sounded like she'd downed a whole economy-sized bottle of Valium. That was real professionalism for you. Underneath it all she must have been twitching like a freshly caught fish. The sounds of the concert behind her almost overwhelmed her voice. "Where are you?"

"Down by the Moon Walk."

"The Moon . . . of course! The exhibition we heard

announced at the radio station." The gal had a great
memory. Too bad she had that ol' stuffy accent that
made her so hard to understand. "Have you found
our subject?"

"There's probably about as many people here as
there are where you are," Boo said, scanning the area
around him, "and most of them are standin' up." A
family of obvious tourists pushed between him and
a stainless steel sculpture, being careful not to touch
him. "It's also pretty dark. The street lamps distort
things a little. This is goin' to be a challenge. I'll try
a findin', but I don't know how it'll do. I'd better not
run down the phone battery. I'll get back to you when
I find 'em."

"You do just that," Liz said, calmly, as though she
was asking him to tea with the Queen. The connection ended. He switched off the telephone and stuffed
it back into his pocket.

The finding spell he liked to use best took a good
pinch of lodestone powder. Boo-Boo felt around in
his coat for the various packets and bundles of cloth
he kept handy. He had a bad feeling that he might
be short on lodestone. The call from Washington
hadn't left him much time to stock up before he had
to meet the jet. His fingers explored the threadbare
recesses of the inside lining of his jacket, coming up
with little bits and pieces. Here was henbane, holy
basil, a small bunch of chili peppers tied with red
thread, and a whistle. There was that last bite of
beignet left over from the stop he'd made at the Café
du Monde with Liz and the group. He chewed on
the stale chunk while continuing to sort out the
contents of that deep pocket. If lodestone powder was
anywhere, it was there. In the meanwhile, he recited
the words of the incantation to himself. It helped if
he got it right the first time.

Nothing in his preparations required that he stand still. He kept moving, hoping to catch sight of Robbie. There was half a hope that Ken Lewis wasn't with her anymore, but Boo-Boo couldn't rely on that. His profile of the missing Ms. Unterburger still would not stretch to make her the mastermind that had engineered small psychic attacks on Ms. Kenmare, let alone sabotaging a whole concert. A pity they hadn't looked closer at the quiet Mr. Lewis. Now that Boo-Boo thought about it, there might have been an offensive cantrip going on to keep them from paying much attention to him. And all that time Boo thought it had been the man's aftershave.

The park had its own soundtrack going. Jazz belted out of the loudspeakers clinging to trees and light poles. You could see people walking along sort of bouncing to the beat. That was healthy, he thought. It was just like he'd been telling Elizabeth Mayfield. Give in to the rhythm, and let it move you with it. Too many tourists came to New Orleans and just brought a bubble of their own homelands along with them. They never got to feel what the city had to offer. Of course, Liz's circumstances were extraordinary. It wasn't often he got to work with an agent from any other department, let alone a foreign national. Kind of nice for a change.

The next fusillade of Roman candles filled the black sky with their lines of white fire. The noise surprised his ears a moment later, almost making him drop the minute bundle in his fingers. He imagined that if there was a correlation going between this display and the mayhem being visited on the Superdome, they'd have a kind of delayed reaction, too. A shame that the delay wasn't enough to give much notice to Liz what was coming before it happened.

There was barely enough of the vital component

left for the spell. He had a hair and a little fluff from the upholstery of Robbie's chair that he mixed in with it, all the while chanting the ancient words, with a few new twists that the government researchers had worked out over the last fifty years. Passersby saw him talking to himself and playing with pocket lint. The other local practitioners would understand, but strangers would leave him well and truly alone. That kind of anonymity was what the Department required of its agents, part-time or full-time.

Eighty percent of the people in the park were stationary, having staked out a good place to watch from. The other twenty percent strolled around. Kids with sparklers ran around sketching glittering arcs in the air. Made a pretty good disguise for the glowing witchlight of the finder spell once he got it going.

Strangers in the thick crowd made plenty of room as he wandered past them. He guessed he was describing such an irregular path that they thought something was wrong with him. He had to look carefully into each of their faces. The kind of heady magic he was pursuing could interfere with perception.

He gave them a reassuring kind of smile, but they backed off anyway.

Within a few moments he located a trace. This might be easy after all. He followed it back to the concrete steps where the two must have entered the park, but from there the trail meandered around and around. Boo didn't like the crazy psychic vibes that he picked up as he went. The girl was messed up somehow. Probably had a lot too many drinks somewhere, making her far too suggestible. Boo-Boo winced as the sky filled with fireballs, picturing the same thing happening back at the Superdome. He followed the silver pointer wherever it went, hoping that his meager supply of lodestone would hold out until he located his quarry.

This was no time to trust exclusively to magic, particularly not when counterspells and black magic were at work. Whenever he spotted an acquaintance in the crowd, he showed them the photo of Robbie. None of them had seen her, but they all promised to watch for her.

Keeping a positive attitude also helped keep the spell strong. There were so many people that he had to dart his head around like a snake to see everyone. Plenty of fellow psychics abounded. All the local fire-worshipers were out in force. They gained strength from a display like this one, and each new surge pulled his magic finder off-line towards one of them. He didn't dare miss the trace he was looking for. He felt sorry for the girl, wherever she was. She wasn't getting anything out of this but grief.

If he had to take an educated guess, he would say that Ken Lewis would have to make his move by the end of the concert. He had an hour to find them— no, forty minutes.

It had better be enough.

"That's good," Ken said, shaking the sagging Robbie. "More rockets! Fill the sky with them! *Beautiful* explosions. Aren't they gorgeous? That's what everyone wants. Fire one!" he said, as a huge green blaze lit the sky. "Fire two! Fire three!" Robbie, her muddy brown eyes fixed on the sky, nodded. Her hands seemed to be working invisible controls. "Ready a barrage . . . and . . ."

"What's a barrage?" she asked, muzzily.

"Twenty-five rockets," he said quickly. Yeah, one for every point in a pentagram, squared. "Twenty-five in a row." That'd shake 'em up in the front rows.

"What color?"

"Red. Blood red."

"But this is a love song," Robbie said.

"Love hurts, baby."

"Oh. All right." Her hands fumbled in the sky, reached for the imaginary laptop computer to one side and put in the instructions. She held her finger poised.

"Now!" Ken shouted as Roman candles popped over their heads. "What are you doing?"

"Time for the laser show," Robbie said. "Can't be late again. Fionna gets so mad." Tears leaked out of her eyes.

"She won't get mad," Ken said, soothingly. "Give her a little spin around. She'll love that."

"Oh," Robbie said. "All right."

"Aaagh!" Fionna shrieked, spinning on her axis like a top. She'd been interrupted in mid verse. That, after the sudden series of explosions that nearly sent Nigel Peters straight through the roof with hysterics, and the imps made of green laser light that threatened the fans nearest the stage. The audience adored the deafening bangs, but the crew backstage was worried about the possibility of fire. The roof was only soft plastic. The danger of deadly fumes and falling, molten globs of plastic began to look like more and more of a possibility. The crew for the Superdome's fire truck had been scrambled to the main floor by order of the Master Control Room operator, who also began to ask if they shouldn't halt the concert and evacuate the building. Hugh Banks, looking years older than he had at 7:30, relayed the message to Liz.

"No!" Liz said, alarmed. Shouts of disapproval came from the arena floor as the fans picked up on her

disturbed state of mind. Quickly, Liz took firm control
of her feelings. "We can't stop now. There is a psychic buildup of epic proportions brewing out there.
That gigantic hall out there is *full* of power. If we
halt prematurely it may be set off. I cannot even *begin*
to tell you what might happen. The best thing would
be if we could force it to dissipate naturally. Give my
associate time."

Banks spoke into his headset, and nodded at her.
"We're all with you. How can we help?"

"Keep the music going, no matter what," she said.
"Let the concert come to its natural conclusion.
Maybe, just maybe the power glut will fade on its
own. In the meanwhile Mr. Boudreau will try to stop
the effects."

The organizers weren't satisfied. Liz wasn't surprised. They were accustomed to being in control of
every facet of an event. To have an outsider dictat-
ing terms to them on top of all the disasters they had
faced before would be intolerable if they decided not
to face reality. If she kept her head all would be right.
She *hoped* it would be all right.

Liz forced herself to keep a lid on the power in
the arena. It was fighting her. What kind of spell was
she fighting? It was *strong*. Malign influence was
pouring into the crowd and giving feedback. Thanks
to her grandmother and MI-5 her training was equal
to the situation, but she simply needed more power
to control than she had. A whip and a chair was no
use against a hurricane.

She grabbed at her purse. The augmentation
powder that Boo-Boo had left for her was right in
front. She tore open the first packet she touched.
Cough drops bounded to the floor, followed by the
sandy remains of a spell to prevent drowsiness. No
problem. She wouldn't need *that*. And as for the

first, if she lost her voice, she'd just whisper the
words to the incantations until her tongue fell out.

"This is a disaster!" Nigel Peters wailed behind her,
tearing at his hair. "What can we do?"

"You can help," Liz said briskly, too busy to be
polite. She simply began to remove everything in her
purse and piled it in his hands until she found Boo-
Boo's packet. "Ah!"

Government regimentation of magical and psychic
phenomena might have seemed to be a foolish enter-
prise, but when they did something, they did it right.
The instructions on the side were in very clear, leg-
ible print. Liz held the envelope underneath the
nearest spotlight to read. Augmentation powder
needed to be applied to the area where enhancement
was required. It worked by the Law of Contagion.
To her delight she saw there were instructions for
group use. That ought to be the answer to her power
problem. She stuffed everything back into her bag
and set it on the floor. She opened the envelope and
very carefully sprinkled it all over herself.

"They're going crazy out there," Peters said.

Liz opened her arms up and held them in the air.
The force gathering around them was like a balloon
pressed against her face, suffocating her. It was
nudging against the walls, beginning to uproot the
supports. If this didn't work, the whole building could
come down on them.

"Nigel," she said. "Calm yourself. Put your hand
on my arm and just concentrate on being open. That's
all you need to do. Can you do that?"

"I don't know if I can just open up," Nigel said,
backing away a pace. "My analyst says I have commitment problems."

That tore it.

"Do you want my old friend to continue to be your

meal ticket?" Liz bellowed. Nigel, startled, halted in place and nodded. "Then, do it!"

"Can I help?" Laura Manning asked. "How about the others?"

"Anyone who can," Liz said, grateful for the makeup artist's take-charge attitude. "Touch me."

"Come on, you lot!" Laura shouted, waving her arm at the others. "Group hug!"

Roadies and stagehands gathered from all over the backstage area. In between renewing her incantations, Liz barked orders at the others who crushed into the cramped space between the speakers.

"If you cannot reach me, then put your hand on the shoulder of the person nearest you. Keep calm. Meditate if you need to. Do not panic! It is necessary to remain calm. If you can't do that, then please move away. Thank you. That is all." She started chanting again.

The others bundled around, trying to find a comfortable handhold. Liz was tugged and pulled in so many directions she felt like the last cashmere sweater at a jumble sale. She tried to catch her breath to protest. Suddenly, Lloyd loomed over her. He bellowed at the group.

"'Ere, all of you! Sort yourselves out *now*." The tugging and pulling stopped. "What do you want me to do?" he asked Liz.

"Join us," she said. "I could use your strength."

"Anything for Fee," he said. "I do love her, you know."

Liz smiled. "I know." The big man put one arm around her from behind and gestured to the others. In no time, he had them arranged in a nice, orderly, spider-web huddle, with more people gathering in.

The cluster of humanity with Liz at its core made Michael do a double-take on his next turn around the stage, but he continued on as though nothing unusual was happening. Bless him, he *was* an angel. Even after getting a hotfoot from little fireballs that had filled the stage, even after getting chased by laser-light monsters, he still kept his head. He trusted her. That gave Liz a warm feeling deep inside.

She was grateful to the rest of the crew as well. Even some of the ones who had been frightened before by the magical demonstration she and Boo-Boo had been forced to perform earlier had dared to join her. The rest were just grateful to have some-one to hang onto while scary things were happening. She didn't mind having a friendly shoulder nearby herself. This was the single biggest magical exercise of her life—perhaps the largest on earth at that moment. She must not fail. She must not. The lives of thousands—not to mention her job—depended upon it.

Liz exerted herself to calm the group around her first. They were full of nervous excitement. If she broadcast the tension they were feeling, then the whole place could go up for grabs. She had a lucky moment while Michael performed a guitar solo at the front. While everyone focused on him, she drew in the blanket of peace for just one moment from the arena to wallop her crew into order. Their shoulders relaxed visibly. As soon as they were properly soft-ened up, she opened up and threw her new, totally revamped and much more powerful calming charm over the crowd of fans.

When she did, she felt evil in the air. The magi-cal charge that built up during a joyful event should be benevolent, or at worst, neutral. There was no doubt at all now that something within reach was trying to change that goodness into malignity. *Stay pure,* she urged through the link, radiating out to the very edges of her web of influence. *Beauty. Justice. Generosity. Calm.* Dark influence licked at the edges of the mass enchantment like a black flame. She must not let it catch in the fabric of it.

The others in her little group, even the least sensitive among them, seemed to feel the pull towards unity and leaned inwards, squeezing the breath out of Liz. The only protest she could make was a squeak. Lloyd heard the faint noise and shoved hard at the nearest offenders, making room for her. Liz gasped in lungfuls of air.

She began to feel hopeless. Though she was grateful for everyone's help, she had little chance of stopping an onslaught of these proportions herself. In spite of the efforts of the band, the malign quality that had crept into the music earlier had taken a firm toehold. While not a deep-seated fan of Green Fire's music, Liz had had to admit that they knew about composition, structure and creating mood. Except for the songs meant to scold, their repertoire tended to uplift, even liberate, the listener. What went into the microphones was positive. What came out of the speakers was growing steadily more negative. Liz found herself fighting a battle she couldn't keep winning for long.

It helped her a lot to have other people's energy to throw at the building wave of darkness, yet what they had to offer was limited by their lack of training. As Nigel had said, he had commitment problems. Others were blocked for just as many reasons. There just wasn't enough power. If she could have made contact with audience members, she might have been able to channel them into creating a more positive cycle. She was afraid to try. Such an action could backfire hugely if word of trouble started going around the auditorium. One whisper of black magic, and 80,000 terrified people would stampede for the doors.

All the people gathered around were depending on her, and her alone. She wished that Boo-Boo was there with her. It was a frightening thing to be left to her own meager devices. She wanted desperately for her mission to succeed. She gave a short, bitter laugh. Yes, she wanted to save the world. Willingness must count for *something*.

Not enough, she thought forlornly. If Boo-Boo failed to stop Robbie and Ken, all was lost. She sensed the bottom of the well in what the others had to give her, and drew hard on her stored fund of Earth power, the last drops of which Boo-Boo had fed her before he went away. Once again she felt herself tiring, almost falling back into Lloyd's strong arms as she surrendered even the last ergs of her own life-force to stop the evil from taking over. She was sorry for Fionna. It must have seemed like an amazing bit of good luck for her to have an old friend assigned to protect her. Too bad that Ringwall hadn't seen fit to send a more able and experienced agent to her rescue.

In a moment Liz would lose her grip on the containment spell, and the whole maelstrom would wind itself up into the largest force of darkness that this city had ever seen. She started to feel dizzy as the drain leached away her very consciousness. In a moment she would collapse like a deflated balloon.

Softly, a trickle of psychic energy began to creep up through the soles of her feet into her body. Liz felt it rise from the floor, running along her legs and body, straightening her spine and flowing out of her hands and her mouth. It couldn't be coming from Boo-Boo. He wasn't this powerful. Liz grew concerned as a mental probe she sent to feel for the bottom of

the well of energy dove down for ages. There was
no bottom. It felt *gigantic*. *Endless*. What incredibly
powerful person could have arisen out of nowhere
to help her? It couldn't be anyone in the company,
nor a member of the audience, yet it poured from
a single source. Who was her mysterious benefactor?

Suddenly, she realized she knew its identity. Not
a *who*, but rather a *what*. The power was issuing from
New Orleans itself. It didn't like this intrusive darkness being pressed down upon it, like a thumb in the
eye. It wanted to bottle up the intruder to prevent
it spoiling the ease of the Big Easy. As much as pure
power could be, this was flavored with spice and
lilting voices—and music. The city, and the French
Quarter particularly, was protecting itself from outside malignity. It saw Liz as the means to protecting itself, and offered the wealth of its own influence
to that end. Liz offered herself gladly as a conduit.

Energy coursed through her every vein, came out
of every pore. She was afraid that it would surge
through her with the force of a fire hose striking a
tissue paper wall and tear her fragile body into pieces,
but it didn't want to destroy her. It wanted to carry
her along, make her a part of it. She opened up like
a camera aperture, wider and wider, until the whole
calm, easygoing identity of that unique city was
coming in through her feet and out through her fingertips. Let *les bonnes temps roulez*. The city itself,
with the driving backbeat of the Mississippi River in
the background like Voe's drumming, provided the
overwhelming music Liz lifted herself on. It was as
though Bourbon Street itself raised up and tied
around the Superdome like a gigantic ribbon of sound.
Not only the goodness of rock and roll, but the cool
breath of jazz, the warm embrace of soul, the heart
of the blues, the edgy ribs of zydeco and the wry glue

of Irish folk music wove together under her hands to form a leak-tight, flexible basket. The music of this great place stood against the evil infecting the acid-folk rock—the ultimate battle of the bands. Her enormously heightened sense allowed her to hear all of these pulses, the good outside holding the bad inside. She could contain the malignance, for now. But she couldn't hold it forever. Sooner or later one of these people was going to want to go home.

Oh, Boo, do something! she pleaded mentally.

Boo-Boo felt as though he was feeling his way blind in the dark. Ken Lewis had shown a distinct talent for concealment. Boo checked with friends, but neither he nor they had seen a good-looking man with a plain girl in blue jeans. When he stopped to consider his throbbing feet, he must have walked up and down the length of the riverfront twice already. He hadn't spotted either of his subjects. The trail wound around too many places. He was frustrated. Liz was back there alone trying to calm a nuclear bomb with a cup of chamomile tea. This exhibition would end pretty soon, as would the concert. Once the crowd broke up, his chances of finding two people in the mob dropped to parts per billion as everybody would make for his or her favorite bar. And that was just to start the night off.

It was beginning to look as though he would have to ask for a search of the waterfront warehouses. His heart sank as he counted the myriad windows reflecting the flying sparks of color. Robbie could be behind any one of them.

He'd give the Moon Walk five more minutes, and then call in the forces. Where could he get a view with some perspective?

The band shell, a modern gazebo, was raised about

five feet above the cobblestone path. If he stood on the railings he would be able to see a good section of the walk. As he made his way through the crowd towards the structure, the magic detector started flashing as it picked up one mighty strong trace. Boo followed it, hoping he had found them at last.

When he had taken no more than six paces, the last of the lodestone powder ran out. The witchlight fizzled and went dark. Boo came to a halt, staring at his empty hand in dismay.

A little boy nearby on the grass looked up at him with sympathy in his large brown eyes.

"Aww," he said. "Here." He offered Boo one from his box of sparklers.

"Thanks, little brother," Boo-Boo said, giving the child a pat on the back. Might do in a pinch. He lit it and held it toward the gazebo, chanting the Words of Finding.

The silver flame ran down the length of the wire and exploded outward in a single, blinding blast. Pay dirt! He ran toward the gazebo, shoving past dozens of holidaymakers with their faces to the sky. Just in the shelter of the slanted roof on the far side he saw a couple of familiar profiles.

Boo-Boo stabbed the auto-dial button on his phone. "Liz!" he cried. "I've found 'em!"

Ken Lewis rolled back on one elbow, watching Robbie operate her invisible equipment. Now and again in his earphone he heard the crackle of confusion coming from the Superdome. He might have had a hard time in the beginning getting the sabotage under way, but now it was going so easy he was sorry he couldn't do it all over again.

He could cause anything to happen that he could get Robbie to visualize. That opened up the range of possibilities for mayhem to well . . . everything. But there wasn't much time left. Once the power had been converted the way Mr. Kingston wanted it, he needed to cause a massive reaction to make it go back into the transmission line and sent off to SATN-TV. A devastating disaster would cause the appropriate reaction.

How best to end the concert? Ken wondered dreamily as tantalizing possibilities danced before his eyes. Should he set fire to the roof and let it cascade down on the thousands of fans in the audience? Blow up the stage and launch goody-goody Fionna into space? Collapse the walls into a black hole? As long as Fionna Kenmare bit the big one, Ken could do what he liked. That had been the only non-negotiable stipulation Kingston had thrown into the contract. A mega-superstar knocked into eternity at the height of her powers and popularity ought to launch boatloads of fear and terror back through the link. And the publicity! Ken could just see the headlines. Every newspaper and television service would carry the story tomorrow. It'd be a blow against good magic all over the world. That ought to be good for another bonus. Plenty of extra hate and fear to feed the Greed Machine. Maybe Robbie ought to set off a ton of fireworks right on the stage itself, and blow them all to pieces.

Wait, he knew the *perfect* conclusion: the Jumbotron! What if Robbie dropped that on the band at the end of the concert? Everyone would be squashed flat, *bang!*

"Honey," he said, very casually, leaning forward over Robbie's shoulder, "you know that big box hanging over the stage? It's in the way. Gary wants you to take it down, right onto the stage."

"Won't it fall on people?" Robbie asked.

"Well, maybe a few," Ken said, picturing the headlines on the paper the next day: *Rock Star Crushed
to Death in Freak Accident.* "Fionna, for one. C'mon,
do it, baby. Just one big tug, and it'll all be over."

"No, I don't like that idea," Robbie said. "It's
dangerous."

"Robbie, it's in your instructions," Ken said. "You
have to."

"No, the fire marshall will never go along with it."
She was growing more agitated.

"Shake it, baby!" he ordered, into a sudden silence
on the riverfront in between jazz numbers coming
over the loudspeakers. People turned around to look
at him. He gave them a sheepish smile. They went
back to watching, and he turned to glare at Robbie.
She shrank away from him.

"All right," she said, in a very small voice. Ken
heard the gratifying crackle of confusion in his earphone. She might not like it, but she was doing it.

"Oooh," the crowd breathed.

"What's going on out there?" Liz asked, from inside
her cocoon. She sensed a frisson of excitement tinged
with fear breaking out from inside the mass enchantment. The building began to rumble underfoot.

Lloyd leaned back and peered out between the
huge speakers.

"More of the usual monsters," he said, as though
he was telling her the weather. "Michael just stomped
a red rocket underfoot. The punters loved it. Hmm."

"What?"

"That 'ere box is moving around."

"Which box?" Liz asked. She experienced a
moment of alarm, which was quickly mirrored by her
support group. Deliberately squashing her feelings,
she let her gaze follow Lloyd's pointing finger straight

up. The Jumbotron! It swayed and moved backwards and forwards on its moorings. Fionna, still in mid-air, had noticed its movement, too, and was waving frantically at Liz.

Liz stood frozen in the midst of her support group. She had always had a horrible feeling that the Jumbotron might fall down. Her worst nightmare seemed on the verge of coming true. If the power continued to rise, not only the band, but hundreds of concertgoers near the stage, could also be crushed by it.

"Boo-Boo," she whispered, *"hurry!"*

"I don't want to make trouble for anyone," Robbie said, her fingers twisting in knots. She had gotten to the weepy stage. Time for a little more liquid courage. Ken poured another splash of tequila in her glass and added a double dose of drugs. "This has been the best job of my life, working for Green Fire."

"Come on, honey," he said, holding out the liquor, "they're no good to you." She drank it without paying attention. She was numb.

"Oh, yes, they are!" she insisted, muzzily. "Lloyd is always wonderful. Nigel is great. I really love Nigel. He called in those secret agents."

"Those spies are there to get you, baby," Ken said, looking into her eyes seriously. The whites of her eyes were bloodshot.

"They can't be," Robbie said, shaking her head. The action was grossly exaggerated. Ken caught her just before she fell over. "They're too nice."

"They're here to take you away," Ken insisted, whispering in her ear. "The government thinks you're a freak. They're evil. They'd lock you up in a little lab if they could. Run tests on you."

"Oh, no!" Robbie protested. "That's what you told

me about the nice man in Dublin. He wasn't a spy. What happened to him, Kenny?"

"You told him to go away," Ken said, with major satisfaction. The guy had been a basket case the last time he'd seen him, slumped outside St. Stephen's Green shopping center off Grafton Street. No more sticking his nose into the Council's affairs for him. Robbie, annoyingly, picked up on his triumph, and started crying.

"I did something to him, didn't I?"

Hastily, Ken offered her more tequila. "Here, baby. Here's something to make you forget all about it."

"Don't wanna forget..." Robbie said, fighting him. She shoved away, put her hands on the ground unsteadily, trying to get to her feet. He'd pushed her too far. Let her relax a little, and work her back to where she could create the big effect he was hoping for.

"Come on, baby," Ken urged her, pulling her down beside him. She slumped into a boneless heap, staring at the sky. "You can't leave. The show's not over yet. You know what I want. Do it. Do it!"

Robbie's voice was almost completely indistinct. He lowered his head to hear her. "The Jumbotron belongs to the Superdome. They'll get upset if we move it."

The fireworks changed tenor as the music shifted from the jazz piece to a martial march. Ken took her face between his hands and turned it toward the show.

"Never mind the Jumbotron. Look at all those pretty flowers!" he said. "Picture ones just like that happening in the Superdome. Big, fiery flowers, with petals that burn the people they fall on. Burning your enemies to cinders. Picture them falling, falling, right on Fionna. Look at them!"

A tongue of light sizzled up into the sky and burst right over their heads into a purple star twice the size of a football field. Robbie screamed and hid her head in her arms.

"They're coming too close. Too close!"

Bad move, Ken thought. He'd given her too much. He held the squirming woman in his arms, trying to keep her from burrowing into the grass.

Some of the passersby had turned around at the frantic scream.

Ken looked at the crowd apologetically.

"Sorry," he said. "She just accepted my proposal. We're engaged!" Indulgent smiles all round, left them alone. Decent people, giving decent privacy. They wouldn't be so nice if he told them *what* they were engaged in.

But he'd miscalculated how much Robbie's system could hold. Her body lay limp on the ground, but her hands were frantically picking at the grass.

"No no no no no no . . ." she murmured.

"Hey, baby." Ken turned her over. She drew her knees up to her chest and screwed her eyes shut.

Ken heard activity nearby, the sound of hurrying footsteps, and looked up to see the agent dressed like a bum heading his way. He shook Robbie by the shoulder.

"Robbie, you've got to finish off the concert hall *right now!*"

"No no no no no no!" She started kicking and lashing out with her arms. Agent Boudreau was getting closer. He mustn't get Robbie. Ken tried to gather her up, intending to carry her away from the Moon Walk.

She smacked him in the face with a wild swing.

All right, so Ken had created a monster—but she was his monster! He couldn't let the agent take her away. Ken wasn't a natural practitioner. His superiors had equipped him with a few easy spells in case of emergency. The disappearance charms were all used up. No way to vanish handily into the crowd. Instead, he had to rely on offense.

He sprang to his feet and assumed a martial arts stance.

Boo-Boo saw him assume a bent-knee crouch with his hands out at right angles. He'd been waiting for something like that. Ken had little magical ability of his own, or he wouldn't have needed Ms. Robbie in the first place. In a moment the agent had taken his opponent's measure. Ken Lewis had wrestled, most likely in high school, and had *maybe* a little store-front karate. He was no match for Boo-Boo in any way that the American agent could think of.

From his pocket Ken whipped out a white envelope and flung it down on the ground between them. It burst with a puff of white smoke.

"Spirits dark, hear me call you, hold my foe still like a statue!"

Boo-Boo almost scoffed out loud. Standard immobilization spell, only you were supposed to hit the one you wanted to freeze with the powder to make it work. Ken had wasted it on maybe an ant hill or a passing caterpillar. Boo-Boo wasn't impressed. The guy was so jumpy he was making stupid mistakes.

But Ken was a dirty fighter. Under the cover of the white cloud, he rushed to close with Boo-Boo, pounding him over the kidneys with his fists. Luckily for Boo-Boo, his old friend of an army jacket, padded with years' accumulation of odds and ends, absorbed most of the force. Boo-Boo twisted out of his hold just in time to keep his ear from being bitten in half. Ken Lewis must have gone out of his mind. Boo-Boo grabbed his wrist and flipped it up behind the other man's back.

"Now, you just hold still," he said. He turned his head to look for Ms. Robbie.

The poor young woman was lying on the ground, mumbling and writhing, her hands waving in the air. Her eyes were fixed on the fireworks, the effect of which she must still be transmitting to the Superdome. Drugged or bespelled, it was hard to say which.

"What did you give her?" Boo-Boo demanded, shaking Ken's wrist. The other gasped but didn't speak. "What have you done to her?"

An urgent beeping sounded nearby.

"Beauray," Liz's voice, much muffled, came from the depths of his pocket, "what is happening out there?"

Ken took advantage of Boo-Boo's momentary distraction to kick out viciously. Boo-Boo took a healthy blow to the shin, but let his weight drop forward. He ended up sitting on Ken.

"Now, what you're doin' is wrong. Y'all want to make it stop before anyone gets killed." Boo looked down at Ken, who was gnashing his teeth. "Or is that just exactly what you want?" He pulled a pair of handcuffs from his hip pocket and snapped them on Ken's wrists.

The everchanging crowd had by now noticed that a fight had been going on in its midst. A few men jumped forward to pull Boo-Boo off his quarry, no doubt thinking he was an insane vagrant. With regret, he stood up over his prisoner and produced his billfold with his Department credentials. The men stood back, surprised.

"Folks, this fellah's in possession of an illegal shipment of pixie dust," Boo-Boo said amiably but with fire in his eyes that showed he meant business. "Y'all want to move along now. Everythin's under control."

To back up his statement, he made a few quick mystic passes of the "These aren't the droids you're looking for" variety. Distracted, the crowd went back about its business. Boo-Boo was relieved.

He had let his guard down too soon.

In the darkness he missed the foot sweeping out from underneath that caught him across the shins. Boo-Boo went flying onto the grass. The cuffs were now around *his* wrists. Pretty slick, he thought.

Ken sprang up. Pausing only to kick Boo-Boo once in the ribs, he fled into the crowd.

Boo gasped, catching his breath around the pain in his midsection. Lewis was gone, but he was not the real problem. Boo-Boo crawled over to Robbie, who was lying on her back with her hands and knees in the air, kicking like a dying fly. Her hair was tangled into a rat's nest, and her clothes were stained and torn. She looked as though she'd been assaulted, but it was all from flinging herself around on the ground.

"Ms. Robbie, can you hear me?"

"Beauray!" his pocket screamed.

Uh-oh. Couldn't let Liz get hot under the collar. The lives of thousands depended on it. Awkwardly with his pinioned hands, he fumbled for the cell phone.

"I'm here," he said. "I've got Ms. Robbie. She's freakin' out somethin' awful."

"And Lewis?" Liz's voice was already calmed down again. The lady was a real pro.

"He's gone."

"Things are still going on here, Beauray," Liz said. "Whatever he has done is running on its own now."

"You still getting the full fireworks treatment?" he asked. He whispered one of the Words of Unbinding, and the cuffs leaped free. His shoes untied and his pants button popped open at the same time, but that was pretty much normal for the course. He refastened them.

"And laser monsters," Liz said, enumerating a list for him. "And fireballs with attitude. And carnivorous rainbows. One of them just bit Mr. Lockney on the arm. But what is troubling me the most is that the Jumbotron is moving. It looks as though it could come down at any moment. You must persuade her to stop before she tears it off its moorings."

Boo-Boo looked at Robbie. She didn't see him. That girl was one powerful channel, but she wasn't in control at all. He had to try and guide her back to reality.

Robbie reeked of liquor. Boo-Boo crouched down beside her and sniffed her breath speculatively. Tequila. Yes, here was the bottle beside her on the grass. But that wasn't enough to cause her to twitch like that. Lewis had to have been feeding her drugs. In spite of those mental obstructions, Boo-Boo had to get through to her. He didn't have much time.

"Ms. Robbie?" he asked. "D'you know me? Beauray. You know me. We got along real well back at the Superdome. Can y'all hear me?"

The girl looked at him without seeing him and rolled over, her legs spasming. He picked her up under the arms. Her hands flailed out and hit him in the face.

"Hey, there," Boo-Boo said, trying to catch her arms.

Some well-meaning citizens in the milling crowd on the pavement saw him do that.

"Hey, you!" a large black man said, jumping up the three concrete steps to the grass. "Get your hands off that girl!"

He attracted the attention of other people who

must have decided that Boo-Boo didn't have any business trying to talk to Robbie. He'd better scare 'em off quickly.

"Any of y'all know CPR?" he asked, putting a healthy measure of panic into his voice. "'Course she's foamin' at the mouth. Dunno if she's got somethin' catchin' or not. Anyone want to help?"

That did it. The ones that hadn't melted away when he mentioned CPR vanished like genies when he suggested Robbie might be diseased. Even the first man to speak was suddenly nowhere in sight. The Good Samaritan wasn't dead these days, but he was worried about incurable illnesses. In a moment Boo had the area near the gazebo all to himself.

"Now, Ms. Robbie, listen to me. You're causin' all kinds o' trouble back along at the Superdome. Y'all got to stop that. Can you hear me? Nod your head if you understand."

Instead, she flung herself at him, pointing at the sudden explosion of pink and gold stars over the river. Boo-Boo grabbed her and started probing her mind gently, using a mind-touch technique he'd gotten the idea for from *Star Trek*. He thought he felt a spark of recognition. Her eyes suddenly met his.

"Ms. Robbie, do you know me? I'm Beauray."

She nodded.

"Good. D'you know where you are? Good," he said when, after a brief hesitation she nodded again. "Can y'all shut down the fireworks at the Superdome?" She nodded. "Good. Can y'all do that right now?" She nodded. Her bleary eyes drifted away from him and focused on the fireworks display. Boo picked up his cell phone.

"That do anything?" he asked Liz.

There was a pause. "No change. That horrid box is still moving."

Boo-Boo helped the girl to sit up. She stared at him wildly. Spittle flecked her lips and she mumbled nonsense. Her hands moved of their own volition, performing a bizarre dance in midair.

"Look, Ms. Robbie," he said reasonably, "if you don't cut off what you're doin', thousands of people are goin' to get hurt. Some of 'em could die. It'll all be your fault."

He could almost see the words bounce off her ear. He had to break the connection between Robbie and the Superdome.

"Nothin' personal, ma'am," he said. He cocked back an arm and caught her under the jaw with a solid right. Robbie dropped to the grass in a boneless heap. Boo crouched over her, keeping passing couples from walking on her. He clapped the cell phone to his ear.

"I just knocked her out. Did that help?"

"No, it made it worse," Liz said, briskly. Boo could tell just from her voice how difficult her task was. "If she is the only one in control, that just set off everything she was thinking of. We have monsters, rockets, musicians in flight *and* the Jumbotron. How is she doing all of that?"

Boo looked down at the unconscious woman sprawled at his feet. "Well, I can't ask her just now."

"But what can we do to turn her off?" Liz asked, and he could tell how she was straining to keep her cool. "The building itself won't take much more. There is only so much power any one structure can contain. This one is more flexible than most, but, oh, Boo-Boo!"

"I know, darlin'," he said, slumping beside Robbie with his head in his hands. He could try force-feeding the girl a Mickey Finn, but if a stiff uppercut didn't work, a knockout drug wouldn't have much more effect. Besides, she was dosed to the eyeballs with something strong. He was afraid to try mixing more chemicals into her system. Who knew what kind of subconscious horrors would swim up from delta-wave sleep? What about a lobotomy? Could cutting off the prefrontal lobe squelch the violent emissions of her brain? An operation, or even a spell to the same effect, would take too long. Time was running out. The quickest solution might be a bullet to the head. He hated to take a life, but he had to balance one girl against the thousands and thousands of others trapped in the Superdome. If someone popped that bubble of power now there'd be a massacre. He glanced out over the river. Maybe sinking the barge with the fireworks would do it.

Thankfully, the fireworks stopped before he could put that into effect. There was a smattering of applause, and the crowd began to break up. He was left alone on the steps of the gazebo with Robbie slumped beside him.

"The show's over. Did that do it?" he asked the phone. "Did the effects stop?"

"No," Liz said. "The place is still shaking itself apart."

Boo-Boo's heart sank. "Then it's all goin' on in her head."

"How can we turn off her *sub*conscious? There are only a couple more numbers to be played. Everyone is going to want to leave soon, and the place is a hermetically sealed drum full of power that will blow if someone breaches the walls."

Boo-Boo's eyebrows went up. He had an idea. The girl had pretty much been following her cues in the beginning. Maybe her subconscious would continue to do it. He hoped he could connect with those ingrained reactions.

"Let's try and reestablish her connection to the

show," Boo said. "Hold the phone toward the band."

Liz nodded to the roadie holding the phone to her ear. He pulled it away and prepared to turn it off.

"No, don't do that," she said. "Hold it out between the speakers so it picks up the music."

Whatever the concertgoing audience thought of seeing a disembodied hand with a telephone at the top of the stage Liz couldn't guess, but Boo-Boo was right. After a few falters, the special effects began again, this time following the cue sheet that the astonished stage manager held in his hand. Robbie certainly did know her work backwards and forwards. Lasers touched the stage. A few Roman candles popped into the air in sequence. The steam box played. At last the show was going according to the plan the producers wanted. The gigantic box overhead stopped swaying. Liz was able to relax her stance for a moment.

It had taken her a short while to appreciate the skill of the young man who had been holding the phone up for her. Not once did he let the instrument slip off her ear or jam it too tightly against her head. He was watching her, moving when she did, and adjusting his grip accordingly. He must also have muscles like iron. Her arms were getting tired being held aloft for hours, and she was trained to hold that pose. It had taken a great burden off her, not having to worry about the telephone slipping off her shoulder and falling down because she couldn't spare a hand for it.

"You are very observant," she told him, and was rewarded with a smile.

"In this business you have to be, ma'am," he said. "You're pretty good at what you do, yourself."

Liz smiled. "I'm beginning to find that out."

Everyone was being so very cooperative. Over the last hour they had formed a special bond. United at first by necessity, they were now freely enjoying all the positive energy running throughout the room and one another. She knew how many people were in the huge auditorium. She knew them all intimately, every emotion, every urge. How many were in tune with the music. How many of them under her overlay of calming magic were excited, terrified, angry, in love, afraid, relieved. How many of them were heading for the lavatory, and how many were coming back. No one was bored.

With the cool beat of jazz running through her veins like blood, she could do anything. The final song was a rocking ballad in a minor key that sent chills up the audience's collective spine even while it thrilled and elated them. The lyrics were an allegory about a mystical underground power that rose up from beneath the earth to destroy humanity because it was destroying nature, but decided to give it one more chance because humans cared about music. If they could understand one kind of harmony, it could learn to appreciate the other. It was a warning, but it had a happy ending. Liz fervently hoped that Robbie could hold it together just a little while longer.

"This is the last number, Beauray," she said into the phone.

"I hear you," Boo said. He shifted Robbie and cuddled the phone closer to her ear. Pretty soon it would be all over.

A tiny, faint beeping began. He realized it was coming from his cell phone. Oh, no! The battery mustn't die now!

It wouldn't. He leaned in close to the receiver.

"Liz, send me a little of that power," Boo said in a very calm voice so as not to alarm Robbie and set her off. She was still out, but her eyelids fluttered, and she was drooling down her chin. He wondered again how much of those drugs Ken Lewis had given her. "Just a tickle."

A tickle was all he got. The small phone grew warm in his fingers. He held it just far enough from Robbie's ear to see the miniature screen. Battery full. Whew.

The music coming from the tiny speaker reached a thrilling crescendo, and died away.

"Okay," he whispered. "Fade to black."

"Beauray." Liz's calm voice issued forth from the earpiece. "It has stopped."

"Whew!" Boo-Boo slumped down on the concrete steps with the unconscious woman in his arms. "Thanks, darlin'. I'd better get this poor young lady back to the hotel. See you at the party."

He pocketed the phone, stood up and hoisted Robbie into his arms.

The park emptied out swiftly. The FBI agent passed within a couple of feet of him. Ken could have reached out and touched his shoulder, but contact with Beauray Boudreau was the last thing he wanted. Or the second last. Ken waited until Boo-Boo had stopped at the street corner with his limp burden, then insinuated himself into a large crowd of happy merrymakers heading north along the riverfront toward a bar near the French Market. He needed a very large drink.

The last thing, really the last thing, Ken wanted, was to have to tell his employer that he had failed. Mr. Kingston wasn't going to like what happened. And neither was the Council. They'd find out sooner or later, but not from him.

He ripped off the headset and stuffed it into the nearest garbage can.

As the final number concluded, Liz watched Fionna settle back to earth as lightly as a feather. Michael ran up to her and threw his arms around her. The two of them spun around the stage, laughing. The fringe of Fionna's dress flashed in the spotlights like electricity made physical. Voe Lockney launched into a fusillade of drumbeats that ended with a crash of cymbals. The sound died away. The Jumbotron stopped rocking. It was over. They'd survived.

The lights dimmed to the sound of wild applause and cheering. Green Fire took its curtain calls. The four members of the band stepped forward to take individual bows, and pointed out the guest musicians and singers for recognition. The applause went on and on.

"Encore! Encore! Encore!" the crowd began to chant.

The musicians looked at one another. Michael shook his head firmly. No. Instead the band waved and bowed to their fans, picking up flowers and small presents that came sailing onto the stage from the audience. Fionna, a huge bouquet of roses balanced on her arm, waved to the teeming crowd like a beauty contestant crowned queen. The band took one bow after another. The crowd didn't want them to leave.

The crew backstage cheered. They'd survived, too.

"It's all over," Nigel Peters said, with relief. He dropped his hand from her shoulder and flexed his arms.

"Not quite," Liz said, keeping her pose.

Peters looked at her in alarm. "What?"

"The question that must be answered immediately is what to do with all the raw, tainted power still swirling around the concert hall. The doors would be thrown open in a moment. We must rid ourselves of the gigantic overload to avoid letting it spill out into the streets of New Orleans."

Peters frowned. "How do you get rid of used power?"

A perfect solution had just occurred to her. Liz smiled, charmed at the simplicity of the answer.

"Why, we'll send it back to the givers, of course," she said. "A tradition of magic says that whatever one does comes back threefold. The concertgoers certainly deserved to have all the love they projected given back to them in triplicate." And whoever was behind poor Robbie being used as a tool deserved what was coming to them, too.

"Attention, please!" she called, as the group around her began to break away. "We're not quite through yet. We need to clear the air before anyone tries to leave the Superdome.

"Aww!" some of them complained.

"Can it!" Lloyd shouted. "Do what she says. Now."

They returned readily to their original positions. Liz looked around at all of them. They weren't really all that eager to give up their chance to have touched real magic. She was their leader in wonderworking. Every eye was on her.

"Now, everybody breathe in. Take in all of the power that has been raised here tonight that we've shared. Keep only what you need for the health and strength of everyone here. Then—breathe out. Push the rest of it back where it came from. Send it back. Send it all back. Ready? Inhale. Now, *push*!"

Liz thrust her arms out in front of her. All the others followed suit. The huge glut of energy went

rushing away from them in a hurricane gale. Anything
not nailed down swirled in the breeze, sheet music,
programs, posters, cables, but the roadies and stagehands weren't afraid this time. They were a part of
it. A grand tornado touched at the edges with green
seemed to rise up from their nucleus, opened out to
the very edges of the arena, and disappeared into the
walls. The power was gone, back where it belonged.
Liz let out a sigh of relief. The ordeal was over at
last.

Everyone grinned at each other like idiots and
slapped one another on the back or caught one
another in energetic embraces. They all picked up
Liz, passing her from one to the other for hugs.

"All right, people," Nigel Peters said, holding his
arms up in the air. "Party time!"

"Yay!" the crew cheered.

The band came off stage, holding up weary hands
in victory salutes. The roadies leaped forward to take
instruments or microphones and hand out drinks as
the group headed downstairs to their celebratory party.
Liz felt triumphant. She'd succeeded, against the
wildest odds, at the first really important assignment
she'd ever been given. She fell in with the band and
found herself beside Fionna.

"I've never been so tired in my life," Liz said.

"And ye didn't do a thing except stand back here
and wave yer arms," Fionna complained. "We're the
ones who did all the real work. Look at me! I had
to sing all me numbers hangin' in the air like the
week's washin'! And I didn't get to wear all my
costumes!"

Chapter 18

"Ken Lewis was your problem all along," Liz told Nigel Peters the next morning in the private corner of the Mystic Bar as they waited for the rest of the company to come down for a belated brunch feast. "He'd been using Robbie as a power conduit to attack Fionna. All the things Fee told you about scratches appearing on her skin and unexpected knocks were true."

"I feel awful not believing Fee," Nigel said, running nervous fingers through his thinning hair. "It's just not the sort of thing you run into every day."

"You were right to be skeptical," Boo-Boo said, in his easy way. "It's not an everyday thing. But once the attacks started comin' in public, he didn't have much of a chance of escapin' notice."

"Lewis was trying things out, working toward the grand climax of this concert, when the main attack would come," Liz said, seriously. "I believe he really meant to kill Fionna. Robbie was unaware of his true intentions, or she wouldn't have gone along with it. She's not evil, she's just . . ."

"In love," Nigel said, sighing deeply. "I know. It's totally hopeless. Everyone can see it, poor kid, but Lloyd's got enough sense to stay where his bread's buttered."

"It's none of my business," Liz interrupted, "but there are real feelings between them. I was . . . rather in a position to know, last evening."

"I guess you were," Nigel said, a little uncomfortably. "Er, how long did Ken have Robbie, er . . ."

"Under his spell?" Boo asked, with a smile. "Most likely's been movin' in on her since he started workin' for you. Lots of your people thought he had it bad for the young lady. His interests in her were purely unaltruistic."

"How do we . . . uh," Nigel's voice dropped to a confidential undertone as he drew the agents aside for a moment, "how do we keep this from happening again? I gave Robbie her job back, but what you were nattering on about this Law of Contagion . . . She hasn't got anything that's catching, has she?"

Liz and Boo exchanged glances.

"Not precisely," Liz said. "But it won't happen again. We've seen to that."

And so they had. Boo-Boo had dragged an exhausted Liz to a little store in a dark street to get the materials they needed for a protective amulet to prevent her from being taken over by malign influences ever again. Both agents were impressed and worried by the different levels of spells they had to delve through when clearing her aura. Robbie was fairly well disenchanted herself, with Ken Lewis, Lloyd Preston, and men in general. For the time being. She might not be vulnerable to love for a while, but she was a vulnerable young woman.

"We have amulets for the entire company," Liz said, indicating a pile of Carnival bead necklaces. "Just to make certain such attacks cannot come through another conduit."

"Here," Boo-Boo said, handing Nigel a string of garish, metallic blue beads, which the manager accepted with a nervous laugh. "This one's for you."

"A little bright, isn't it?"

"The more garish the better," Boo-Boo pointed out, "to scare away bad spirits, y'know."

As the members of the company filed sleepily into the bar on the way to the dining room, Boo-Boo stepped forward to loop a necklace over each of their heads. Liz handed him fresh ones as each new person arrived.

"Souvenir of N'Awlins," he said, pleasantly. "What we call a lagniappe, a little somethin' extra. Enjoy."

"Hey, thanks, man," most of them said.

"Is this extra *special*?" Laura Manning asked, with a wicked glint at Boo-Boo as he placed a bright gold necklace around her neck that went well with her dark skin.

He grinned at her. "Y'all might say so." She leaned over and kissed him.

Liz had an armload of protective necklaces in every color imaginable for Fionna to wear with every outfit. When the star finally arrived, Boo-Boo lavished amulets on her until the exhausted star looked like a carnival float. Liz held back a couple of the leftovers to take home to HQ for analysis. It never hurt to have more examples of protective magic in the grimoire.

"You're all safe now," Liz assured Nigel.

"At least from an attack like that one," Boo-Boo said, genially. Nigel didn't look reassured by Boo-Boo's qualified promise.

"But how did Lewis get a nice girl like Robbie to work for him?" he asked.

Liz looked grim. "She believed that Ken was doing magical work on her behalf, ostensibly to help her gain Lloyd's love. She didn't catch on as to why she wasn't winning her man. She put it down to Fionna's stronger magic. Frustration was why her power levels could build so high."

"That wasn't all her, y'know," Boo-Boo pointed out. "She was gettin' a power feed from somewhere else. An untrained practitioner like herself couldn't generate that much without bein' detected. That was why it took us so long to figure out it was her. Now, she'll just have to work out her love troubles in some other way. She might still be jealous of Ms. Fionna, but she won't be wired into a negative-energy pool any more by an unscrupulous bastard like him, y'all will excuse the language."

"Poor kid," Nigel said. "But what was it all for?"

"Power," Liz said. "Eighty thousand bodies' worth. When you have that many like-minded people in a room, they generate psychic energy that can be tapped by someone who knows what he's doing."

"Like radiation?"

"Sort of," said Boo-Boo. "Ken had a hookup to a satellite receiver feedin' into the control room, wired to Robbie's chair. Since the energy had touched her once, it would continue to have an effect on her. It was attached to the transmission lines in the press room, right next to the control room. We were in there, and never connected what was happenin' to what we were lookin' at."

"This is still too fantastic for me," Nigel said, shaking his head. "Dark sorcery, beamed here via modern technology. And we'll never know who was behind all this, huh?"

Liz held her tongue. Boo-Boo had kindly shared with her the early-morning report of the very bizarre destruction of a television station in the northwestern United States. The agent, a stringer named Ed Cielinski, reported that some new equipment installed at SATN-TV that gave off evil vibrations had been acting oddly over the last few days. Some time after he'd gone off duty the night before, the whole place was trashed, like a rock group's hotel room. His employer was discovered sitting on the floor in the middle of the ruins muttering to himself. So far as he knew no one had been hurt, but the place was a mess. The department was investigating, and would share its results with OOPSI.

"I'm afraid not," Liz said at last.

"I had no idea we were harboring a dangerous criminal," Nigel Peters said, shaking his head. "We were lucky he didn't turn up for the concert itself."

"He did almost as much damage by remote control as he would have if he was right there," Boo-Boo said.

"You can say that again!" said Gary Lowe, coming over to hand Nigel a drink. "We had everything planned to work without Robbie's effects, and he went and bollixed it all up by vanishing. It's a good thing I know how to run a light board, or the whole thing would have come off in darkness."

"In more ways than one," Boo-Boo said.

Gary Lowe gave him a puzzled frown. "Well, it made my job twice as hard, doing that along with overseeing everything else."

"The concert was wonderful," Liz assured him.

"Thanks. One vote of confidence, anyhow."

"Well, I've fired Lewis in absentia," Nigel Peters said. "He'll never work in the industry again."

"You can't really tell future employers why," Liz

said. "This matter is now covered by the Official Secrets Act."

Nigel gave her his nervous smile. "In this biz, honey, all I have to do is say he's too weird. I don't have to explain myself."

"That's mighty convenient," Boo-Boo said. "Weirdness covers a wide range of sins, don't it?" He felt through his pockets and came up with a grubby square of pasteboard. "If he does turn up at all while you're in the United States, call my department."

Nigel took it with gingerly fingers. Liz produced a card of her own, pristine white and snapped it into the manager's palm. "The same goes for our territories and the EU," she said. "He's a wanted man, now. On both sides of the ocean."

The others in the bar were discussing the concert, sharing their impressions of how things had gone. Instead of being frightened from having been in the presence of incomprehensible magic, the roadies and members of the band had taken it all in their stride. Some of them seemed honored that it had happened to them, their band. Liz marveled at the elasticity of human nature. Of course, Boo-Boo had had a lot to do with it. He'd jumped right into the thick of the conversation, making jokes.

"I wish it would happen all over again," one of the stagehands exclaimed.

He was shouted down by his fellows. "Oh, no, you don't!" Robbie Unterburger insisted.

The special effects technician had come out of her experience feeling as though she'd had her aura washed. Refreshed after a night's sleep and a good detoxification treatment by Liz and Boo-Boo, she looked prettier and happier than Liz had yet seen her. She was transformed, laughing and joking with her peers.

"Oh, you were a lot of help, taking off like that," the others teased her. Nigel had been purposely vague in describing Robbie's part in the magical attack to the others. "You didn't see what happened."

"There's seven cities left on the tour," Robbie said, defending herself. "I dreamed up some new effects that will knock your socks off."

"We're not so sure we want to hear about your dreams," Hugh Banks said. "We've seen what your nightmares look like."

"So that's that, now," Fionna said, appearing at Liz's shoulder. Fee had deep circles under her eyes carefully covered by concealer stick. The green in her close-clipped hair had been freshly touched up to enhance the vivid makeup job on her face. Liz wondered if Laura Manning had gotten any sleep at all.

"Yes," Liz said, turning to her familiarly. "I'm glad we could help."

"Thank the good Lord it's all over," Fee said, gulping a drink that Lloyd brought to her. "Well, you'll be going now. No need for you to stay."

"That's right," Liz said. "Straight back to London. My orders came this morning. My employer is pleased that we were able to isolate the threat so quickly."

"After all, you were just doing your job," Fionna said.

Liz schooled her face not to show her astonishment. The ungrateful wretch couldn't bring herself to say thank you. That was the least she could do. Liz guessed she was still embarrassed that Daddy had called in her old school chum to pull her very public fat out of a particularly strange fire.

"It was a splendid concert," Patrick Jones said, jumping in. He'd been eavesdropping, and was clearly embarrassed by Fionna's gracelessness. "You should see the reviews. We're all very happy."

"Well, we're going in to breakfast, now," Fionna said, swinging away on her heel. Liz made as if to follow her. Fionna stopped short and looked down at Liz with disdain. "It's a *private* party," she said pointedly. "You can go now."

Furious, Liz withdrew without a word. She had thought after all their hard work Green Fire might at least invite them to breakfast. She watched Lloyd open the door at the rear of the bar. Fionna sashayed through it without looking back, leaving Liz smarting.

Oh, well, Liz thought, trying to be philosophical about the situation. Fionna Phoebe Kenmare Kendale was safe and well. After all, wasn't that why she had come in the first place? She was a government agent. She received a paycheck. She shouldn't expect rewards.

She wasn't doing a very good job of convincing herself. Of all the miserable females who ever walked the earth, Phoebe Kendale took the biscuit.

"Don't worry," Boo said, coming up beside her and touching her arm. "I've got somethin' better for you." He tilted his head toward the door. They left the rest of the band exulting in their successful appearance.

But they did not escape unobserved. The sharp eyes of Michael Scott spotted them as they were about to leave. The slim figure rose from its place among the others, and followed them into the lobby.

"Wait," he called out to them. Liz stopped, hopeful. Michael strode to catch up. He smiled at them.

"That group of ingrates won't say thanks, but I will. You were, well, marvelous. Miraculous, really."

"All part of the job, sir," Liz said, briskly. She was still a little hurt by Fee's indifference.

"No more of the 'sir,' please, Liz," he said, with the little smile she adored. The golden lights in the lobby lit up his hair like a halo. "It's Michael to you, now and forever. Fee may be a tough bird to handle—and I'm dyin' to know how you know so much about her—but we love her. She's special. You've done good work, both of you."

"Thanks," Boo-Boo said. "Happy to have been of service."

"Give me your cards. You're both welcome at any of our concerts whenever we pass through. If you can still stand us, that is."

"Of course I can," Liz said, in love with him all over again. "I didn't get to appreciate this one properly."

"If it wasn't for you, it wouldn't have happened at all," Michael said firmly. "I might not still be here to thank you. Perhaps one day we can sit down and talk about what happened—what *really* happened. I'll be getting back now. God bless." He bent and gave Liz a kiss on the cheek, shook hands with Boo. He slipped away again into the bar. A little of the light seemed to go out of the room with him.

Liz sighed. Well, perhaps there were a *few* rewards for virtuous agents.

Augustus Kingston shuffled disconsolately through the ruins of Studio A. The girders were still in place, but the acoustic ceiling tiles had cascaded down in pieces all over the floor. His beautiful television station had been destroyed, along with his plans for world domination.

It had looked for a while as though his place in the Council was assured. When the members had arrived, dressed in their red silk robes over thousand-dollar power suits, he'd had the stage set for success. He'd been proud of his attention to detail. The altar was the same one they used for the afternoon talk show. The thirteen black candles in holders made from the skulls of small animals were cast of human tallow. Everything had been just right. He was ready to catch the whole ceremony on videotape.

There they'd stood, waiting for the chosen hour. Kingston had quivered with anticipation under his postulant's robe of red-dyed camel hair. The needle on the special receiver rose higher and higher until it pinned on the right side of the meter. Then the power came pouring into the studio.

The Council members expected to be bathed in glory, but it was more like standing in a meteor shower. Sparks shot everywhere, setting fire to his precious props: the altar, the black silk hangings, the posters, and worst of all, the gauge that told them how much money the ongoing telethon had raised for Satan. He remembered the disbelief on their faces as they could smell the sticky, gooey love wrapping around the rush of power, three times as much as they expected. Howling, the men batted at their arms and robes in disgust, unable to bear the purity. The love and happiness were overwhelming. The men, powerful black magicians in their own right, started spinning in circles, unable to stop. Some of them floated up to the ceiling, pursued by animals made of brilliant colored light. The Council was getting their power, all right, but not an erg of it could be used for evildoing.

Kingston tried to turn the receiver off, but he couldn't get near it for the force of the energy flow. The grand master had ordered the members to channel all their black sorcery into it, to try and get a hold of the wild magic and send it away. The transmitter had overloaded. Sparks began to shoot out of its base, then it rocketed through the roof. The rest fell in on them. The power burned up everything in the studio, followed by a rush of water power that drenched the ashes. All the equipment in the place just overloaded on goodness. One by one the cameras blew. Kingston himself had narrowly escaped being riveted in the gut by a 70mm zoom lens that went through the wall into the lobby.

Within minutes, it was all over. Without saying a word, the Council, covered in confetti, crumbled acoustical tile and broken glass, had filed out into the night. The last to leave had been Eldredge Mooney. He'd given Kingston a look that could have killed.

After seeing the morning national news Kingston almost wished it had. Fionna Kenmare was completely unharmed. Nothing out of the ordinary seemed to have happened to her. Green Fire had enjoyed a triumph in New Orleans. The reporter was particularly taken with the special effects which were, she said, "just like magic."

Three million dollars down the tube. The plan had been so perfect! How could it have failed? What the hell had happened to his focus person and his conduit?

The receptionist's voice came thinly through the hole in the wall. The public address system had blown out with everything else.

"Telephone for you, Mr. Kingston."

Nervously, Kingston picked up the telephone receiver.

"Hello, Eldredge. Yes, I was expecting to hear from you. No, I can't explain it. You can't blame me for that. I had everything set up just the way we planned. It would all have worked if . . . No, we can't use her again. What'd be the point? I hate to admit it, but even my own viewers are going to lose interest because nothing happened to the woman. They'll think everything reported was part of the show. After this she'll be so popular that any attack on her will only enhance her and affect us negatively. Well, there'll be another victim. We'll strike again. What about my membership in the Council?"

"You must be out of your mind!" Mooney bellowed. Kingston removed the receiver from his ear to frown. "Don't ever call me again!" The connection went dead, and Kingston found himself staring at the phone.

"Well, to hell with the rest of you, too!" he snarled.

It was all going to be so beautifully evil, and now his dreams were wrecked. Kingston looked at the mess, not even knowing where to begin cleaning it up.

What in hell was he going to do for the morning broadcast?

Liz scraped up the sweet apricot sauce on the deep plate with her fork.

"This is very nice of you," she said, looking across the white tablecloth at Boo, whose clothes looked shabbier than ever in the genteel ambience of the dark wood paneled restaurant. "Even I've heard of having breakfast at Brennan's. I'm surprised you were able to get a reservation. There's quite a crowd here."

"Oh, I know someone," Boo-Boo said.

"You always do," Liz said, smiling impishly. "Forgive the impertinence, but are you certain you can afford this meal? I would be happy to split the check with you."

Boo gave her a cheerful smile. "My superiors approved the expenditure. They're feelin' pretty good today. Department BBB gets to keep its budget intact for another year. I made it clear how much you'd contributed to the success of my mission."

Liz ate the last of the Bananas Foster instead of

biting her tongue. She was *not* going to overreact again.

"It was *my* mission, after all," she said, pleasantly, and was gratified to see Boo-Boo's bright blue eyes harden slightly. They'd never agree as to who should have been in charge. She sat up, remembering a detail, and fumbled in her purse. "Here's the cell phone. Thank you very much for the loan. I rang my chief. He's passing along the good word about the outcome to Lord Kendale."

"Well, all's well that ends well," Boo said, "as your Shakespeare said."

Liz let out a sigh, sitting back for a moment as the hovering waiter refilled her cup with excellent coffee. As soon as he was gone, she leaned across the table.

"You realize that all we've done is stop *this* conduit. There might be others out there. Kenny Lewis disappeared before we could question him."

"There's always somethin' or someone out there," Boo said, shrugging. "Y'can't keep on worryin' every minute. We've stopped this round, the end of our assignment. If it starts again, we'll stop it again. That's all we can do. Anythin' else is chasin' our tails. I think Miss Fionna is safe, now. They won't try it on her again."

"I agree." Liz couldn't help but feel that if she'd had a tail, it would be wagging. Her assignment was over, and it had been a success. Boo-Boo paid the check with a shiny gold American Express card and escorted her out to the curb where a taxi was waiting. He helped the driver sling her bags into the boot. "Do you know, I've only been here three days, but it feels like I've been here for years."

Beauray Boudreau grinned. "That's N'Awlins, darlin'. It creeps into your soul, and it never lets go."

"I hope I can come back sometime, and just be a tourist," Liz said wistfully.

"I hope you can," Boo-Boo said. "It'd be my pleasure to show you around." He leaned over and gave her a peck on the cheek. "'Til next time, darlin'. Keep an eye over your shoulder. There's always somethin' out there."

"Stay in touch," Liz said, squeezing his hand impulsively. "If you ever need me, call."

"Same goes for you, darlin'," he said. "We're friends now."

Boo gave her a brief wave. Then, he turned and shouldered his way into the dense crowd on the street. Within a few steps he'd disappeared into the mass of tourists and genuine characters that were as unmistakably a part of New Orleans as the jazz. Just like Boo.

"ICE cold Coca-Cola!" shouted a vendor pushing a cart along the street.

"Lucky Dogs! Get your Lucky Dogs!"

Liz smiled and settled back in the seat as the taxi drove away.

TIME SCOUTS CAN DO

In the early part of the 21st century disaster struck—an experiment went wrong, bad wrong. The Accident almost destroyed the universe, and ripples in time washed over the Earth. Soon, the people of the depopulated post-disaster Earth learned that things were going to be a little different.... They'd be able to travel into the past, utilizing remnant time strings. It took brave pioneers to map the time gates: you can zap yourself out of existence with a careless jump, to say nothing of getting killed by some rowdy downtimer who doesn't like people who can't speak his language. So elaborate rules are evolved and Time Travel stations become big business.

But wild and wooly pioneers aren't the most likely people to follow rules... Which makes for great adventures as Time Scouts Kit Carson, Skeeter Jackson, and Margo Carson explore Jack the Ripper's London, the Wild West of the '49 Gold Rush, Edo Japan, the Roman Empire and more.

"Engaging, fast moving, historically literate, and filled with Asprin's expertise on the techniques and philosophy of personal combat, this is first-class action SF."   —*Booklist*

"The characters ... are appealing and their adventures exciting ..."   —*Science Fiction Chronicle*

The Time Scout series
by Robert Asprin & Linda Evans

Time Scout	87698-8	$5.99	___
Wagers of Sin	87730-5	$5.99	___
Ripping Time	57867-7	$6.99	___
The House that Jack Built	31965-5	$6.99	___

MERCEDES LACKEY
Hot! Hot! Hot!

Whether it's elves at the racetrack, bards battling evil mages or brainships fighting planet pirates, Mercedes Lackey is always compelling, always fun, always a great read. Complete your collection today!

The Bardic Voices series:

The Lark and the Wren, 72099-6 ✦ $6.99 ☐
The Robin & The Kestrel, 87628-7 ✦ $5.99 ☐
The Eagle & The Nightingales, 87706-2 ✦ $5.99 ☐
The Free Bards, 87778-X ✦ $15.00 ☐
Four & Twenty Blackbirds, 57778-6 ✦ $6.99 ☐

The SERRAted Edge series:

The Chrome Borne (with Larry Dixon), 57834-0 ✦ $6.99 ☐
The Otherworld (with Mark Shepherd & Holly Lisle), 57852-9 ✦ $6.99 ☐

Bard's Tale novels:

Castle of Deception (with Josepha Sherman), 72125-9 ✦ $5.99 ☐
Fortress of Frost & Fire (with Ru Emerson), 72162-3 ✦ $5.99 ☐
Prison of Souls (with Mark Shepherd), 72193-3 ✦ $5.99 ☐

Bedlam's Bard (with Ellen Guon), 87863-8 ✦ $6.99 ☐
Knight of Ghosts & Shadows (with Ellen Guon), 69885-0 ✦ $5.99 ☐
The Fire Rose, 87750-X ✦ $6.99 ☐
Fiddler Fair, 87866-2 ✦ $5.99 ☐
Werehunter, 57805-7 ✦ $6.99 ☐

Available at your local bookstore. If not, fill out this coupon and send a check or money order for the cover price + $1.50 s/h to Baen Books, Dept. BA, P.O. Box 1403, Riverdale, NY 10471.

Name: _____

Address: _____

_____

I have enclosed a check or money order in the amount of $ _____

Got questions? We've got answers at

BAEN'S BAR!

Here's what some of our members have to say:

"Ever wanted to get involved in a newsgroup but were frightened off by rude know-it-alls? Stop by Baen's Bar. Our know-it-alls are the friendly, helpful type—and some write the hottest SF around."

—**Melody L** *melodyl@ccnmail.com*

"Baen's Bar . . . where you just might find people who understand what you are talking about!"

—**Tom Perry** *perry@airswitch.net*

"Lots of gentle teasing and numerous puns, mixed with various recipes for food and fun."

—**Ginger Tansey** *makautz@prodigy.net*

"Join the fun at Baen's Bar, where you can discuss the latest in books, Treecat Sign Language, ramifications of cloning, how military uniforms have changed, help an author do research, fuss about differences between American and European measurements—and top it off with being able to talk to the people who write and publish what you love."

—**Sun Shadow** *sun2shadow@hotmail.com*

"Thanks for a lovely first year at the Bar, where the only thing that's been intoxicating is conversation."

—**Al Jorgensen** *awjorgen@wolf.co.net*

 ### Join BAEN'S BAR at
WWW.BAEN.COM
"Bring your brain!"